wandering warrior

wandering warrior

DA CHEN

To Victoria and Michael
Our kungfu kids

Acknowledgments

I thank the following people for their contributions to the making of this book:

Sunni, my beautiful wife and masterful in-house editor, for tirelessly helping to sharpen the book into a miracle.

Victoria and Michael, for inspiring me to write for those who still believe.

My mother, for your simple smiles that are my daily nutrients.

My father—your loving spirit still shines like a sun.

William and Alice Liu, for your love that is as generous as the Yangtze.

Elaine Koster, my super agent, for faith, guidance, and friendship.

Marissa Walsh, my editor at Delacorte, for your literary insight, artistic vision, and editorial skills.

And Beverly Horowitz, my publisher, who was the first to open the door, inviting me into this prosperous garden where children's books are grown.

PArt 1

和尚男童

OLD MONK AND THE BOY

"THE FUTURE EMPEROR shall bear five black moles under each foot," the monk Atami read reverently from the sacred ancient scriptures. He would look up at the innocent boy that Luka still was and continue. "This rare emperor descends upon this holy land only once every five hundred years."

"What does that mean?" Luka would ask.

"It means that you are destined to be the next Holy Emperor and the living god of all the Chinese people. Even among all the emperors before or after, you will stand out like a giant and bring the greatest blessings to this Central Kingdom called China." There was more to that passage but Atami didn't mention it, at least not yet. Then the monk would always bow and pray and offer a short admonishment. "Don't ever let others know who you are."

"Why?" Luka would ask.

"Because the Mogoes are afraid of you."

"Because I'm so big?" Luka stood up and pushed out his chest.

"No." Atami smiled. "Because when you are enthroned, all the Chinese will rise up against the Mogo invaders, who have taken our land and slaughtered our people. These mountains, these rivers, our people, our cattle, our grain, those maddeningly beautiful flowers . . . all await your coming." Tears would roll down the monk's cheeks as Luka listened quietly.

For as long as Luka could remember, Atami had carried him on his back while they traveled from one tribe to another, carefully avoiding any sign of the Mogo forces and pretending they were just two of the many wandering beggars. The first few steps Luka had taken had been on the rocky face of the Liao-Shan Mountains, trailing behind the monk's long shadow. The first few words he uttered had been "Please spare some food," Atami's usual opening line. They had journeyed a thousand *li* and crossed a hundred rivers.

Atami worried that Luka might not live to maturity in the face of the harsh reality of the Mogo occupation and the year-round famine gripping the land. But he prayed and wandered and begged on. Luka's extreme intelligence and rapid growth amply reassured the monk, whose only conviction was that the emperor should and would live. And Atami intended to raise him the best he could in the traditional Chinese way, notwithstanding the ironic footnote in the holy history, that this little emperor did indeed carry the blood of that unfortunate race, the Mogoes.

They lived like father and son and loved each other so, but when they were alone, it was always "Your Holiness" this and "Your Holiness" that. Atami carried China's sacred treasure on his back and did not intend to dent it in any way.

At the age of three, Luka one day called Atami Baba. Father.

"I am not your baba," Atami corrected him, disturbed. "I am your servant. You are the Chosen One, Your Holiness."

"But I don't want to be the Chosen. I want you to be my father. Why aren't you my father?"

"Your Holiness, one day I will tell you who your baba is. But for now we have to go on begging so that we can live."

They would have food one day and go hungry for three, roaming the lonely mountain roads and deserted windy tribes. They ate frozen cats, dead dogs, tree bark, and rotting snakes. They fought for prey with wild animals, and were often chased by the vultures themselves.

"When can we stop begging?" Luka asked.

"When the Mogoes leave China and you sit on the throne in the Forbidden City," Atami replied, referring to the royal palace in Peking, the capital of China.

"But they are all over China."

"Then you beg until the day you die."

"I don't want to die."

"You won't as long as I am alive. The day of your enthronement shall come. It is your fate, and those black moles under your feet prove it. They are Buddha's mark."

Once an old lady opened her door to offer the wandering monk some leftover *wawato,* corn bread. When Atami bowed to thank her, the dark face of Luka, who rode on his back, revealed itself. The old lady, a fair-skinned Chinese, spat in the monk's face and turned away.

"Please spare some food for the child," Atami begged.

"For a crossbreed? Never!" She slammed her door.

"What is a crossbreed?" Luka asked.

"A peach growing on a pear tree," the monk replied. They walked on.

On the road, they saw dead people everywhere lying with dead animals. Thieves robbed thieves. Beggars killed beggars. The living robbed the dying and wild animals chewed upon the dead. A severe famine was eating people young and old, for the ignorant Mogo rulers had ordered them to give up planting rice and grow barley and wheat instead. The seedlings had withered hopelessly and rotted in the muddy fields on the plains, where wet rains came with howling typhoons and misty seasons lasted forever. Some villagers were rumored to have eaten their own children, others their dogs. Atami could only pray, look to the sky, and go on with the life he was destined to live, no matter how hard it was. He had to live so that Luka could live. They climbed mountains and waded through valleys, hand in hand, day and night, till they reached the outskirts of Peking, where the promise of food and survival beckoned.

There Atami taught Luka the ancient Chinese scripts and had him memorize all the verses when he was four. Every day at sunrise out on the edge of Peking, Luka sat inside a little tent Atami had patched together to shield out the wind and the sun. With his legs crossed at a short table, he nibbled away at the insect-like writings. Luka found those ancient words fascinating. They recorded the creation of the world. First there was the void of nothingness. All silent. Then came the torrential rains that filled up

5

the ocean. When the rain stopped, land was formed. But his favorite was the hand-drawn paintings of eight auspicious Buddhist symbols: the parasol, the banner, the conch shell, the golden treasure vase, the knots of eternity, the golden wheel, and the lotus flower. He often wondered what it would be like to perform the traditional dance of *Yian Ge* in bare feet and sleeves rolled up for the celebration of autumn harvest or if he would ever be allowed to do so as a Chosen One. When the daily monotonous chanting of the ancient scripts bored him, he would let his mind slip away to the adventures of playing a long trumpet, loud cymbals, and noisy drums—all of which existed only in his imagination.

Atami got up even earlier. He was the sun before the sun and the moon after the moon. He fussed around their little tent, noisily making black tea and, on good days, some *wawatos*. He chanted his long prayers while fetching water from the sunken well in the backyard overgrown with weeds, then off he went to beg for food. As light cast its last rays, he would enter the tent on his quick feet, his back hunched, clutching his precious bundle to his chest. Even as his eyes shifted fearfully to see if anyone had followed him, he hummed a happy tune for the bounty of the day.

"Come eat, Your Holiness," he would say, opening up the bundle. Usually it would be *wawato* crumbs, some sour rice, or half-eaten fruits.

Looking up from his books one day, Luka announced, "Your Holiness is not eating today."

"Why?"

"Your Holiness should go out and get food himself now because he is a big boy of ten years."

"But you need to do your studies, Your Holiness. You are already behind what would have been expected of you."

"Forget the studies. From today on I am going out to beg."

"But this is work. Holy work. Sacred work. The best work you could ever do for yourself, the people, and me. I am begging you." Atami was on his knees.

"Don't worry, I will learn at double the speed. That way I can spare some time to help you."

"But the sanctity of your spiritual studies cannot be hastened. One word at a time. Every phrase has meaning and significance. Only through quiet, undisturbed meditation can you achieve that enlightenment we all aspire to."

"If you don't trust me, you can test me. Come on, test me now."

Atami agreed to this, for testing his pupil was his favorite chore. The monk asked a hundred questions and Luka not only answered them satisfactorily, he also pointed out that two questions were actually redundant and begged for two more to fulfill the day's quota.

"Outstanding, Your Holiness."

"Can I go now?"

"Absolutely not."

"Why not?"

"No Holiness has had to beg before."

"No Holiness has been this hungry before."

"What am I going to do with you? You are beginning to show rebelliousness. That is not a good sign, Your Holiness. You are the tradition. You cannot break the tradition. If you do, I will have sinned a thousand times. I cannot take that blame. Please stay at home, study, and let me take care of you," Atami pleaded, on the brink of tears.

"Okay, okay. If it means so much to you."

But the following day, as soon as Atami left, Luka sneaked out of the little tent. He stretched his lazy limbs and took a deep breath of fresh mountain air. He had often peeked through a hole in the tent and watched the tail of Atami's robe disappear every day, but he was at a loss as to where to go now that he had taken his first step toward freedom. He jumped over the fence marking off their little yard and was soon on a Peking street. A din drew him to a dusty market square. Chinese people in their traditional robes, buttoned on the side, their waists tied with sashes, squatted throughout the busy fair, their garments draping the ground as they haggled, bargained, bought, and sold.

Everything Luka could imagine was for sale here. Nomads hawked animal skins and lamb butter. Valley farmers peddled *wawatos* and vegetables. Red-combed roosters stretched the limits of their leashes as they paced around on webbed feet. Ruby-eyed rabbits nibbled away at their bamboo cages. A thick snake, wrapped around a wooden pole, hissed at passing eagles. Woven tapestries showed the colors of the mountains. Rugged hand paintings captured the sounds of the rivers. Live cows mooed.

Dead cows' carcasses hung, dripping, next to piles of cracking tanned leather and goat meat, goat milk, goat bones, goat fat, and precious goat manure for fertilizing.

A group of nomadic cattlemen from the northeastern mountains burst into a lively song, dancing with their quick feet to the music of a four-stringed guitar called a *pipa* and a two-stringed violin known as an *erhu*. A dozen valley farmwives, wrapped in their bright-colored dresses, echoed the song's chorus. Children ran among the thickening dust, under men's legs, over rooster cages, between chewing yaks, and into the ample bosoms of scolding mountain mamas.

Why should I sit at home when there's so much happening here? Luka thought. He had to learn his trade, the trade of life. As he looked left, then right, he saw two boys, one with bare feet, the other with a dripping nose. They snuck up behind a bearded merchant who sat dozing near his fat fur racks, where many hairy animal skins hung. The barefooted boy slipped his small hand into the merchant's hip pocket and pulled out a thick money bag. The merchant twitched his pointed nose, opened his eyes, and slowly turned his groggy head until he saw the little rascal smiling at him.

"What are you doing?" the old man asked, rubbing his nose.

"Nothing," the boy answered.

"Get lost!"

"I'm out of here." The boy slipped the bag he was holding behind his back to his friend, who ran off into the crowd, then retreated slowly, backpedaling. Just as he was about to run, he saw Luka, who had been an unwilling witness to their heist, and gestured for him to be silent.

The old man, patting his hip and discovering his money was missing, jumped up and grabbed the boy, shouting, "You little thief!"

"You filthy accuser!"

"Give me back my money!" He searched the boy, finding nothing.

"Go clean your poisonous tongue!"

The old man tightened his grip. A crowd formed around them.

"The boy is innocent," one woman offered.

"He's guilty!" said another.

"He was born a thief!"

"He killed my rooster the other day!"

The old man took out a little dagger. "I'm going to cut off your dirty fingers so you can't steal again."

"I'm innocent!" the boy cried.

"I don't believe you."

"Cut him, Laoren!" a voice shouted. "He stole my onion the other day."

"Don't cut me! I didn't steal your money. That boy did." The thief pointed at Luka, who was still standing a few feet away.

Laoren let go of the thief, smiled, and walked over to Luka. The crowd followed him. "Where is my money bag?"

"I did not take it," Luka said loudly.

"You're lying. You work with him, don't you, you Mogo bastard?"

"I am Chinese, not Mogo. And I am not a bastard. My name is Your Holiness."

The merchant grabbed Luka's face, squeezing it with his fat fingers. "Your Holiness!" Laoren scoffed. "Did you all hear that?" The crowd laughed.

"That's my name. Why are you laughing at me?" Luka shouted angrily at the crowd.

"How dare you shout at me? I haven't even cut off your fingers yet."

"I am not a thief. You can search me."

He did, flipping Luka onto the dirty ground. He patted him up and down, in his crotch and under his armpits.

"I told you I don't have it. Let me go," Luka demanded.

"Not so easy. I'm going to keep you here until you tell me where the money is."

"But I am innocent."

"The sun shall tell."

Laoren tied Luka to the rack of furs with his hands behind his back. Beneath the burning sun, Luka stood with his eyes closed, chanting memorized verses. He was tired and thirsty and his hands hurt. Laoren asked him to confess again and again, and slapped him when he didn't. Luka got angrier and angrier and abandoned his original plan to point the finger at the thief. He stood there with his mouth zipped.

The old man eventually dozed off again. Luka's face dripped with sweat and dust. He chanted on with his dry mouth, closing his eyes and shutting out the world. When the sun's rays slanted, the two thieves returned. They snuck behind the merchant and untied Luka, and before the old man could awaken, the three were at the far corner of the market.

"I'm sorry for what I did but you just made two very good friends," the barefooted boy said. He extended his dirty hand to Luka, who took one good look at the thief before jumping on him like a small tiger.

"Sorry? Let's see who is sorry now!" Luka shouted while striking and biting him.

"What did you do that for?" asked the boy who was about Luka's age.

"He almost cut off my fingers for the sin of theft you committed!"

"Sin?" the runny-nosed kid asked. "What is sin?"

"Doing something you shouldn't do," Luka answered.

"How about that? Doing something you shouldn't do," the thief sneered.

"Who are you to be talking to me like that? I am Your Holiness."

"Yeah, yeah. So am I."

"Why did you frame me?"

"To save my fingers."

"You are a sinful boy!"

"If you keep using that word, I'll have to hurt you."

"I am going home now and do not wish to see you again in this life or the next."

"This life or the next. You really are a little monk, aren't you, Your Holiness?" the tall boy said.

"He talks like one," the shorty said.

"Come back," the tall boy said as Luka turned to leave. "Aren't you hungry?"

Luka stopped and turned around. "Very."

"Here, take this money and buy a dozen *wawatos* for your family." He pulled a large note from the stolen money bag and gave it to Luka.

"A dozen?" Luka repeated in awe.

"Yeah, maybe even more at this hour of the day."

Luka was tempted. A dozen! A half-eaten *wawato* was reason enough for Atami to sing and dance when he unwrapped his bundle. Then Luka remembered a verse in the script prohibiting the acceptance of a thief's loot. "I can't take it."

"And why is that?"

"Another sin."

"Brother, the way this boy talks we could change our last name to Sin." They laughed.

"Goodbye," Luka said curtly.

"See you later," the pair shouted back. "The money is yours if you want it. Any time, Your Holiness. We owe you."

That night, Atami spanked Luka for the first time. He had been worried sick when he had returned and found Luka missing. Convinced the boy had been captured, he had been about to race back to town to look for him when Luka had stumbled into the tent, sweaty, dirty, and bruised. Atami's heart was torn.

After putting the shaken boy to bed, Atami broke into tears and prayed. "I could have lost him, my fragile emperor. What should I do? I can't be with him every second. Please, my heavenly Buddha, enlighten me with a sign." He crawled to his shrine, determined to keep on praying until a holy answer was given. But soon fatigue overcame him and he dozed off. Guilt woke him up again and he mumbled, "No answer, no sleep."

Each time he dozed off after that, he poked his forearm with a burning incense tip, shocking himself alert. But soon, even the pain of burning gave way to a snug snore and he dropped the chunky incense on a piece of paper, which started to burn. Awakened by the smoke, Atami slammed his right hand on the fire and smothered it. As he jerked his hand away from the half-burned paper and dusted off the ashes, his eyes caught a drawing Luka must have sketched when daydreaming. The island of unburned paper showed a dancing monk—one leg flying high, both arms stretched out—much like the description in the Book of Heavenly Joy. The eyes were too big, the ears too long, but there was genuine joy expressed on the face.

"Thank Buddha!" he cried. "One stone to kill two birds—settling his mind and defending his body." Atami folded the picture into his pocket. He blew out the lamp and was snoring within a second.

The following morning, Atami woke Luka before sunrise.

"But the sun isn't up yet," said the groggy boy.

"We have new lessons to cover and we won't be able to fit them into your busy routine without getting up earlier."

"What lessons?"

"Lessons that will cleanse your soul and tame your temperament."

Luka yawned. "Are you adding another book of history and culture to my list?"

"No, I am going to teach you something that will help you with your studies."

Luka's little mouth sagged in disappointment. "It sounds boring."

"It's not. I will be teaching you kung fu from the legendary school of Xi-Ling."

Luka's jaw dropped. He was stunned. His sleepiness vanished, leaving in its place a broad, incredulous smile. "You mean Shaolin kung fu, Wu Xia, *cha-cha-cha, hai-ya* kung fu?" Luka fired back, kicking and punching.

Atami was taken aback by the child's display of such secular knowledge. "Where did you learn about that?"

"Oh, in the Book of Evils." Luka lowered his eyes and took a quick peek at the monk.

"The study of the Book of Evils is supposed to warn against all things evil and vicious. You seem almost to delight in its contents."

Luka lowered his eyes again guiltily.

Atami sighed and said sternly, "This is not to satisfy your childish whims but rather a heavenly choice of a secular solution. I was enlightened in my desperate prayers last night. An inch of deviation calls for a foot of correction. Do you understand?"

"Yes, I do," Luka replied. "But who is going to be my master in these new lessons?"

"Your humble servant," Atami said, bowing.

"You?" Luka said, shocked.

"Yes, Your Holiness."

"But you're . . ." Luka struggled to explain what was wrong with the picture.

"How do you think we survived the fire when the other thirty monks perished? Kung fu is a gift from Buddha. A kind monk, Master Gulan, from the Xi-Ling Mountains, sheltered me and taught me his sacred art, not because I was strong but because I was weak."

"You never told me."

"I never intended to inform Your Holiness of my humble skills. I have long sworn to Buddha that I will use these skills only to fend for you and for our peaceful existence. By teaching you what I have to offer, I'll honor that vow because the purpose of the learning is spiritual. The bodily exertion will lighten your head and purify your heart. Buddha has shown me."

"When can we start our lesson?" Luka practically danced in eagerness.

"Not yet. There are a few things we need to remember before you begin the journey of kung fu."

"Whatever the rules and principles, I will obey."

"Mean it with your heart and swear it with your life," Atami said.

"I do."

"Good. Now get dressed." He threw Luka a thin white robe. "I stitched that while you were sleeping. From now on, that will be your practice attire."

Luka put it on and checked it over. "It fits well. Thank you, Atami."

"It is not much, Your Holiness. I made it out of my sheet."

"No wonder it feels so soft and comfortable. But what are you going to cover yourself with at night?"

Atami was touched. "Let's worry about you first. We will start now."

Luka hopped out of the tent, then jumped right back in, shaking. "It's too cold out there."

"You will grow accustomed to it."

Luka hugged himself and wondered how.

They walked to a clearing beyond their wooden fence where the moon hung behind a leafless winter tree, making its slow westward descent with yawning fatigue. A distant wolf howled sadly for the waning night as the wind cut through Luka's robe.

Nervously, Luka tugged at Atami's robe. "But doesn't our teaching warn us against all violence and encourage benevolence toward all living creatures?"

"Who is teaching you violence? Kung fu was developed so that we might transcend the mind and discipline our urges. It has long been misused, but I'm very pleased that you asked. Shall we kneel and make a pledge to Master Gulan?" Atami lowered himself to his knees. Luka knelt also, facing him.

"Master Gulan, you have left the legacy of *Jin Gong* in my

keeping," prayed Atami. "Today, I present to you the future emperor of China, whom I deem the most worthy to inherit the tradition of our art and your pure soul, and without whom your legacy shall be no more. His Holiness hereafter swears that he shall never pass on the knowledge of *Jin Gong* for as long as I, his master, lives." Luka repeated Atami's oath.

"Each time I face an opponent, let me see only the face of Buddha," continued Atami. "And each time I raise my humble, unclean hands, let your principle of tolerance be my best weapon."

Luka paused in his repetition and asked, "Does that mean I can't hurt anyone without hurting our Buddha?"

"Yes, it does." Atami smiled. "Now, lesson number one: horse stance." He spread his feet and crouched.

Luka imitated him, squatting with his legs spread, as if riding a horse. The monk frowned and shook his head, walking around the boy. "Why does your horse have a big belly?"

Luka sucked in his stomach.

"Now your horse has a dragging butt." Atami pulled him up by the collar. "Ah, that's perfect. Stay that way. I'm going to the tent to do my chores now."

"How about me?"

"Wait for the sunrise."

"Just standing still like this?" Luka asked.

"Yes, Your Holiness. Soon you should feel yourself taking root in the ground."

"But I'm cold."

"You will be sweating soon if you keep your horse galloping, but not trotting." With those cryptic words, Atami crossed the yard and disappeared back into the tent. Once he was inside, a silhouette of his kneeling body appeared against the tent wall.

Soon Luka was trembling and his teeth chattering. His arms grew heavy and his legs sore. He would never have imagined that kung fu involved so much pain. The descriptions of kung fu he had so cherished in the Book of Evils had only glorified the kung fu fighter's exploits—how masters could split rocks, jump walls, and fly off roofs. Nobody had written about this horse stance thing.

His whole body continued to shake and his back ached. His stomach pushed out and his back slackened. Remembering Atami's words, Luka sucked his belly in again and held it for awhile. *Galloping? Rooting? What did he mean?* Atami had never been more mystifying. Luka let his mind wander, imagining himself riding a real horse, a white one. A trot soon became a gallop and the sandy dust whipped at their feet. Luka could feel the horse's hardened muscles and strength vibrating through him. In their windy chase, they became one and Luka felt warmth showering over him.

Atami's calloused hand tapped his shoulder. "The sun is up, Your Holiness. You did it."

"Yes, I did. And I'm sweating!"

"Did you feel rooted?"

"I don't know. I imagined that I was riding a horse, and felt a part of him."

"Yes, you were rooted," Atami said with satisfaction. "The horse was your roots."

Luka shook his head, amazed. "Why is rooting so important?"

"Because if you are rooted, when someone pushes you, you will sway but not fall."

The scripture reading that day was unusually smooth. Luka felt as if his mind were a dry sea that could drink up a skyful of torrential rain and not even burp. And the daydreaming that usually accompanied the waning sun in the afternoon was replaced by the eager anticipation of tomorrow.

The next day Atami woke him up even earlier and taught him the cat stance.

"While a horse stance is heavy, a cat stance is light, ready to strike." Atami kicked Luka's feet closer together. "Think of yourself as a cat with quick paws," he said, then went back inside the tent.

When he returned to announce the sunrise, Atami asked, "Do you feel like a cat now?"

"A mountain cat," a sweaty Luka replied.

"I'm very pleased with your progress."

"What will I learn tomorrow?"

"Tomorrow you will learn how to develop *Qi*, inner energy. Without *Qi* one is strengthless."

That day, Luka felt like a soaring eagle as he breezed through some of the most difficult passages of his required reading. Although his legs and arms were sore, it was a happy pain, a taste of an exciting world beyond his readings that set him free.

On the third day, Atami filled two cloth bags with sand and

strapped them to Luka's legs. "From now on, you'll live with those bags as if they were a part of your body."

Luka dragged his feet. "They're heavy."

"No. Not nearly heavy enough," replied Atami. "I promise to add more sand as your strength grows."

The ten pounds of sand soon felt like a hundred. And the weight seemed only to double when Atami instructed him to jump onto and off of the top of a short wall. Pain ripped through his legs all the way up to his groin, so that even going to the outhouse was excruciating.

"How are the sandbags going to help me?" Luka asked.

"Simple. Once you are free of them, you can fly."

Luka was inspired.

The monk never forgot for a single moment that this exercise was just the means to a holy end. As he added more sand to Luka's bags, he also expanded the scripture lessons. Yet the exertions seemed only to increase the boy's intellectual capacity and appetite. In the short order of six months, Atami judged Luka was ready not only for the studies of sacred philosophy, which normally took a much older mind to master, but also for the lessons of *Tie Sha Zhang,* Iron Sand Hand.

Atami gathered two barrows of fine sand and ordered Luka to plunge his straight fingers into them. Luka's nails chipped, his skin flaked, and his fingertips bled. But he saw the pain as a test of faith.

The final test came one day when Atami heated the sand, but

Luka plunged his fingers in with even firmer resolve. Atami nodded silently, but tears welled in his eyes. The boy's easy grace and shadowless quickness reminded him of his old master, Gulan, and the essence of Xi-Ling style. Luka would make a wonderful successor to the legacy. But would the legacy be good for him? For the gift could only beget peril.

Since he had begun training, Luka's appetite had quadrupled. To Atami's dismay, he could never seem to find enough food to feed the young tiger. Atami stayed out in the streets even longer every day, trying to find food.

One moonless night, Atami returned limping badly, and collapsed once inside the tent.

"Are you all right?" Luka asked, holding him.

"Don't worry about me. Worry about yourself, Your Holiness. I'm afraid you will have nothing to eat tonight. The dogs from the Mogo army compound snatched our food and bit my ankles. I have come home empty-handed, and I might not be able to go out tomorrow if these bites don't heal. Please forgive me."

Atami didn't get up the following day. Even when the sun shone on his skinny behind, he still slept soundly. Luka shook him, but Atami only opened his eyes briefly before closing them again. The monk felt hot and his legs were red and swollen like thick tree trunks. Luka decided that it would not be a good day to do his studies. Remembering the only other people he knew, Luka wandered back to the market and soon found the two rascal thieves smiling at him.

"Look who is here," the tall boy said.

"Your Holiness," the short boy said with a smirk.

"You looking for us?" the tall guy asked.

"I am."

"Well, how long has it been? Ages, it seems. But we still remember you. It's your lucky day. Usually we're pretty busy, but today we're on vacation," the tall guy said, looking at his buddy, who nodded with approval. "A long-awaited vacation. What's money for if you can't buy a little rest for your dirty feet?"

"Have you got a name?" Luka asked.

"I'm Mahong. It means *big feet.*" He wriggled his toes in the mud.

"And I'm his brother, Mahing. *Nose.*" The little guy swiped away dripping mucus.

"Mahong and Mahing."

Mahong nodded. "Easy to remember, huh? We're the best pair this side of the mountain. Can we help you?"

"I need the money you offered me before. You said it was mine any time."

"So it was a sin to take the money a season ago, but not now?"

"You may say so, Mahong."

"What are you gonna do with it?" Mahong asked, counting out a few notes and passing them to Luka.

"Whatever I want to do."

Mahong grabbed the money back. "Wait a second. A couple things you shouldn't do. You are too young to smoke and too little to gamble."

"I am not doing any of that."

"Good, because when that day comes, I will personally show you how to do it." He flipped a pipe out of his pocket and slipped it into his mouth. Mahing filled it with a pinch of tobacco and lit it for him. They took turns puffing on it. "Want some?"

"No."

"How about a drink?" Mahing pulled out a small bottle of liquor. "The best money can buy." He uncapped the drink and tossed a big slosh into his mouth. His face wrinkled in pain as he gulped it down. "Oh, Your Holiness, I feel heavenly."

"How old are you both?" Luka asked, disgusted by their bad habits.

"Twenty-something, if you add us together," said Mahong.

"About right." Mahing nodded drunkenly, then burped.

The trio sauntered to a steamy food stand, where Luka bought ten *wawatos* and some fruits.

"I can carry that for you," Mahong said.

"I don't need help," Luka said. "And I can go home by myself from here."

"We will walk you home," Mahing said.

"Don't you have a home to go back to?"

"Nope, never had one before." Mahong shrugged.

"And never will," Mahing added, shrugging too.

"You don't have a home?"

"Do I have to repeat myself?" Mahong asked.

"Come with me, then."

"Are you sure?"

Luka nodded, hoping Atami would not mind.

But Atami could not mind. His fever was still high and he rolled deliriously on the sheepskin bed, talking nonsense, alternately chanting and groaning in pain.

"Nice digs here," Mahong commented, lowering himself in.

"We should get ourselves a roof like this one of these days," Mahing said. "What's the matter with your father?"

"He is not my father."

"Then who is he?"

"My servant."

"Your servant? Right, and I'm the emperor."

"He was bitten by the army dogs yesterday when he was looking for food."

Mahong, the smart one, blinked, thinking. "I know a cure for that."

"You're not a doctor," said Mahing.

"I am in this case. I was bitten once by a hound. Remember, we'd had nothing to eat for days."

"What is the cure?" Luka asked.

"Tomorrow I will get it for you."

"But he might die tonight!" Luka exclaimed.

"Nah, he won't. Look, I'm alive and I didn't take anything till days later. I thought I was going to go on to the next life, but then a miracle happened."

"What miracle?"

"You wait and see tomorrow."

The three ate a good meal and took turns watching the sick monk.

The next day, Mahong set out early and came back with a small, covered bamboo basket. "How is he now?"

"Still sleeping."

"Good."

Mahong pulled a green snake from the basket and gripped it close to its head. He aimed the hissing serpent at the monk's right ankle. The snake struck the monk twice, then went limp in his hands.

"Good, I got the right snake, Mahing," Mahong declared. "The same type that bit me."

"You mean you weren't sure it was the right snake?"

"Nope, you never are sure till it goes limp. This type of snake spits its poison and dies."

"You gave Atami *poison*?" Luka asked.

"What did you think it was? A kiss?"

"You didn't tell me it was poisonous. Now he is going to die!"

"Believe me, he won't die," Mahong assured Luka as if he were a seasoned doctor, tossing the dead snake on the ground. "If you hadn't done anything, then he would have died. This is exactly how I got cured. I was lying there in the weeds waiting to die when a snake like this came up and bit me. The next day I was up and running like Mahing again. Right? You were already making a little casket for me, huh, Mahing?"

"Yeah, I was. Don't remind me." He shuddered.

"You're such a crybaby. I'm just trying to tell this guy to stop worrying about his servant. Believe me, he'll be fine by sunrise."

So they waited and ate dinner again in the tent. Mahong wanted to smoke, but Luka chased him out. The two thieves settled for booze and slept like puppies, snoring away in each other's arms till sunrise.

It was to this sight that Atami opened his eyes. "What happened to me?" Atami asked Luka. "And who are they?"

"You almost died. The tall one is your doctor."

"My doctor?"

"Yeah, see that snake there? That was your cure. It bit you."

"Snake venom to cure the bite from a dirty dog?"

"I had to do something."

Atami examined his wounds. They were almost healed, and the swelling had subsided. He felt as if he'd just had a good sleep. He studied the dead snake carefully and opened a thick book of Chinese medicine, where he found that his cure was one rarely used, since the patient often died from the treatment. Too little venom, and one died from blood poisoning. Too much, and the poisonous spit would rot one's bones and melt one's skin.

"I could have died twice!" the monk exclaimed.

"But you were saved," Mahong replied, having just woken up.

Atami grabbed the three boys in his arms, hugged them, and kissed each of their foreheads. "Thank you for saving me. You don't know what you have done."

"We do, we just saved the life of a servant," said Mahong.

"How can I ever repay you?" asked Atami.

"Go get us some Oolong tea," said Mahing.

The monk smiled and made the darkest Oolong tea for His Holiness and the two rascals.

SOON THE BOOKISH wisdom of a thousand years lost out to the antics of two untalented, barefoot, runny-nosed artisans. Telling himself that a short break from his prayers would not hurt anyone, Luka would meet his friends outside the tent. They welcomed him by jumping on him and throwing him to the dirty ground, which he allowed, for he enjoyed the roughhousing.

"What do you do that for?" Luka asked them one day.

"Wrestling? All Chinese men wrestle. It's like burping," Mahong explained.

Mahing belched out a fat one.

"See, he can do it any time he wants to, even in his dreams. Isn't that something?" Mahong said.

"Right, that's something. Fellas, I have to study."

"What on earth are you studying?" Mahong asked.

"Does it have anything to do with the Your Holiness crap?" Mahing added.

"Something like that. But it is important to me."

"And we're not important?" Mahong asked, curling his toes.

"You are."

Reassured, they jumped on him again and hugged him, smacking him with odors he couldn't name. Only two were newly recognizable: cheap tobacco and foul liquor.

"Good grief!" Luka said, fanning his face. "You could kill a dog with that breath."

The duet shrugged.

"We'll show you something new today," Mahong promised.

"What is that?"

"Well, we showed you where to steal for a living."

"The market?"

"You're pretty good," Mahong said. "Today we're showing you where to beg for a meal."

"Good, then I'll be able to help Atami."

"Did you notice that I used the word *living* for stealing, while one only begs for a meal?"

"I don't understand."

"No problem, I forgive you. Your Holiness's mind is all clogged up with holy crap. My point is this: stealing is a profession, while begging is expediency at best." Mahong arched his brows.

"At best is right," Mahing confirmed.

"Okay, show me the place."

"What's the hurry?" Mahong asked. "Remember: stealing is always preferred, and begging is the choice of no choice. You got that?"

"Why?"

"Why? Begging is for losers," Mahing reasoned. "Do you know how many beggars we got in this town?"

"How many?" Luka asked.

"Thousands," Mahing said.

"And do you have any idea how many get their heads cracked, legs broken, and fingers cut off for a rotting leg of lamb?" Mahong asked.

"How many?"

"All of them. If you don't believe me, check this out." He pointed to Mahing, who bared his back, revealing a long, swiping scar. One brother theorized, the other demonstrated. Always a duet.

"What happened?"

"A knife thrown on a hot summer day," Mahong said. "Nothing he'd want to repeat." Mahing nodded.

"My goodness."

" 'My goodness' is right. But that was then, this is now. We are thieves now. Don't you just like the ring of it? *Thieves.*" Mahing narrowed his eyes.

"Yeah! We're pirates without ships," Mahong added.

Luka couldn't help probing these fascinating minds further. "Why does that make you feel good? It's taking what is not yours."

"No, it's beyond that, way beyond. It takes skill, trickery, timing, but most of all, courage. Begging, you only get what is given. Stealing, however, you take what you want," Mahong said.

"That's deep, Mahong. I never thought of that," Mahing said with wide eyes.

"Well, we complement each other, don't we?" Mahong said.

"Yeah, we do."

Luka didn't know whether to laugh or cry. These two brilliant criminal minds obviously had not considered the sinfulness of stealing and the severe punishment awaiting them down those fiery steps to hell. Life was but a blissful journey to them. They sauntered along like two romantic heroes, swapping war stories, laughing out loud, and spitting against a wind that sent the phlegm right back into their faces. He followed them silently along the main streets before they took a curve down the market square to their final destination. Along the way they touched a vegetable stand, causing the peddler to throw a bucket of water at them, and fondled a mother goat's sagging nipples for fun, which led the beast to kick wildly. Nothing in this world could keep their hands still.

Mahong slowed down. "This is the Mogo army base," he whispered.

The three stood in ascending order, looking. It was as if a fabled kingdom had fallen from the sky and landed on this dusty street corner of Peking, outlandish and alien.

"Well!" Luka took a long breath.

A massive stone wall rose before them. The entrance was shut, its doors heavy like thick lips vertically clenched. Two stone lions sat by the door, not in welcome but with frozen angry growls, guarding the compound's secrecy. Along the wall top walked armed soldiers partially hidden behind barbed wire, their eyes stabbing this way and that. The white flags blew limply in the wind.

"What do you see there?" Mahong asked Luka.

"I see beggars along the foot of the wall," Luka said.

"Not bad. His eyes aren't hooked by the fancy smooch." Mahong slapped Luka's shoulder. "What else do you see?"

"I see weapons pointing—at us."

"Are you sure you're only eleven?" Mahong was impressed.

"Yeah, but I should be fifteen," Luka replied.

"Did you hear that, he should be fifteen?" Mahong slapped his shoulder again. "You know what? You could be fifteen because you know crap. And it takes crap to survive in this world, pal."

"Don't call me pal."

"Okay, okay. Your Holiness."

"What do you see there?" Luka asked Mahong in return.

"I see hate. I see blood. I see many things that ain't right. That's what I see," Mahong said. "I see Chinese getting their butts whacked every way I turn. Someday I want to whack that evil general called Ghengi."

"Who is General Ghengi?"

"Who is Ghengi?" Mahong asked, astonished. "The Mogo vulture who calls himself our emperor. He's bothered many of our women. That's all I can say about him. His window is the one in the center. See it?" Mahong pointed his dirty finger at a huge, ornate window on the top floor of the building. "Someday, I will personally make him suffer."

"You do hate him."

"I got every reason to hate him."

"Why?"

"His men killed our parents in a riot."

"They did?"

"And you know what? He's here to kill us before we grow up. That's his job: killing all the Chinese till we are no more, so the Mogoes can take over all our mountains and land. But someday we will fight back."

"Someday soon," Mahing confirmed. "Let's get some food over there."

"Wait," Mahong insisted. "Do you know what is inside there?"

"No," said Luka.

"A loose army, that's what they are. Warlords. You know what they do inside that compound every day?"

Luka shrugged.

"They wait for the orders from above. Lazy armies do lazy things, and evil things. What do you call that . . . ?"

"Sinful things."

"Right, sinful things. They throw banquets in there, and eat tons of good food every day." Mahong paused to swallow. "They have beef, pork, eggs, fish, barrels of lard, opium, silk, satin. . . . Everything goes in there, and I mean everything. And what do we do out here? We starve like those old dogs dragging their half-chewed legs."

Luka nodded. He understood.

Hordes of beggars and dirty orphans rested along the base of the wall, bathing in the warm sun that shone only briefly each day, waiting for the army's garbage cart to come out. The sun was straight above their heads when the entrance opened. A fat Mogo cook pushed out a cart of rotten leftover food. The beggars sprang to their feet and surrounded it like flies around hot manure. With a smirk on his face, the cook dumped the garbage into an open manhole to the total dismay of the famished beggars.

"Don't dump it! Feed us, please!" shouted a shaking voice.

"That's good food! Let us have it!" another screamed.

"Now that's begging, if you care to know," Mahong said calmly.

Luka was too caught up in the scene to hear him. He went closer to the crowd and saw the back of a familiar figure—Atami, who was fighting to squeeze in. *It can't be him,* Luka thought. The rickety figure turned only for a brief second. It *was* him. Luka's heart tugged with pity and sadness. Atami knelt in the dirt, slurping liquid he had scooped with his hands from the cracks on the ground. Then he stuffed a dusty chunk of meat into his mouth. He was like an animal attacking his prey, filling his mouth so urgently that he nearly choked himself. When a group of orphans rushed over to him, he lay down on a pile of cabbage that he claimed as his own, covering it with his skinny frame to make it clear he would not share. The orphans surrounded him, picked him up, and threw him off the juicy site.

With his friends in tow, Luka ran over to Atami, who was crouched down in pain. Kneeling down beside the monk, he asked, "Are you all right?"

"I am," Atami said in surprise. "But what are you doing here? Please go home, Your Holiness."

"Forget 'Your Holiness.' I just saw the most horrifying thing in my life. I can't let you beg for food like this anymore."

"What are you going to do? This is the life I have accepted. Do you understand?"

"No, I don't. Why did you let those orphans hurt you like this? Why didn't you fight back?" Luka asked.

"If I fought back, someone might recognize my fighting style, and we would be in danger. Besides, this is nothing, just a food fight. It happens every day. We are friends when we are not fighting. See, I still managed to hide a few chunks of good cabbage under my robe." The monk revealed a corner of his long robe, smiling as blood oozed from his cut lip. "We are going to have a good meal tonight."

The fight for food at the trash cart soon turned into a battle. The cart crashed under the weight of hundreds of hungry people. Crawling out from under half-naked knees, the fat cook emerged, crying. Two long rows of Mogo soldiers marched out of the grand entrance and bore down upon the mob with *qiangs*, steel-tipped spears, shouting and poking randomly at the frenzied crowd.

Luka saw a tall young turk aim at a beggar's ramshackle wooden shelter and use it for target practice. A shrieking old man crawled out of the hut as if bitten by a snake, his arm bleeding where the weapon had struck him. The crippled man knelt before the soldier, begging him to stop stabbing the hut. "My dying wife is inside and cannot move."

"Why can't she crawl out like you, idiot?" the tall Mogo shouted.

"She is paralyzed from her waist down."

"A cripple and a paralyzed one. What else?" The soldier laughed as he continued to poke the thin wall of the hut. The woman's cries of pain were loud and clear.

The cripple turned to the sky, still kneeling. "Please, Buddha. Please give us a slice of hope. Where are you?" His words faded into sobs.

An officer, identified by the *da dao*—big sword—he carried, appeared beside the young soldier. "You want Buddha?" he asked the old man.

"Yes. Please, Buddha, give us hope and make these soldiers leave our land," he cried again.

"You want Buddha, you'll get Buddha." The officer swung his sword, whacking the old man's left temple. The cripple collapsed to the ground.

"Dump him and burn the hut," the officer ordered before leaving.

His soldier grabbed a torch and set fire to the hut.

Atami jumped before him. "Please, I beg you to let me carry the woman out. Please, sir." His head was on the dirty ground, kissing the earth. The soldier smiled darkly and spat on Atami before kicking him in the flank with his battle boot.

Once, twice, three times.

Atami stayed motionless like a turtle. Not a sound, not a cry. Luka knew that he would be fine. Atami had put on his armor. His inner self would be safe under the protection of his invisible shell, which was made possible by his lifelong practice.

Other beggars cried out for him, lamenting the defenselessness of the peace-loving monk. They waved their hands, they shouted, but they dared not move an inch toward the soldier to stop him.

I guess they do care for each other, Luka thought, their outcries shaming him for his own inaction. *Atami will be fine,* Luka told himself. *I must exercise restraint.* It was what Atami would want him to do: to be calm in the eye of a storm. But his fortitude would soon falter.

From the corner of his eyes, Luka spotted six tall soldiers marching urgently toward the kneeling monk, *qiangs* in their hands and bundles of arrows strapped at their waists. Their boots stirred up the dust.

"You're supposed to be burning the huts down. Remove that monk," bellowed the leader, identified by the red band across his forehead.

"I can't. He won't move," the soldier replied.

"Make him."

"I've been kicking him, sergeant."

"You dummy! Why are you kicking him when you have a *qiang* in your hand?"

"Oh, yeah." The soldier stopped kicking, dusted off his boot, and raised his weapon high in the air, the steel tip pointing at Atami.

"Go for the neck!" one of his comrades shouted.

"I'm going for the head!" he shouted back gleefully, bringing the *qiang* all the way up for maximum thrust.

He must have heard it! Luka screamed in his head. *He must have heard it! Why isn't he moving? Is his armor hard enough to shield against such a powerful weapon? Is that frail body able to tolerate the assault coming his way?* In his mind the answer was yes because he knew that Atami had been training for moments like this all his life. But his heart ached, crying No!

All the ropes that bound Luka mentally broke loose. He employed the leopard's leap, his arms stretched out like the beast it was named after, with his legs trailing behind. He took off from five feet away, leaping over a few beggars' heads. For one brief moment, Luka was horizontal, shooting forward like an arrow toward the soldier, whom he would surprise from the back.

The beggars he passed over stared at him in shock, and the soldiers paused in alarm.

The tip of the *qiang* was falling with urgency, closer and closer to Atami, who still knelt like a dead turtle hugging the earth. It was only inches away from Atami's shiny scalp when Luka touched the ground, landing at the soldier's feet, and plunged his iron fingers into the soldier's *San Gu,* the hidden spot of vulnerability that Atami had taught him about, located in the back of a man's lower leg.

The soldier felt a shock of debilitating numbness shoot up his thighs, crotch, and shoulders before he collapsed. The blood-stained blade missed Atami's head only by a silk thread.

Atami woke up within his armor, his head jerking around like a mole testing his surroundings. He hadn't been disturbed by the chaos surrounding him, for within, he was at peace. It was Luka's presence that had stirred him.

What have I done? Atami wondered. *I have gotten the boy involved. He should have known that a thousand* jin *of weapons could not move me under the armor. Now the whole point of the armor—seeking peace instead of battle—would be forfeited, and Luka would be sucked out of the security of his childhood into the intricate web of the world.*

Atami wished he were a mother eagle, able to sweep the innocent child under his wings and soar up into the sky and far away into the mountains. But the soldiers were closing in. Escaping with Luka now would only provoke those determined to pursue them to their demise.

I must fight now before the six soldiers stab the young boy to death. I shall fight even at the risk of revealing our identities.

Drunken Monk was the tactic to use. And since he had to deal with only six puny opponents, he didn't even need to be very drunk.

In the Xi-Ling parlance, Drunken Monk meant to imitate an uprooted tree dancing in the wind, going everywhere and heading nowhere. His steps would be wobbling and his posture noodling, his arms twirling like a windmill and his head dangling like a melon. All parts would be moving, but none in the same direction.

Atami got up and stumbled drunkenly into the arms of the first soldier. The man, disgusted, grabbed his shoulders and pushed him around. Atami looked like a flopping fish, tossing his head back and forth, his arms flapping. With one big forward swing, Atami butted the soldier's forehead and unleashed enough *Qi* in that brief embrace to render his opponent unconscious.

The next target was a soldier with a mustache. Atami, not a

hairy man himself, had never liked anyone with grassy growth. He staggered forward and howled into the air, swiping his right arm—the one to avoid—and plunging his thumb between the man's shoulder blades. The man drooped forward as if he were melting.

The third target would not be an easy one, for he watched Atami's drunken charade with hawk eyes. He dropped his *qiang*, knowing that a long arm could not fight a short war, and pulled his dagger from the heel of his boot. He sliced a cross before him in warning.

Atami let out a string of tipsy laughter, waltzing closer in his random dance. He tripped over a little twig and his butt landed on the soldier's right foot. The brittle toes beneath him crumbled like dry cake under the force of Atami's grinding Iron Tailbone.

With three more to go, Atami had to hurry, and he grew even more out of control. He spun on the ground and in one sweep downed two enemies, who landed on top of each other.

The red-banded leader was the last one standing. He was not amused. Five men down. One frail monk, drunk. What had he been drinking? The leader backed away as Atami crawled toward him like an earthworm slithering in mud. As the leader turned to run, Atami pointed his index finger at the fleeing man. It emitted a beam of his inner *Qi*, which rocketed the man into the hardened face of the fortress wall.

Wham! The wall shook upon contact.

"Wow! Way to go!" Luka marveled.

"Don't worry. He won't remember what happened to him," Atami said.

From the corner of his eyes, Luka saw his two friends in action. They threw stones and rocks at other soldiers who were coming their way, shouting the dirtiest curses he had ever heard. Their strategy worked: the pelted soldiers chased after the two rogues. Luka knew that his friends would be safe. They would give the soldiers a run for their money before losing them in the dusty alleys of Peking.

He turned back to see that the fire had engulfed the hut. He could feel the burning heat and almost peed in his pants when he saw the woman crawling out of the hut, which was collapsing under the heat and flames. Luka raced to the hut and grabbed the woman. With all his strength, he pulled and pulled. The woman was struggling, but to no avail; her legs were paralyzed. For the first time, Luka felt the approach of death.

Atami arrived to help and they dragged the woman out just as the hut collapsed.

"Your Holiness, a life is worth saving even if it is half dead," the monk said.

"Yes, Atami, and thank you for saving mine."

Atami replied, "It was you who tried to save me first."

Luka hung his head. "I'm sorry. I thought I could, but I realize now that all I did was cause more trouble for you."

"That you did," Atami said, though he wanted so much to praise the boy for his bravery and selflessness. But he realized that a warning, instead of praise, would do him more good at this point.

"Your Holiness, always remember: your gift can be a blessing or a curse. Sometimes it is both."

He let Luka chew over the words a moment. Then he said, "Let's carry the woman to the edge of town and hide her in the shade."

Luka squatted down and lifted the woman's two burned legs over his shoulders. With the monk carrying the rest of her, they left the yard and struggled toward the edge of town. As they walked, Luka's knees shook and his arms grew numb, until he collapsed when they were under a dancing willow tree. He pinched his nose to block out the sickening smell of burnt flesh. "What should we do now?"

"Don't worry, she has passed on."

Luka jumped back from the unmoving body.

"It's okay, she is better off dead. I will pray tonight and the next three days for her spirit to completely leave her body. Then I will plan a Heavenly Burial for her."

"Heavenly Burial? Isn't that a Tibetan tradition?"

"It is indeed," said Atami. "She was Tibetan by descent. Her family had been driven here by the Mogoes. We have to bury her in the way of her ancestors or her spirit will never rise up to heaven. Would you like to witness that sacred ceremony, where the dead will be flown off to heaven forever?"

Luka nodded sadly.

"Remember what the Mogoes have done to innocent people. One day you will right the wrongs."

• • •

On the day of the Heavenly Burial, a large crowd gathered at the foot of a hill. Luka huddled with Mahing and Mahong.

"Hey, you were divine out there. That Mogo soldier ate dirt," Mahong said.

"Well, thanks for leading those soldiers away."

"Yeah, we make a great team," Mahong replied. "So what's your secret, Your Holiness? Maybe you can teach us a thing or two and we can fight with you against those Mogoes next time."

"It was nothing."

"Oh, it was something, believe me. We were there."

"I'm sorry," Luka said. "It is not mine to teach."

"And why is that?" Mahong asked, upset. "We got money."

"There are things money cannot buy. I have made a pledge to my master not to pass on his teachings while he is still alive."

"Hey, any agreement is made to be broken," Mahing said.

"Not this one," Luka replied.

In disappointment, the brothers rested their chins on a piece of rock and looked on. The ceremony began.

The diced chunks of the deceased woman, bloody and smelly, were laid out on the smooth slope of a rocky hill. The crowd at the foot of the rock was sad and solemn while clouds thickened above them. The only sound heard or felt was the whacking wings of hundreds of hungry vulture eagles. They circled about the bounty, darkening the already dark afternoon sky.

Atami chanted with a Tibetan monk, their heads low, their knees on the rocky ground. With the stained chopping knife by his side, the Tibetan monk begged those sacred eagles to descend and take what was left of the useless body, freeing the woman's spirit to ascend to heaven. Then the praying ceased. The crowd was quiet, not daring even to breathe, as the eagles swooped down.

Suddenly, Luka heard strange whooshing sounds. The eagles shrieked pathetically as they plummeted to earth.

Arrows darkened the sky. More eagles dropped, landing as messy and as bloody as the diced human flesh they had been about to devour.

More arrows, and more . . . until the eagles had all fallen from the sky. Not a squawk was heard; not a feather moved.

From behind a bush, a white flag sprang up. The Mogoes.

A platoon of *qiang*-carrying young soldiers jumped out of hiding and surrounded the pious Chinese gathered at the site. It was an ambush!

A voice boomed in the distance. "THE HEAVENLY BURIAL IS A SUPERSTITIOUS CEREMONY VIOLATING THE MOGO IMPERIAL PENAL LAW. ALL PEOPLE ARE TO DISPERSE QUIETLY AND IMMEDIATELY."

My enemy, Atami realized, recognizing the voice. He heard that cold voice every night in his nightmares. *He has found me again!* And he knew how. The battle at the fortress a few days back must have given him away. Where was Luka? Atami's eyes swept over the crowd.

Luka's shock was replaced by an outrage that shot all the way to the top of his head. He knew how sacred those eagles were re-garded in the ancient scriptures. They were more than just birds: they were a spiritual linkage to the distant past, to the very begin-ning of China. Seeing the eagles now, lying in the throes of their bloody death, Luka felt shaken. He wanted to throw up, but noth-ing came out. He wanted to cry, but there were no tears. His two friends didn't know what was happening to him. They thumped his back as he heaved.

"Are you sick, Your Holiness?" Mahing whispered.

"No, I'm not sick. I'm furious. Those eagles are our ancestors, did you know that?"

"Yeah, yeah, but it's not worth dying for them. Stay down," Mahong urged.

Luka threw their arms off his back and climbed onto a boulder. From his thin frame, a thunderous voice roared, "You barbarians! You killed our sacred eagles!" His words echoed among the moun-tain peaks, stirring the crowd. They too stood up fearlessly.

"Barbarians!"

"Barbarians!"

The quiet valley was flooded with outcries.

As the young boy stood atop the boulder addressing his people, Atami felt a fleeting moment of pride. What a majestic emperor Luka was, and how much he resembled his grandfather, the old emperor. But what was he doing up there? Did he know that his deadliest enemy was here hunting for his prey? What righteous-ness, what stupidity.

"People, my Chinese people, we cannot tolerate this invasion anymore!" Luka picked up a bloody arrow and charged toward the smiling Mogo soldiers.

At first they couldn't believe that such a little boy would dare do such a thing. But he was for real. He shouted the battle cry of ancient Chinese warriors, his robe flying in the wind as he ran barefoot, arrow raised high.

He has gone crazy, Atami thought. So too the other Chinese who picked up arrows and followed in Luka's path.

The Mogoes weren't smiling anymore. They aimed and unleashed more arrows, this time into the crowd heading their way. A dozen people were hit and fell.

Arrows whizzed by as Luka dodged left and right. *As long as he is rooted, he will be okay,* Atami thought.

The boy might have lost his mind, but not his gift. He zigzagged to a bank of boulders where archers were shooting. With one leap, the boy took off and landed on the screaming soldiers. Instantly, the arrows stopped raining and the soldiers cried in pain. A brief moment passed. Then all was quiet and still.

Fearing that Luka had been killed, Atami ran toward him. Then, amidst the swirling dust, the boy stood up, his face stained with blood. "Stay down!" Atami shouted. Luka turned to see the monk approaching.

What have I done? Luka thought. *And how am I going to get out of here?* he wondered as dozens of soldiers closed in on him. His head swiveled around and he saw his only route out—the end of the slope at the top of the cliff. Atami shouted, "Crawl up there!" Luka turned and quickened his strides, attempting to scale the last ten feet to the top of the slope, beyond which he knew was a sudden drop of forty feet down to thorny bushes. He would be bruised or even broken, but at least he would be alive. Atami was right. But that last ten feet was a steep, difficult climb. Even his *Tie Sha Zhang,* his Iron Hands, bled at the exertion of gripping the rock. When he was finally on the precipice, Luka took one last look back at Atami, who shouted, "Go with the flow and bury yourself among the waves."

Just as Luka was about to jump, Atami saw a sniper hidden behind the trunk of a thick tree take aim at the boy. Atami could see only the tip of the sniper's arrow, not the face of the assassin, but he knew who it was: the only man who could sniff out the identity of Luka.

You might think the tree shields you from detection and shelters you with protection, but Ghengi, you bastard, nothing is safe from the magic of Jin Gong, *least of all its archenemy.*

Atami drew out his *Jin Gong* dagger, concealed in a secret sheath up his sleeve, and kissed the tip. It was more than a weapon to him, for it had been handed down from one Xi-Ling warrior to another for hundreds of years. This dagger was blessed with a life of its own; it could see in darkness and detect its target beyond physical barriers. Each month, Atami blessed it with sacred prayers so that it retained its power and sharpened its knowing soul.

Atami threw it.

It would have been a futile throw had the dagger not been able to seek out its target with its own eyes. It did not fly straight but slithered like a snake, left and right, in an unpredictable manner to confuse its target. It came to a screeching stop in front of the hoisted arrow and stared at it. Then, with a kiss of its tip, the dagger killed the arrow, which fell to the ground in pieces.

"Aye!" Ghengi screamed from behind the tree.

The dagger turned and saw its enemy. It noiselessly sliced through the archer's right shoulder, severing the arm precisely and neatly from its joint. One could only imagine Ghengi's suffering from the agonized cry that followed.

The *Jin Gong* dagger knew it had done its job and that having leaped off the cliff, Luka was safe. It swept around the tree and faced its master, awaiting Atami's command. With a sweep of his arm, Atami called the gold dagger back to him. It flew in an arc and landed in his hand like a tame falcon after a deadly hunt.

All the soldiers rushed to their commander, tending to his bleeding shoulder. All except one, Ghengi's lieutenant, the best archer in the fortress. He hoisted another arrow and traced Atami's movement.

At the cliff's edge, the monk leaped up after Luka. Had he gotten there even a moment earlier, Atami could have saved the boy from the fall. But it was too late—forty feet too late. Luka tumbled down from one rock to the next, bouncing with painful cries. Atami's heart ached, and in that moment of tenderness, he became vulnerable. His emotions pulled all his energy around his heart. His back was left unprotected.

Ghengi's lieutenant was another kung fu man, well known in the Mogo mountains. He could not have gotten near the renowned Wu Xia master under any other circumstances, but now the moment had come. The lieutenant unleashed his poisoned arrow into the back of Atami's heel, cutting the monk's tendon. He knew that this was what his master, Ghengi, would have wanted him to do. The monk would not die, but neither could he run away anymore.

When Luka woke up again, it was night, and his two friends were breathing into his face. He saw broken walls and a shabby roof beyond them.

"Where am I?" Luka asked.

"An abandoned temple." Mahong's voice echoed.

"Why?" Luka asked.

"The Mogo patrols are everywhere looking for you. There are reward notices posted in every corner of the town. You're safe here."

"But not sound," said Mahing.

"What happened?"

"Atami was taken away by the Mogo soldiers. He was lucky. Many others died like those eagles."

"Where is he now?"

"No one will ever know."

"Ever?"

"They said he was heading to prison, but usually they behead captives the moment they're out of sight. And then they tell you the prisoner died of illness in prison and here is your lousy jar of bones."

"It can't be." Luka started to cry.

"Get a grip on yourself. Crying isn't going to do you any good," Mahong said.

"He was like my father."

"Father? We will find you another father if you want."

"I loved him, he raised me. I have to take revenge!"

"Would you stop crying? Act like a man!" Mahong slapped Luka's right shoulder and Luka slumped over.

"Oooow!"

"What hurt?"

"My shoulder."

"Let me see." Mahong, the self-anointed bone man, pushed aside Luka's shirt and inspected his shoulder with a wrinkled nose. He urged Luka to let go of his right arm and swing, just swing.

"It hurts when I try."

"I can see that, and it refuses to follow your order also."

"What's wrong with me?"

"It popped out."

"What should I do?"

"If you leave it, you will be in pain forever."

"Or?"

"Or I can fix it."

"Fix it how?"

"How is not your business."

"I don't trust you."

"Are you forgetting something? Who cured your servant that time when he was dying of dog bites?"

"You."

"Thank you."

"But this is different."

"Once a doctor, always a doctor," Mahing said in support of his brother.

"Easy for you to say. Why don't we let him fix you?"

"All right, I'm sick of your disrespect. Fix or no fix?" Mahong demanded.

Luka winced in pain. "Fix it, please."

"That's my boy. Mahing, get me the poison."

"Poison?" Luka asked.

"A brand of liquor, you scared rabbit. It will kill the pain as we fix your arm." Mahing pulled out a small bottle, but it was empty. "Oops!"

"Empty?" Mahong kicked his brother.

"I was nervous. The poison calmed me down."

"Now we can't fix his arm," Mahong said with disgust.

"Why not?" Luka asked.

"You'll die of pain if we do it without the numbing."

"I can take it," Luka said.

"Yeah, yeah, but we also need the liquor to keep the swelling down or your shoulder will swell like a tree trunk and rot like a melon."

"Where can we get some more?" Luka asked.

"From Laoren, that greedy fur merchant," Mahing said. "But nothing from him comes cheap."

"You got any money?" Mahong asked.

"I am penniless," Luka said. Then his face brightened. "Wait, I can sell this necklace." He pulled it out from under his shirt and wrapped it around his nose.

"A necklace?" Mahong took it and examined it. "Where did you get this piece of treasure, my little Holiness?"

"My mother."

"You never told us you got a mother."

"Where else would I have come from?"

"I don't know, from the rocks in the mountains?"

"My mother was a pretty woman, Atami once told me."

"I'd love to chitchat with you about your pretty mom, but my belly won't let me. Let's get to the bottom of this. Is it gold or silver?"

"Genuine gold."

"There are Mogo characters engraved here. Can you read any of it?"

"Sure, it says *batoo,* the Mogo word for *dragon.*"

"Why are there Mogo words on it?" Mahing asked.

"I don't know." Luka scratched his head.

"Do we care? My little Holiness, this is very impressive. Let's go pawn it for the liquor."

"But wait it's the only thing I have of my mother's."

"Forget that for now. We need to save your life. We'll get it back when we have the money. Let's go." Mahong carried Luka on his back and the Ma brothers raced breathlessly through the darkness of the night. They dodged the spots where Mogo night guards patrolled, traveling only by the narrowest lanes until they reached the merchant's house.

"What do you want?" The merchant peeped at them through a tiny keyhole in the squeaky red door of his storefront.

"I want to pawn this gold necklace," Mahong shouted.

"I don't trust you. Get lost!" The merchant's eye vanished from the hole and out poked the tip of a sword.

"Please let us in."

"No way, you thieves. Get lost!"

"Here. I'm passing the necklace through the hole for your inspection."

The sword was removed. Mahong pushed the jewelry inside and winked at his companions.

"This is worthless crap. Where did you get this from?" shouted the merchant from inside.

"Oh, the mother of His Holiness gave it to him."

"What holiness?"

"Here he is." Mahong pushed Luka before the hole, taking off his fur hat. "See, he is Your Holiness."

"Another filthy thief. Who is your mother?"

"A pretty woman called Zuma," said Luka.

There was a long pause. Then the merchant opened his door and let the three boys in.

"If you are who you claim to be, take off your shoes." The merchant grabbed Luka and inspected his profile.

"Come on, do as the man asked you to," Mahong urged Luka.

The two pushed the boy on the floor and each pulled one boot off. The old merchant flipped Luka's stinking feet up and gazed at the ten black moles, five on each sole. Then he helped Luka put the shoes back on.

"How much do you want?"

"How much? I want to pawn it for some Poison brand liquor and one hundred *yuen*," Mahong said.

The old man's eyes rolled. "A bottle of Poison and fifty *yuen*."

"Nope, can't do it," Mahong said. "Make me a better offer."

"My previous offer plus a good meal and a place to spend the night." Sounds of the searching Mogo patrols outside drifted through the window.

It was an offer none of them could refuse, least of all their stomachs.

"What are you cooking?" Mahing asked.

"Roast lamb and lots of *wawatos* with some liquor and fine tobacco. I got them all."

"Deal," Mahong said. "Pass the Poison now."

The merchant used a long pole to fetch a dusty jar from the top shelf. He handed it over to Mahong and said, "Fire away."

As Mahong popped the lid, a pungent aroma of concentrated liquor filled the air. "Are you ready, Luka?"

When Luka frowned, the brothers took matters into their own hands. Mahing grabbed Luka's head, Mahong pinched his nose, and down they poured the nastiest-tasting stuff Luka could ever have imagined. It exploded into his nose, throat, and the rest of his body. The effect was quick. He felt throbbing at his temple. His head lolled to the side and his pain was soon forgotten. As Luka dozed lightly, Mahong grabbed his right arm and jerked it. With a crunch, Luka's shoulder popped back into its socket.

"Now swing it again," Mahong ordered.

Half-awake, Luka did so. This time, the pain was gone. In his daze, Luka smiled, little pearls of tears wetting his lashes. The two barefooted doctors smiled back.

"I guessed it right again," Mahong said to Mahing. "It was the right twist."

"You mean you weren't sure?" Luka asked.

"Had I twisted your arm to the west, it would have been limp forever. Lucky for you, I twisted it east."

What followed was the ugliest feast ever to occur in the land of poverty. Grabbed handfuls of lamb meat, oily and slightly burnt, were stuffed down throats without much chewing. No time for that. Soon Mahong was noisily sucking the gooey marrow from a leg bone while Luka licked up the last bit of *wawato*. Mahing held an empty liquor jar in midair waiting for the last drop to land on his wagging tongue.

All the while, the merchant was humming, smoking, and polishing the newly acquired necklace engraved with the official Mogo seal. He had just made the deal of his life. He smiled and threw the kids another full liquor jar. The three celebrated the end of the feast with an echoing round of bubbling burps.

As soon as the boys had fallen asleep like little piglets in the warm earthen bed called *kang*, Laoren noiselessly slipped out the back door. He locked it from outside and headed for the nearest Mogo patrol stationed in the market square.

AT SUNRISE, A terrible noise awakened Luka and the two brothers. At first Luka thought it was a dream, but he was soon proven wrong as ten young Mogo soldiers rushed into the storefront, tied the boys up, and stuffed their mouths with foul-smelling cloth. Mahong shrugged and garbled a question. The soldiers ignored him and threw the trio into the back of a locked carriage, which took them under the morning stars to a little jail behind the army compound where they kept petty thieves. The warden dumped a bucket of cold water over them and they were untied only to wait in a small cell.

"Laoren betrayed us!" Luka said.

"That old root. I'm going to cut his tongue out the next time I see him," Mahong said.

"Let's think of a way to escape first." Luka looked around the seamless cell and sighed.

"We're trapped. I'm sorry. I shouldn't have drunk the Poison," Mahing cried. "Now we're going to die."

"We're not," Luka said.

"How can you be sure?" Mahing asked.

"Because we are too young to die."

"That's a lousy reason," Mahong said.

The warden appeared again, this time with a nameplate for each. They compared the wooden plates hung around their necks. As long as they were together, they were happy, if not brave and confident. Fear filled their hearts and choked their throats. It was serious this time.

The worst part was not knowing what would happen to them and no one was telling. The uncertainty was killing them, even Mahong, the experienced daredevil. As for Mahing, he would be happy just being the shadow of Mahong. Being separated would be worse than death itself. Their companionship was the only treasure the brothers possessed in this world. Silently they waited for their destiny.

Hours later, two soldiers came to take them. The thin one looked mean and the tall one looked rough. They forced the three down the long hall out into the street. There stood two horse-drawn carriages with the imperial army insignia—black stallions—printed on the side. These were the carriages used to transport criminals.

"You two will go to the first carriage," the tall soldier told Mahing and Mahong. "And you over to the second one," he said to Luka.

"Where are you taking me?" Luka cried.

"Shut up," the thin man ordered.

"Somewhere far, I hope," the tall one added with a grin.

"I don't want to go alone! Throw me in there with them," Luka shouted, but he was ignored. They stopped near the back of the carriages, where their arms were untied.

"They're going to Water Prison, I'm sure," one bystander shouted.

"They're going to the prison in Lanka," said another.

"Poor orphans."

"Dirty thieves."

Some threw rocks at them, while others spat in their direction.

"Stay where you are and enjoy your public reception. Your drivers will be here soon." The two soldiers went to sit on a bench near the entrance ten yards away.

In the crowd, the old fur merchant appeared with beads of sweat on his forehead. He pushed his way through the ring of spectators and surreptitiously stuffed a folded piece of paper into Luka's hand. "Read it and you will know," he whispered.

"What is it?"

"All I can say is that I am sorry. Read it later, not now."

Luka was both curious and moved by the old man's strange behavior. When the two drivers came, Mahong and Mahing were dumped into the first carriage and Luka was pushed alone into the second one. With their eyes, the friends said goodbye. No tears. They didn't know if they would live to see each other again or what destination they were being sent to. Luka would miss them, those rascals, for his life and fate would never offer another pair of friends half as good or as loyal.

Luka watched until he could see them no more. Had he known where he was heading, he would have said goodbye to Peking and its mountains, and taken a last long look at the Forbidden City. But he didn't.

PART 2

友友真友

CELL MATES AND SOUL MATES

因
友
真
友

LUKA HID THE merchant's letter in his inside pocket as soon
as the carriage pulled away from the shouting crowd in front of
the army base. Each day Chinese were hauled away from there,
and the village children saw it as the daily big event. They threw
things at the prisoners and chased them in the dust that followed.
Luka sat in a corner of the carriage on the icy floor, thin and
small, away from the window, so that the rocks and water would
not touch him. He did not know where he was going, nor did he
care. His Atami was gone, as were his two friends. This town
was going down as far as he was concerned. He might do better
in another. Atami had taught him not to chew on the same
bone forever.

As soon as the carriage was a safe distance away, Luka pulled
out the note from the old merchant. It read simply:

> *Dear Holiness,*
>   *I am convinced beyond doubt that you are the little*
> *emperor we have prayed for. And if it is so, in your*

final days, I, as one of your humble flock, owe it to you to reveal the secret you were born with. Your father is none other than the Mogo emperor Ghengi. You may question me, or even punish me in heaven for having told you so, but this truth is as big as the Tai Mountain.

Zuma, your mother, was a tender flower of the mountain at sixteen. She used to come to my fur store and admire my beautiful things, of which I have too many. One day she was said to have been abducted by Ghengi. Nine months later she had you. Gossip or rumor. I got my eyes and ears around here.

Had you not been on your way to death, I would not have dared insult Your Holiness with this dark secret. I am pious, and the pious do only the righteous thing. Even though I, as you know, have committed many sins—including tipping off the Mogoes to your whereabouts, which led to your capture and the possibility that you will never be back at all—I have said my prayers before Buddha many times, and I will say many more to cleanse myself of such wrong. I swear to you as you are still breathing and living that I shall repent. Please bless me in life and death. And please do not send me to hell for this small mishap, for men are prone to many follies, as you would have come to know. I wrote this letter hurriedly so that you will die knowing the truth. Please find me a place in heaven when I leave

*this world, and forgive me for all the ill profits I made
during my career of fur trading and for this one-time
windfall of reward money. I could not help it. It was all
too tempting.*

                                                    Laoren

Luka was jolted out of his seat.

His mother, the most beautiful woman in his mind, with the ugly, evil Ghengi? And worse yet, Ghengi might be his father? That monster? Luka was angry and confused. More, he was scared. *I am going to die. I am going to die. Why am I going to die?*

It took him awhile, sitting in the corner of the carriage, to figure out that there was something irreconcilable between him and Ghengi. He was supposed to be Ghengi's son, but he lived in hell while Ghengi lived in paradise. Ghengi had gotten rid of Luka's mother and Atami. Now it was Luka's turn. He was a sore in the Mogo's eyes. That he understood.

The same dreadful thoughts repeated over and over in Luka's mind as the carriage jolted along the rocky road. He thought they might take him to a desolate mountain peak with lots of wild animals. They might hang him, or worse, bury him alive, so that the dogs would dig him up and chew him to a painful death. He threw himself at the back door of the carriage, but it was thick and solid, with locks all over it.

Hours went by and days passed. The end wasn't as near as he had anticipated. The carriage just rolled on and on. They descended from the northern plateau along hundreds of *li* (similar to miles) of lonely, pitted roads down to the flat land of the south near the foot of the Tai Mountain. And the journey almost killed him.

Food was only a few pieces of sour bread with a jar of water the driver scooped up from ditches by the roadside. The little window allowed him fleeting glimpses of white tigers and nameless wild predators and prey running alongside the carriage. The air felt wetter, the trees were thicker, and the leaves grew broader as they dropped inch by inch in altitude. They finally arrived at a small town.

"Where am I?" Luka drummed the wall of the carriage, shouting.

"Ghost Town," the Mogo shouted back through the crack in the carriage, which clanked along on the cobbled street. "People come here to be condemned."

The carriage lurched to a sudden stop and the door was unlocked and thrown open. The bright sunlight shocked Luka's eyes. Two thickly built Mogoes grabbed him by his arms and dragged him into a heavily guarded chamber. He was given a prison uniform and taken to a hearing room, where one old officer sat and smoked a pipe. The space was filled with the pungent smell of his tobacco.

"What is the charge?" the judge asked the officer.

The officer whispered into the judge's ear, and the judge's eyebrows rose all the way up his prominent forehead.

"Born to die, huh?" the Mogo judge said.

"I didn't do anything wrong," replied Luka.

"You don't have to do anything wrong." He slammed his gavel. "Under Penal Code Section 99, you are now sentenced to death by hanging. Normally, you would be executed in ten days, but given the local ordinance and labor shortage, you are to serve in labor reform for another six months. Therefore your execution is delayed for that length of time."

The verdict exploded in Luka's head. "Your Honor, please . . . ," Luka cried.

"Remove him from my courtroom, guards!"

Luka's knees felt weak and his head dizzy. The words *death by hanging* rang like the thunder that accompanied a shuttering typhoon. Struggling against the guard's grip like a trapped animal, he didn't even feel pain as the Mogo clubbed him on the back of the head.

When he awoke, Luka found himself alone in a dark cell. He leaped to his feet from the narrow bed and touched the cold, sweaty surface of the walls around him. Each step he took was followed by a deep echo. The nauseating odor of moss, mold, and urine surrounded him.

Luka despaired, but only for a moment. Then, he grit his teeth and let out a guttural cry. He would cure himself with the inner strength that came with his *Jin Gong* training. He saw only the sunlight. In the darkest night, he was determined to find the beacon that would always shine. And he would live. Luka took the six-month delay as an omen, a fortunate one, for the longer he had to live, the better his chances of escape.

The next day, the jailer's gong woke him up. Rubbing his eyes, he moved with the rest of the prisoners in a slow procession sadder and gloomier than that of a royal funeral.

As he exited the prison, Luka looked around, sizing up the place. The gray stone walls were topped with spear tips and had to be at least twelve feet high. Outside, below the wall, ran a peaceful ditch pretending to be a canal. On top of the south wall sat a lookout from which hidden arrows aimed at the prison windows. Guards with *qiangs* roamed about, smoking and chatting. Barren hills sat as a backdrop fifty yards from the prison wall.

Ahead of Luka, a guard whipped a prisoner, who yelled in pain. Luka turned to face front and fell in step behind the man. The sea, though miles away from the prison wall, loomed like a rising dome, gleaming with the promise of sunlight. Luka sighed at the realization that he lived between two of his favorite natural makings, the great sea and the mysterious mountains. In either direction he could disappear into forever like the fish or the tiger. But to get there would take planning and persistent effort. Six months! A few inches a day. If he was to find a way out of this death trap, he would have to start right now. There was no time to rest. But where and how to start?

The work camp for the condemned was as quiet as a tomb. The guards patrolled frequently. Luka saw around him sad eyes emitting nothing except despair and blankness. The old man next to him on the assembly line, who passed the basket of wet soil for the dam, looked more like a skeleton than a living human. His eyes were sunken and haunted, his legs, scarcely clad with the prison blue, were covered with red wounds that oozed green pus. He had more flies buzzing over those red, gory, teary craters on his bony calves than a dead swine lying in wet mud. The old man hardly paid any attention. Only when one of the flies accidentally got lucky and landed right on the heart of the sore would the man jump, not instantly but with a delayed reaction, only to squat down afterward in great pain that radiated to his colorless face. But even then, he would check over his shoulder first to see that no guards were looking, otherwise he would remain upright, gritting his teeth and shaking in agony, enduring the poking and clawing of the wanton fly drilling the softest spot and licking off the juice of his rotten flesh.

Luka could only convey his sympathy with his eyes and shake his head quietly. Each time the old man squatted down, Luka took the load of soil and walked to the next man in line. The first time he did this, the old man stared at him with his dead eyes and murmured, "You're new here, aren't you?"

"Yes."

"If that dog Warden Otto sees you helping me, he'll punish you."

"Thank you, but I think you need help."

Hearing Luka talking to his neighbor, the warden ran over and slammed the handle of his *qiang* down onto Luka's bare right foot. As Luka crouched in pain, anger shot through his young head and the veins in his temple throbbed. He picked up a rock the size of his fist and threw it at the back of the warden's head.

The whole camp stood in silence as Otto went down on his face, eating dirt. As soon as two other guards picked him up, the warden grabbed a bow. Arrows flew out at Luka.

Luka thought he was hit when a sheet of dirt forced him backward to sit on the wet ground. Patting his body all over and not feeling any pain, he struggled to his feet. He was met by the thumping weight of wooden *qiang* butts raining down on him. Luka defended himself with his hands, arms, and legs, but something smashed his right temple and he landed on his back in a nearby ditch.

A sharp whistle was blown and order was restored. The prisoners were whipped away to resume the assembly work around the hill, while Luka was left to lie unconscious in the mud, where he stayed for the rest of the day. Of all the people at the camp, only the old man stole a few secretive peeks at him in sympathy for the young and ignorant.

When Luka awoke, the day was waning on the seaside town, and he was surprised to find a group of young girls staring down at him with wide eyes. They wore dark blue blouses and baggy pants made of coarse cloth. The only features distinguishing them from boys were their delicate frames and feminine voices. In a fog, Luka waved to them, that little exertion hurting him all over. His eyes came to rest on a tall, elegant girl around his age whose sweet smile soothed his dizzy head. Her eyes were intelligent and big, her nose narrow and straight, and her face long and thin with high cheekbones. For a moment that seemed like an eternity, their eyes met and locked until Luka blushed.

"Are you the new death row boy?" she whispered.

"Yes, my name is Luka. And you?"

"We are orphans who work in the uniform factory here." She tilted her head toward a shabby bungalow that stood in the west. "We saw you here and thought you were beaten to death, but we fed you some water and now here you are, alive."

"We've got to go. The warden is coming!" another girl whispered.

In the distance, Luka saw his fellow prisoners marching toward him, the sunset behind them.

"Here, this is for you." The tall girl pressed the stem of a flower into Luka's hands.

Luka was moved. He sat up and tucked the flower into his pocket. "What is your name?"

She turned around, showing three numbers stitched to her back.

"Three-three-three?"

"But my real name is Hali." She smiled sadly and whispered, "Lie down quickly and pretend to be asleep."

Luka did as he was told, and the girls rushed off like a swarm of butterflies in a summer garden.

"You orphans! Stay away from the prisoner," Warden Otto shouted.

Luka stole a last look at the angel. As their eyes met again, Luka's heart thumped like a little fist above his empty stomach. He saw not the dull, faded color of her uniform but a beautiful rose budding defiantly in cold winter.

Two prisoners carried him back to his tiny cell, which was half underground. As a thread of moonlight penetrated the narrow window near the ceiling, Luka laid the flower on his pillow and knelt on the hard earth of the floor. He clasped his hands together, worshipping the kind, demure moon goddess. He meditated, blocking out his misery, and tried to breathe in the mountains from beyond the cell walls. At this calm moment, he could almost smell the fresh mushrooms and touch the morning dew resting on the leaves of ancient oak trees.

Yet ultimately, there was nothing to do besides sleep. His young body screamed out to reach the outside world so freely given to him and now was so far away and unattainable. He tried to steer his mind away from his pending execution and challenged himself to think of any way to escape, but a heavy, gloomy sense of death hung low in the air. For the first time, Luka was scared, not of death but of being alone among the living dead.

But Luka was determined to discipline himself. He sat with his legs crossed like the monks in the mountains and meditated. Then he exercised. The first night he slept eight hours, overcome by the unusually heavy workload. The second night, he cut down to six and practiced *Jin Gong*. All the while, he concentrated on one thought only: escape.

On day three, around midnight, he heard his cell door open. It was Warden Otto, with his butcher's face and double chin. Then quietly, almost like a ghost, the old man with the rotten legs snuck into the cell, carrying an empty night pot to replace Luka's used one.

The old man kept his head low and his eyes fixed on the ground.

One hand carried a kerosene lamp that illuminated his pale face. Luka did not seem to exist as far as he was concerned. With effort, the old man picked up the old pot, left the new one there, and trailed after Warden Otto. The door slammed and the lock clicked.

Luka watched the whole incident silently but with interest. That was it! He smiled in the darkness. Tomorrow he would work on the old man.

The next morning before sunrise, the inmates fell into line in the courtyard again. The dogs were barking and the guards pacing, whipping some prisoner who had stepped out of line.

Luka, as usual, walked behind the old man who coughed weakly and rubbed his hands for warmth, his slight frame shaking like a sieve. The cool air of the southern fishing town, nippy for an old man, was refreshing and exhilarating for Luka. He couldn't wait for an opportunity to communicate with the old man, and finally nudged him in the back while the guards were lighting their smokes.

"Hey, you changing pots every three days?"

The old man ignored him.

Luka nudged him again.

This time the man turned around and stared at Luka with angry eyes.

"Come on. Just nod, yes or no."

The old man narrowed his eyes and his nostrils flared. For the rest of the day, he refused even to look in Luka's direction. Three nights later, the man came again with a guard. This time, the old man winked at Luka before he left.

A week went by and nothing happened. Then one day, the work camp suddenly became noisy with the sounds of Chinese instruments. A group of young children from the nearby school were performing their school play for the guards, whose lives were almost as deadened as the prisoners'. While they sat for the show, only one young guard was left watching the fifty prisoners who were still working. But soon, even this last guard was so taken with the children's performance that he too sat down, lit a smoke, and hummed to the tunes.

Luka was surprised when the old man seized him by the sleeve and whispered, "How long is your sentence to be delayed?"

"Six months."

The old man rolled his eyes, calculating silently. "Too young to die." He shook his head, looking lost.

"I have a favor to ask you."

"Shhh." The old man looked around. "Do not talk to me. I will talk to you. Check your night pot tonight. Now look away."

Luka picked up his hoe and resumed digging as the guards returned.

That night when the old man entered, following Warden Otto, Luka remained very quiet. As usual, he lay on his bed, pretending to be sound asleep.

"Get up," the warden ordered.

Luka jumped off the bed and stood before him rubbing his eyes. "Yes, sir."

"Put up your arms." The warden patted him down quickly, spun him around, and stormed out.

Quietly, the old man changed the pots. At the door, he turned his head, winked at Luka, and left. When the footsteps died down, Luka moved like a night mouse to the pot and turned it over. There was nothing there. He puzzled over it for a brief moment, then opened the lid. There, at the bottom, he saw a cloth bag. In it was the broken head of a small hoe, and folded into a little square, a note. Luka opened it urgently and read the shaky calligraphy again. *Dig west to the pothole outside the wall.*

It was the direction to the back of the cells. The idea pleased him but the distance did not. Every day as he returned from work, Luka counted the steps from the front entrance through the courtyard to his prison cell. It was a good fifty yards. As far as he could tell, the distance from his cell to the surrounding back wall had to be at least thirty-five steps; a whopping voyage for the tiny hoe. But the key concern here would be the quality of the soil. If it was the loose red soil that prevailed in the south, the digging would take less time. If not, the soil would be harder, and there was the possibility that some parts might be grainy rock.

As Luka grabbed the hoe from under his straw pillow and weighed it in his hand, a mysterious power swept over him. It was not a magical tool, but it was the only thing he had and all his convictions in life, his dreams and his future lay in this meager tiny hoe. Atami's words rang in his ear. *You were born to overcome and excel. There is greatness in you!*

It was after midnight when the moon crept through the tiny

window. He pulled aside his bed, faced the moon, which was setting in the west, and dug the first chip out of the ground. From that night on, he slept at most four hours a day. His body clock woke him up, and he dug until the moon had set and the sky showed silver. Then he slept until the knock at the cell door rudely woke him for a breakfast of soupy porridge.

At the work camp his energy level was high and he didn't show any sign of fatigue. He smiled more, even hummed a few bars of his northern melodies. At the end of each day, he would pick up that flower left for him at the crossroad. Each day brought a different bloom and each bloom signified life rather than death. How he wished to catch another glimpse of that girl. But he never did. The only trace of her was the fragrance of the petals and the freshness of the dew.

One day, during the five-minute lunch break, Luka was humming over a bowl of moldy yams. The old man stared at him from his bowl and stepped hard on his right foot. "Shut up."

"Why?"

"No one in here is supposed to be so lighthearted," he hissed, smacking the back of Luka's head.

"Thank you," Luka whispered. Again the old man had saved his neck.

Every night Luka advanced about two and a half inches. The dampness of the dark red soil allowed him to dig with little noise. Fifteen days later, he had opened up an L-shaped tunnel under his bed that would allow him to sleep in it curled up. And what joy it was to lie down there for a brief rest, close his eyes, and dream about the outside world.

One night when Luka had just crawled into the hole, he heard heavy footsteps thumping down the hallway. He froze with fear, for there were always unannounced inspections on this ward. If the steps were coming his way, he would have barely enough time to climb out and pretend to be asleep. And there was no way he could change his clothes covered with the dirt he had been digging.

Quickly, he wriggled out of the hole like an earthworm and moved the bed over to cover it. One leg of the bed got caught in the hole. He cursed himself for being so sloppy and lifted the leg out. The steps came closer, and then stopped. Luka knew they were for him but had no time to wonder why. He stripped off his clothes and stuck them into the night pot filled with his waste. When Warden Otto yanked open the door, Luka was standing naked, bowed over his pot. He had stuck his index finger deep into his throat and was throwing up whatever was left of his meager dinner.

"Unannounced inspection. Stand still," Warden Otto shouted.

"I can't. My stomach hurts."

The room reeked of his puke and the warden flinched at the smell. He looked in every corner of the room with his lantern. The warden lingered at the bed and was about to check under it when Luka fell on his back and puked again, right on the warden's foot.

"Cut the crap and clean this mess off my feet!"

"Okay, okay, sir," Luka mumbled, rubbing his quilt over the warden's shoes. Otto slapped him and left, pinching his nose. Long after he was gone, Luka murmured his thanks to Buddha for the rest of the sleepless night.

因
友
真
友

ANTICIPATION OF DEATH was worse than death. One was languid, the other instant. Despite his optimism, Luka couldn't help feeling depressed at times, though he was driven to a kind of madness for survival. He was like a young mountain tiger trapped in a pit, looking death in the face, clawing the steep walls only to slide back down with bloody paws.

Every night when the moon started its eastern climb, shedding a slice of light through the crack of his tiny window, Luka would stand on his bed and let the light wash his face. With the moonlight upon him, he could smell the mountain flowers scattered in the endless valley of the northern plains. Thoughts of these and all the things that mattered in his life spurred him to crawl again into that small tunnel he had dug so deep into the foot of the western mountain.

It had been four months since he had started the tunnel, yet he was nowhere near where he should be. His original estimate of progress had been far too optimistic. The passage had been choked with rocks and he was a month off his plan. He was getting anxious, and at times dug so furiously that he thought his arms would fall off. The first few days of his digging, his blisters had been big and ugly and had burst into rotten red openings, but Luka had dug on. What was a little blister in the face of death, and what was a little pain to the joy of life? His blisters had soon hardened into calluses. On the occasions he rubbed his face with those hands, he jumped at his own touch. They didn't feel like his hands anymore, but rather like seasoned tiger hides. He gently rubbed the five moles under his feet. They were meant for something, the monk had said, for he was the Chosen. Luka smiled and found strength pouring back into him and sleepiness vanishing like the shadow of a ghost.

Each time he pulled out his secret weapon to start his nightly labor, he thought of the good and kind old man who had passed him the little hoe. He didn't even know the prisoner's name, only his number—788. Each morning, walking behind him, Luka felt the burden of debt he owed the wobbling man.

One morning, 788 walked with a new charge of energy. His hands did not shake as much as usual and he seemed to be an inch taller. He even let his arms swing normally, back and forth, not like his usual wooden gait. Of course, the sun was bright and a nice sea breeze was rustling the leaves of the nearby tree. But it was just another doomed day in this town. Nothing unusual to make the old man skip like a little child.

At the curve, 788 turned and winked at him. It was a good wink with a little story in it. Not a yes or no wink or a good morning or good night wink. It said: *I have good news.* A mystery. Luka was itching to know it.

At noon, the fat cook scooped lunch from a big wooden barrel with a dirty ladle. He was always in a hurry and angry for no reason whatsoever. If you were lucky, you caught the whole ladle. But often, he would spill only half of it and move on to the next empty bowl. You couldn't complain, for if you did, you would get nothing at the next few meals. The practice fit the prison policy just fine. Feed them enough to keep them alive but not enough to make them strong so they can escape. A model prisoner was one with ribs you could count, a sunken stomach you could see, and shrunken cheeks you could feel. No light gleaming in the eyes and no strength to desire anything. 788 had been a perfect example of that policy, living a dead man's life.

But the walking dead man wasn't himself. He sat close to Luka and looked left and right before pouring half of his meal into Luka's bowl as he usually did. "I'm getting out," the old man almost sang.

Luka was shocked by the wonderful news. "When are you leaving?".

"Soon, but . . ." He paused, looking out for guards, his old habit, which Luka thought was going to accompany the man for the rest of his life. His voice trailed down to a bare whisper of sound. "You just wait and see. I might be able to help you. Silence now, the dog is coming."

Though there was nothing this old man could do for him, Luka was happy, so happy for him. He had said more within a minute than he had in all the months they had been stacked together. His voice had changed. Color Luka thought the man had never had

had somehow returned to his skin. The whole afternoon, Luka saw him digging and humming. And occasionally, smiling. A smile to himself. What freedom—or just the expectation of it—could do to an old man was amazing.

Night fell again. Luka, as usual, stood on his bed, waiting for the touch of the young moon. Then his nightlife resumed. He was only twenty feet deep, while he should have been twenty-five. At this speed, he would be hanged soon and all his efforts would have been in vain. He could taste death in his mouth. Maybe it was the taste of blood, but he could sense it and it was disgusting, choking him. He wanted to scream at the top of his lungs at the injustice of the world, but he could not lest someone hear him. Tears trickled down his face. He rarely cried, not even when he had been given the death sentence, but today brought an added loneliness that he had never felt before. It was 788's news. The old man, his nervous state, his thieflike existence, would be gone and Luka would be left alone, knowing nobody, only the hateful faces of the wardens. He would be left with only the rats that sometimes visited him in his sleep, the snakes that swam in the ditches he stood by every day, and the brief touch of the moonlight. Though he was truly happy for the old man, his sadness increased.

But Luka was born to endure and persevere. He slapped himself for being such a wimp, picked up his hoe, and dug on. He praised himself for being able to block out his emotions and attack his target logically and rhythmically, as a good mountain man would, trapped in an unexpected avalanche in the mountains. Coolheadedness . . . that was it. So, coolheadedly, he dug on for hours.

Almost near daybreak, Luka came to a wall of wet and hard rock. He stopped only briefly to study it. It was a seamless piece of rock, the first of its kind he had encountered so far. He wasn't going to be stopped that easily. So he dug upward. Still the rock. Then downward, then left, and then right. He made the tunnel six feet wide. Still there was no end to the rock. He wondered if it was just the tip of an enormous boulder. If that was the case, he was a dead man. The plan itself had hit a rock. By then he was too tired to feel anything anymore and could only lean against the cool stone, feeling totally defeated and lost. *Curse the rock!* With that thought he crawled back to his little bed and fell into a dreamless sleep.

The next morning, for the first time in months, Luka felt hopeless. There was a rock sitting heavy in his heart, pushing his mood lower and lower. The morning gong, which had been to him a symbol of life, now sounded like a death toll. He didn't even look at his bowl of breakfast. He felt physically and emotionally full.

When Luka saw 788 again, the old man looked especially tired. A few times Luka tried to talk to him but 788 just turned away and looked elsewhere. It was strange that he should behave that way. Luka needed the old man's advice. When he turned to nudge the old man again, he saw that he was fast asleep during the little rest time they had.

788 repeated his strange behavior over the next few days.

Luka was now burning with desperation. Each night, he revisited the rock. And each time, he was more convinced that there was nowhere to go. He wished he had the strength to blast through the rock and make a hole out of this misery, but that would never happen. Every night, before he unwillingly closed his eyes for the luxury of sleep, he scratched another day off his makeshift calendar on the wall. Another futile day, another day closer to his demise. Would he feel anything? Would he become a ghost or would he just be a puddle of ashes, eventually blown away by the breeze and gone forever? Come from nothing, returned to nothing?

That night Luka cried himself to sleep.

THE NEXT MORNING, 788 was not to be seen. He must have been released. In front of Luka stood another inmate, number 787. He was a middle-aged man with a hunched back and shifty eyes. How could 788 be gone just like that, without any notice or trace?

Later, as he was scratching another day off the wall, Luka heard thunder in the east. A storm was coming. According to local fishermen, eastern thunder meant the gathering of rain from the sea and sea winds, which would blow inland. Lightning sliced the sky.

Luka's thoughts were suddenly disturbed by a noise coming from the wall against which his bed was laid. He closed his eyes, concentrating. In the lull, he heard it again. It was coming closer and closer. Luka glued his ears to the wall and realized that the sound was not coming from the wall but from the floor. Someone was digging!

He waited with alarm and joy warring in his heart, and held his hoe in his hand, ready to jump the intruder when the sound was but a skin away from the floor under the bed. Luka quickly moved the thin bed and hid behind it. Finally, with a cracking thud, another hole in the floor opened right next to his, as someone tunneled through. A face covered with dirt popped up. It was none other than his beloved old friend.

"788!" Luka dropped his hoe and helped him up. "How in Buddha's name did you do it?"

"I have been working on it for a while. Come now, I want you to visit me."

Luka jumped into the hole.

"Pull the bed over."

"Where am I going?"

"My place."

Luka crawled behind the old man along the narrow but quite neat tunnel that 788 had dug.

"How did you make the tunnel so smooth?" Luka asked, climbing out of the tunnel into 788's cell.

788 held up his hands. His fingers stood like ten thick metal nails.

"Your fingers?"

He nodded, just looking at Luka as if he were seeing him for the very first time. Then he took Luka's hand and guided him to sit on his bed. "Do you know who I am?"

"I know you are my savior."

"That's insignificant. I know you. Your name is Luka."

Luka was shocked. In this hell called prison everyone was known only by his number. "How did you know my name?"

"Guess." A rare grin was creeping onto the old man's face.

"Cell record?"

"No, not at all." The old man broke into a full smile. "I felt the presence of you on the very first day of our encounter."

"You did?"

"And I was much pleased to be confirmed of my sense by the moles under your feet."

Another shock. "My moles?"

"Remember the day you were passed out in the ditch, feet up in the air? I couldn't believe my eyes."

Luka clutched his chest, fear squeezing him and Atami's words ringing in his ears. *Never let anyone know who you are.*

"There is no cause for alarm." 788 put his hands on Luka's shoulders.

"Who are you?"

"My name is Gulan."

"Gulan?" He knew that name. *Where did I hear it?* Then it came to him. That sacred name had only been mentioned once, on that very special night when Atami had initiated him into the art of *Jin Gong.* Luka shot out of his seat and grabbed the man. "You are my master's master?"

"Grandmaster, then." The old man nodded with a grin.

Luka dropped to his knees, bowing his head to the floor, kowtowing. One, two, three times. "Forgive me, Grandmaster. Your humble disciple has been blind. Please punish me. I have been rude, ignorant—"

"Up, up! And stop banging your head, you will break it." He held

Luka's face in his hard hands, studying him. "My Holy Boy. Oh, you *are* my Holy Boy."

"Forget Holy Boy. Please tell me why you are here?"

"To save our Xi-Ling kung fu." He wrinkled his nose and narrowed his eyes as if looking into the darkness of his past. "You see, our brotherhood has long been a sore spot for Emperor Ghengi, for it is in our blood to fight the injustice on earth.

"Fifteen years, ten months, and three days ago, on one dark night, all our Xi-Ling warriors found themselves besieged by the Mogo imperial garrison troops. They accused us of committing treason."

"Why?"

"For being in alliance with the deposed Chinese emperor, Lulan. It all started when Ghengi found out that one of my ablest masters had secretly joined the resistance force to fight the Mogo invaders. His name was Mudana Mutami Atami."

"My Atami?"

"Yes, a very patriotic Atami." Gulan nodded and continued. "He became the old emperor Lulan's highest-ranking general. Atami led the great Chinese forces from one victory to another."

"But Atami never told me any of this."

"There are many things he kept from you for your own good," Gulan murmured. "Soon, tragedy would befall them. Mind you, it was not due to any lack of bravery or courage on Atami's part. Rather, it was due to his soft heart."

"What do you mean?"

"For years, Atami fought the Mogo imperial forces, leading his troops by day, guarding the old emperor and his family by night. He traveled with them over high mountains and across turbulent rivers. It was during those long journeys that he fell in love with the emperor's beautiful daughter, Zuma."

"My mother?"

Gulan nodded. "Yes, it was an error of the heart, beyond the calculation of his clear mind. There was no fault in loving one as worthy as Zuma. But the misfortune lay in the fact that Zuma was also the object of admiration of the Mogo emperor Ghengi."

Luka was in the tailspin of a whirling storm. The revelation was too much for him, and the suspense was killing him. "What happened?"

"Atami was too much of a monk. Their love for each other could only be kept a secret. She was afraid of risking her father's disapproval and of threatening the future of a great general. So they were always apart, Atami fighting battles and Zuma hiding from the Mogoes. But their hearts were always together. Love tortured them.

"Then one day Atami was informed that Zuma was missing and that her horse had returned riderless to camp. Alone on his horse, Atami set out to find her. He fought and killed the soldiers in his path, searching for her. But when he finally found her, Zuma, your mother, had already been taken by Ghengi." Gulan bowed his head and Luka's fists clenched.

"But there was more tragedy to come. There had been a deadly ambush back at their camp while Atami was gone. All the tents had been burned, the horses slaughtered, and his men killed. The old emperor and his family all died in the blaze."

Tears glistened in Luka's eyes like raindrops, and the old man wiped them gently away with his sleeves. "Atami escaped with Zuma and hid in the forest. They wandered and wandered until the night of your birth. It was on a cliff that your life began." His face darkened. "It was also on that very cliff your mother's life ended."

"How? How did she die?"

"She flew off the cliff like an eagle and thus was forever freed."

Luka was shaken with uncontrollable sobs. Yet in his mind, he saw a beautiful mother eagle extend her graceful wings and in one swoop glide down into the depths of a green valley.

"With her gone, you are the only heir left in the long bloodline of the Lu Dynasty. Atami named you after your grandpa, Lulan, and devoted his life to raising you. In all his letters to me, he poured out his love for you and described in the minutest detail what you looked like: your swordlike brows that signify fortitude; your straight, tall nose—authority; wide mouth—generosity; hooked chin—defiance; soaring ears—power known to the four corners of the earth; and those moles—that precious heavenly sign designating you as the rarest and greatest of all emperors."

"But what does all this have to do with you and your imprisonment?"

The old man chuckled. "After the fall of Emperor Lulan, Ghengi demanded Atami's surrender and your return. With our Xi-Ling temple's protection, Atami fled, swearing to keep the little flame, you, alive so that one day China will rise again. That's when the Mogo imperial forces came to our door. They demanded that we turn you and Atami over or face annihilation."

"What did you do?"

"What would you have done, Luka?"

"Fight!"

"A thousand versus a hundred thousand?"

"I thought one Xi-Ling warrior could take a hundred."

"We can. But the annihilation would start with our women and children, down nine degrees of blood relations."

"So what did you do, Grandmaster?"

"I learned the lesson of water: be soft, but unbreakable. As their leader, I surrendered myself on the condition that all my warriors be spared and their families set free."

Luka knelt and hugged the old man in silent homage as the grandmaster stroked his hair lovingly.

"I could not let three hundred years of tradition die. But I also did it for a selfish reason."

"What reason is that?"

"To perfect *Yin Gong*."

"Silver art?" Luka asked.

"Yes, it is the ultimate art of Xi-Ling. It crystallizes the essence of the many styles of kung fu—the strength of Southern Fists, the power of Northern Kicks, the suppleness of Eastern Swings, the enormity of Western Winds. The silver art takes its power from the moon, transforming us from earthly mortals into zodiac beings, and the golden light of *Jin Gong* extracts its strength from the sun, propelling us into fireballs of life that shine forever. When *Yin Gong* and *Jin Gong* connect, one can be anywhere and do anything his mind wishes. Only the sun and the moon are our limits."

"I know of *Jin Gong*," Luka said.

"From Atami, no doubt, for he was charged with the task of perfecting it. When we meet again, the old glories of Xi-Ling will be brought to an unprecedented height."

Luka's head dropped in sadness.

"What is it, my boy?"

Luka told Gulan about the fatal Heavenly Burial. "They took him away and I think they killed him." He could not hold back his tears.

The old man's eyes also filled with tears, but he was smiling, which perplexed Luka.

"Why are you smiling, Grandmaster?" Luka rubbed his eyes.

"He cannot be dead."

"How can you be so sure he is alive?"

"I have studied every wrinkle on Atami's face and know his fate like the back of my hand."

"You can tell fortunes by one's facial features?"

Gulan nodded. "Atami is going to live to be a hundred, that old root. He has the longest chin I have ever seen on man or beast."

"What a happy prediction, but I can hardly believe it," Luka said sadly.

"Have faith, my boy. We are going to find him soon so that my silver will be wedded to his gold. I am sure that by now he must have done his job and perfected his art. My poor boy, I don't know how I will be able to thank Buddha for your arrival and have you share this glimmer of hope with me. From now on, you are my charge. I will care for you as Atami would."

A forgotten feeling returned to Luka. For the first time in a long, long while, he felt like a child again.

Outside the cell, the night was fading and the day breaking. A sliver of light from the eastern horizon pierced the window slit, chasing away the darkness.

"We've got work to do for the next two months before they hang you," Gulan said.

"We?"

"Yes. I am passing to you the art of *Yin Gong*."

"The art of *Yin Gong*? But isn't that just for you and Atami to know?"

"Finding a suitable heir for our knowledge and tradition is also our sacred duty. Besides, I doubt that Ghengi's pardon is without some dark purpose."

"I am most grateful, Grandmaster." Luka clasped his hands and bowed.

"Tomorrow night, at moonrise, we will start your lessons here in my cell."

LUKA HAD A song in his heart the next day and could not wait for the sun to set. The world around him suddenly regained its colors—deep, crystal-clear hues that had escaped his eyes for so long. Birds sang again and crickets charmed anew. The river chatted noisily, one ripple to another. Even his prison mates seemed to return to life.

That night, a beam of moonlight illuminated Gulan's cell. Luka sat facing the old man on the floor, in silent meditation.

Gulan started his lesson. "*Yin*, silver, is the color of moonlight. That's why we practice this now, with the silver light over our shoulders."

Luka nodded.

"Many warriors have misunderstood the essence of kung fu. It is not about *without*. It all comes from *within*. To demonstrate, hit me."

"Excuse me?"

"That's an order. Stand up."

Luka sprang into a horse stance, pulled his fist back, but hesitated.

"Indecisive! Can't you take an order? Hit me right here at my *duntian*." Gulan pointed two inches below his navel.

An order was an order, but still, the man seemed little more than a skeleton. How could Luka punch him in the belly? It would break him in half.

"You think you can break me in half, don't you?"

"Yes, I am afraid I will."

"Then do so."

"I can't."

"You are wasting the precious moonlight."

"Okay, okay."

"Do it with all your might."

Luka ground his teeth. This was harder than he thought. He pulled his right fist as far back as he could and delivered his most powerful blow. But something strange happened.

Gulan's *duntian*, soft like mud, sucked his fist into the wrinkled skin, wrapping around his hand like an octopus's arm. Luka tried to pull his fist free but couldn't. His hand was drawn in deeper and deeper and wrapped tighter and tighter until the pain rippled all the way up his arm to his shoulder. His head began to ache from within. When he began to shake helplessly, Gulan pushed out his *duntian*, propelling Luka across the cell and pinning him against the wall for a good five seconds. Only after Gulan unwrinkled his *duntian* completely did Luka drop to the floor.

"Ouch!"

"I could have twisted your arm off with little effort."

Luka rubbed his back, then his fist. "What makes you so powerful?"

"My *Yin Gong,* the *Qi.*" Inner energy again.

"How did you get that?"

"Good question. Let's see, I have devoted four thousand two hundred and twenty-six nights in utter concentration and isolation, away from the red dust of the world."

"That's almost twelve years!" Luka exclaimed. "Will it take me that long?"

"No. For you, with your willingness and diligence, fifty days."

"But how can I learn in fifty days what you have attained in twelve years?"

"You can't. I'm giving it to you."

"Giving it to me?"

"Yes, on one condition."

"What is that, Grandmaster?"

"You will have to empty your body and cleanse your soul in the next fifty days before I can infuse you."

"How do I do that?"

"Through the practice of *Wu* philosophy. Nothingness."

"Nothingness?"

"Imagine yourself as a bamboo flute, hollow at heart. When the flutist blows into the hollow flute, it leaps to life and beautiful music flows. I am the flutist with the breath of *Yin Gong* and you are the flute, empty and ready."

"I am ready to begin."

"We will begin cleansing ourselves with meditation. Sit against the wall, facing the moonlight. Stretch out your arms and open yourself to the goddess moon. Think nothing but silver." Gulan placed a wrinkled book on the floor. Each page of text was accompanied by diagrams of a monk in various positions and contortions.

"One last thing. Once the transfer begins, it cannot be stopped," Gulan said. "An aborted attempt will bring total loss of the art."

"I promise I will not pause for one single second once on the road."

"Be warned. Every night of chanting and meditation will cause severe pain and bring drastic change within you, at times at the risk of your life. Are you sure you're ready?"

"I am, Grandmaster," Luka said firmly.

"Thank Buddha. Xi-Ling has hope."

In the whisper of Gulan's chanting, Luka closed his eyes and found his mind opening and responding to the silver moonlight as never before, as if the chanting were the key to the rusty lock in his head. He felt himself lifted up, almost out of his own body, free to fly out the window into a moonlit world where he glided between huge gorges. A few times, he felt as though he were returning to his old self, though he remained acutely aware that his body had not really moved an inch but was still sitting on the floor. Then Gulan's chanting would deepen and Luka would continue his dreamy flight. When he woke up, poked by Gulan's elbow, it was daylight once again.

"You must go now. I hear them coming with the breakfast buckets."

Luka cocked his head. "I don't hear anything."

"You will."

"Is it your *Yin Gong* ability?"

"Let's just say my senses are widened."

At work, Luka yawned, feeling exhausted from the lack of sleep. The sun burning his back didn't help. Nor did the warden's whipping him when he nearly dozed off into the ditch. Others were puzzled, since Luka used to beat them at every chore, but Luka was too sleepy to care what they said and thought about him. Why couldn't the sun go down a bit faster so he could crawl back to his cell to get a wink of sleep before the next moonlight session?

The second night Gulan had to pin him to the wall to keep him awake while he chanted. No matter how hard Luka tried to keep his eyes open, they rolled uselessly like dead oysters. By midnight, Gulan had to punch him to get a few minutes of wakefulness before he dozed off like a water buffalo, saliva trickling down his cheeks.

"This is not going to work," said Gulan.

"Do what you have to do to make it work, pleazzzzz . . . ," Luka said, starting to doze off in mid-sentence.

Gulan pulled out a long strip of linen from under his bed. One end he tied to Luka's earlobe. Then he rose up in the air like a flying monk, his robes fluttering amok, and tied the other end to a beam on the high ceiling.

"Are you flying, Gulan?" Luka asked.

"How else would I be able to get up here?" He landed like a mosquito. "It's called weightlessness, my boy. It'll come as you gain your *Yin Gong*."

Each time Luka dozed off, the cloth strip would tauten with a painful reminder. With each pull, Gulan's chanting rose to a higher pitch, but all came to Luka only in patches like passing clouds.

"Hang in there, Luka," said Gulan.

But soon, even the trick of tying his earlobe no longer had any effect on him. He resorted to biting his own lips, first upper lip, then lower lip, till they bled.

"Survive the night or you'll never be cleansed enough to reach the door of *Yin Gong*."

Luka bit his lips even harder and concentrated. To his surprise, he began to feel the heavy sleepiness lift like a light white cloud blown by a breeze. A flow of energy came from Gulan's fingers to his, tips to tips, slowly warming the rest of Luka's body.

"Thank you for giving me your warmth," Luka said before parting for the day.

Gulan nodded without a word.

A complete cycle of the moon passed, but the time went so quickly that all Luka noticed were the sunsets and moonrises and Gulan's growing weakness. He was speaking less and looking thinner with every passing day. At the end of each night, Gulan would slump into his bed, wrinkled like an empty bag drained of air, breathing thinly, saying goodbye only with the tip of one finger.

One night Luka said, "Grandmaster, we must stop. You are dying. I don't want this. I don't want *Yin Gong* anymore."

"My Holy Boy, the choice is not yours anymore, nor is it mine. *Yin Gong* must live and this process cannot be stopped or all will be lost."

When the new moon was born again, Luka began to feel the subtle changes taking place inside him. The sun was redder than ever, but he didn't feel as hot, and the red soil beneath him did not burn his bare feet as it used to. Though the warden gave him twice the load to push to the landfill, Luka managed the double weight in record time. He hauled a hundred loads before lunch, and the puzzled warden gave him one additional break, a reward unheard of before that day. Luka napped under a tree, but a loud whistle from an arriving ship woke him up.

"Did you hear that?" he asked 787, the prisoner who had taken Gulan's spot.

"Hear what?"

"That ship coming into port."

"You are very strange lately." 787 cast him a disdainful look and pushed on past with his barrow.

"You mean you can't hear anything?"

787 spat at him and was gone.

When he rejoined the stream of laborers that afternoon, Luka sniffed the air and asked the warden, "Do you smell that?"

"Smell what?" barked the warden.

"Something burning."

"I'll have your ears burnt if you keep asking everyone this and that." The warden brandished his whip at Luka. "Get back to work."

Five minutes later, flames and smoke spat upward in an angry roar, darkening the sky. The bungalow that housed the clothing factory was on fire.

Luka cringed with fear. Hali and the other orphan girls! Were they trapped in the building or had they managed to escape?

As all the prisoners stopped what they were doing and turned to look at the fire, the warden whipped their heads and backs until they resumed the work at hand.

How Luka wished he could be there for the girls, but the warden's eyes were on him like nails. Luka had to turn away from the burning bungalow. All he could hear was frightened shrieks and the shouts of Mogo guards. That evening on his way back, Luka was shocked to see the clothing factory reduced to piles of dark charcoal. Only half of one wall still stood as stubborn smoke lingered, filling the air with the stench of burnt fabric.

At the crossroad that day, there was no flower.

That evening, Gulan was not surprised when Luka told him that he had smelled the smoke half a *li* away even before the flames had darkened the sky. "You're emptier than you were before, that's why you hear better and see farther. And you should be able to remain cool in heat and warm in cold."

"No wonder the sunlight has softened on my skin."

"The tolerance will come in handy when you visit your Peking again. The snow there is brutal, I heard."

"You mean I could be shirtless and not chilled?"

"Inner fire radiates through you."

"Thank you so much, Grandmaster. I feel like a new person with added energy flowing through me. And I haven't slept for days."

"Then you are ready to start the infusion soon." Gulan coughed, nearly tearing his flimsy frame apart.

"Are you all right?" Luka asked.

Gulan nodded. "Let's continue."

On the eve of the fiftieth night, Gulan turned to the last page of verse and read the last line. "So *Yin Gong* has fallen from heaven, passing its final bridge of life and death. . . ."

As he finished, a drop of blood trickled from his mouth. He pressed his hands to Luka's, tip to tip and palm to palm. The waves of warm *Qi* shocked Luka at first and then shook him. The current was full and vibrant.

"So enters the soul, so ends the bridge . . . ," Gulan gasped.

When Luka opened his eyes again, he saw the wrinkles on Gulan's smiling face double as his teacher withered before his eyes. He fought to pull away, wanting to stop Gulan's rapid aging but could not. As Gulan held Luka's hands in a death grip and continued to blast his *Yin Gong* into his veins, Luka's body felt lighter and lighter while his heart pumped with new vigor.

"We are one now," said Gulan. "The wind and the rain will separate us not."

Luka felt a final shock of electricity; then Gulan released his hands and fell forward. Luka rose like a kite without string, flying higher and higher, spinning around and around.

I am flying now. I am flying.

His head hit the ceiling. "Ow!"

"Careful, young man. If you don't know how to fly, then don't," Gulan whispered, sitting up. "Come down now."

"How?"

"*Yin Gong* works at your will. You are the master and *Yin Gong* your servant."

Luka grimaced, willing himself down. The next moment he slammed into the ground forcefully, eating the dirt floor.

"Your control will get better with a little exercise," Gulan murmured. "Here are the verses. I am passing them to you. Guard them with your life till you decide to pass them to another worthy of your trust."

Luka received the book with a bow.

"With the knowledge of *Yin Gong*, so do you also receive the *Yin Gong* dagger as your weapon." Gulan pulled a tiny dagger from inside his sleeve.

"It looks just like the one Atami had," Luka said.

"They are a pair. Atami's is gold, male, while mine is silver, female."

"Does it work like Atami's?"

"Yes. It's an extension of *Yin Gong*. Your wish is her command."

Luka made a mental note of Gulan's use of *her*.

"You must bless her with a verse from the book once every

cycle of the moon. Otherwise she will turn blunt and deaf to your command. And every thirteen years, she should meet the gold dagger like a woman greeting her husband. It has been almost that long since I parted with Atami." The way Gulan spoke about the little dagger as if it were human made Luka feel strange.

Luka received the dagger with both hands and studied it carefully. It was a beautiful but small weapon, its handle embedded with a red gem shaped like a tear. "Thank you, Grandmaster. What are you going to use now that you have given it to me?"

"Do I look like someone in need of any weapons?" He coughed a bit more. "Remember, the dagger is also useless if her master doesn't blow *Qi* into her."

Luka nodded, remembering Atami kissing his dagger before each use.

"Be careful with her. She is a *Shen Dao*, a spirited dagger from our founder. They don't make daggers like these anymore."

"I'll cherish it—I mean her—with my life."

"So you must, for that's how much she cherishes you." Gulan nodded and then sighed. "How I wish I had time to teach you all seventy-two dagger moves, but time is running out. They just received the order from Peking authorizing my release tomorrow. The timing couldn't have been better."

"Oh, Gulan, what am I going to do without you?"

"I am taking you with me."

"You are? But how?"

Gulan only smiled.

• • •

The next morning Gulan was picked up by two wardens, one of whom said, "Please forgive what we have done to you, Wu Xia master. We are forced to be cruel to all inmates. Otherwise we would be punished severely."

"Let bygones be bygones," Gulan said.

"What does that mean?"

"It means to forget what is past."

"Let be-gones by be-gones."

"No, it's bygones be gone-by," said the other.

"Would you mind carrying this trunk for me?" Gulan asked. "I'm feeling awfully weak."

"Sure." The young one picked it up and dropped it instantly, underestimating the weight of its contents. "Ouch! What is so heavy?"

"I'm taking a prisoner with me," Gulan said.

"You're kidding." The older warden shook his head. "Let be-gones by be-gones. You are such a kidder. Bringing a prisoner with you. That's the funniest joke I've ever heard in here, and I've been here for twenty years."

The two guards, who now thought themselves buddies of the Wu Xia master, carried the wooden trunk on their shoulders and planted it in the back of a carriage waiting at the prison gate. It was Gulan's only piece of luggage.

Only when the carriage began to jump along the dirt road did Luka let out a huge sigh through the little airholes Gulan had poked for him to breathe through. The trunk was, after all, only a trunk, but Luka knew freedom was but a short while away. He felt happy, grateful, and terribly lucky, even though he was still curled up like a shrimp. Yet his thoughts turned to Hali, the girl with the flowers. Was she still alive? And would he ever see her again?

THE PRISON CARRIAGE drove them as far as the busy docks of Jiushan harbor. Only when the squeaky wheels had faded into the dust did Gulan unlock the trunk.

Luka blinked at the brilliant sunlight that bathed the wet port city. He was surprised to see Gulan dressed in a gray shirt with a silk sash tied around his waist, and a pair of baggy gray pants that narrowed at his ankles. He even wore a pair of new boots. Except for his cheerful eyes, he looked so different that Luka hardly recognized him. The old, sad-faced 788 was gone forever.

"You look . . ."

"Radiant? Freedom can do that to you."

Luka reached out and hugged Gulan, knowing well that it was not something done between a master and his pupil. But the master hugged back just as tightly, and that embrace became their silent celebration of the world.

"Take off your prison uniform," Gulan ordered.

"But what am I going to wear?"

"Anything but that." Gulan fished a little bag out of the trunk and handed Luka a bundle of old clothes. Luka put them on and discarded his old prison garb into the bag.

"Sorry that you have to wear my old clothes," Gulan said, "but I figure anything is better than your prison rags."

"Not at all, Grandmaster. It feels heavenly."

Luka donned an old robe and cap. Both were tight, and when he lifted up his arms to scratch his head, he heard a ripping sound: his muscles had burst through the flimsy seams.

In the busy port, they blended right in. Seas of fishermen, hungry for the touch of solid land after their voyages, surged into a dirty, smelly bazaar, where hundreds of peddlers shouted for their attention. Luka and Gulan could not have come to a livelier spot on this planet.

"Go look around while I rest my feet," Gulan said. He sat down on a rock under a small tree.

Luka hesitated, unwilling to leave him.

"Go on. I'll be fine."

Luka shrugged and wandered off into the crowd. He was mesmerized by the colorful world of the marketplace. But his glee as a freed man would last only as long as his stomach—a huge empty reservoir—was filled. For the last few months, the prison's tasteless, meager food had quieted and suppressed the easily excitable cells that lined his stomach. Now, at the teasing of a thousand flavors, his stomach regained its natural sensitivity, was reacting to the pungent smell of the world violently. The hungry walls gnawed at each other in vain. Lodged at the middle of his body, his stomach tossed and churned angrily, poked his heart, pulled his spleen, and squashed his kidneys. Had it been able to travel upward, it would have choked his airway at not being fed. It was an ambush, a revolt . . . no, worse, a *coup d' etat.*

His body was in a state of anarchy. His mouth watered, his stomach shouted at his throat, and his leg bones were melting like the fat of the poor animal in the pot. He blamed all this on his hungry eyes, which took everything in. His nose was just as blameworthy. Even his ears reached for every sound of slurping, burping, chewing, teeth clicking, and the oh-so-happy sigh after swallowing. Everything surrounding him conspired to choke him with deeper hunger. His mind, the only sensible part of him, receded weakly against the tide of hunger. He was going crazy. He was crazy.

Before he could do something irrational like grab a chunk of bloody, oily meat and run, something bit his ankle. He squatted down to find an obnoxious mutt sitting on his tail, licking his chops, looking innocent and bored.

"Hey, why did you do that?"

The mutt blinked a couple times and looked away.

Luka patted the little fellow, grateful to him for pulling him away from temptation. "What do you want from me?"

The mutt looked up with big sincere eyes, caught the hem of Luka's robe with his teeth, and started dragging him along.

"Wait. Where are you going?" Luka was amazed by this little guy, who would not go away. He stood up and saw the badly written sign that, in his extreme hunger, he had not seen. MOUNTAIN DOG STEW. BETTER THÁN OUR SNAKE STEW!

Luka's heart shrank at the declaration. How repulsive. Had he eaten anything from that pot, he would have spat it all back out. Dogs were the hunter's friend, the herdsman's brother, the foe of his foe and friend of his friend. Luka followed the mutt, who was busy guiding the way under people's legs and along a dirty wall to finally stop at a hut in an isolated corner of the marketplace.

The hut was stitched together with straw, and sheltered a pile of watermelons that were ripened with fragrance and pregnant with seeds.

What lay temptingly inside those pregnant mother melons made him squirm. He could just imagine how best to approach such a voluptuous fruit. Smack it open with his hard head, slurp it up with his silvery tongue, and suck out the melting meat into his volcano throat, ceasing only when a burp was so eminent that if he did not stop, the whole thing would just come back out. He would then wash his face with the juice that pooled in their empty shells.

The dog's barking, however, jolted him from his daydream. The mutt stood before him with a man's shirt. It must be his master's clothing. What was the mutt trying to tell him? That he was watching the hut and his master was gone for a while?

Luka checked the surroundings. The hut was removed from the chaos of the bazaar, but the din of the market still drowned out the whacking sound he made as he smacked his head into the melon he had taken. He slurped it with such a loud, ugly sound that the mutt, sitting at his feet, had to step on him to quiet him down.

The dog looked happy and gave Luka a bored yawn when Luka burped to announce that he had swallowed all the evidence of his transgression. He wiped his mouth with his sleeves, then bent down and tried to kiss the mutt, but the dog avoided him as if he knew Luka hadn't been cleaning his teeth very diligently. The mutt also seemed to be aware that Luka had his master to feed as well: he pushed another melon to the boy with his front paws, licking it with its tongue.

"You want me to take this to my master?"

The mutt blinked three times, which Luka took as a yes.

With a melon on his shoulder, Luka bowed goodbye to his furry friend and whistled through the crowded market square, heading back to Gulan. A large crowd gathered beyond the food stands, watching some sort of street performance, but Luka had no interest. Another fake kung fu man was selling fake belly-worm powder. They were everywhere in the country, he thought.

Fighting through the crowd, Luka was alarmed to see that the rock upon which Gulan had been sitting was empty. Gulan was nowhere to be found. Where was he?

Gulan's wooden trunk was still there, awaiting its master's return. Deciding to wait, Luka sat down on the rock and placed the ripe melon beside the trunk. He then realized something was seriously wrong. A leafy branch, freshly torn from the young tree shading the rock, lay on the ground. With it lay an arrow that must have severed it. As Luka picked up the arrow, his heart skipped. A black horse was carved into the wood—the symbol of the emperor. The Mogo garrison force was here!

As he turned and looked for other clues, Luka's right foot stumbled on a brick. A character had been hurriedly drawn on it: *run.* It was Gulan's writing.

Run? Run where? He couldn't leave the old master all alone. He was weak and probably dying. *Where are you, Gulan?*

Calming himself, Luka willed his senses to expand. The instant serenity that came from within surprised him. He was like dry hay catching fire. In one puff he was aflame. In wonderment he marveled at this new life within him. And in that peace he could hear Gulan's heartbeat. *I found him,* he sang in his heart. The grandmaster was nearby, for the beat was loud, nearly deafening, yet the rhythm was unhurried. Slowly, Luka sensed other sounds—the stomping hooves of heavy horses, the shouts of a hundred mouths.

Luka had little time to think and even less to prepare. He ran like a tiger, with big strides and silent footfalls, darting among the thick mob that blocked his way with every step he took. Within seconds, he was standing in an outer ring of onlookers, peeping through a tall wall of pigtails and bronzed shoulders with peeling skin. He caught glimpses of five pompous garrison soldiers, who circled on their tall, proud stallions. The men lashed their whips at somebody in the center of the circle.

Poor Gulan, he was so frail after giving his *Yin Gong* to Luka. Those five brutes would make him a meatcake.

As Luka had feared, it *was* Gulan whom the five trotting horses chased. But his grandmaster was no meatcake. He was whirling in the circle like a tornado. He had taken off his silk sash, and he used it as a weapon, whipping and slashing it around as if it were supple steel. The ever-thickening crowd was amazed at how alive the sash had become. It shot out like the tongue of a huge serpent, struck the forehead of the first horseman, and threw him off his horse with a force that was hard to credit to such a harmless piece of silk.

Yin Gong was still within his master. Luka was overjoyed and pushed forward, ready to join the fight, when an old farmer pulled his collar and warned him, "Hey, careful, boy. You don't want to get in between the old man and Ghengi's lieutenants."

"I've never heard of them before," Luka said.

The farmer spat at the horseman nearest them. "Abin, the eldest, with the long beard, is the chief lieutenant and a famous archer. He captured that warrior monk, Atami, with an arrow."

"He is the one?"

"Yes, and he's also deadly with a doubled-edged sword. Babu is the ugly one with a two-headed *qiang*. His nickname is Q. You figure out what it means. Candra is the one on the black horse. He has the quickest hand at the whip. Dogo, the fourth guy, handles his two *daos* (longswords) like chopsticks, and Egol, the one whom the old monk knocked off his horse, can use anything, but he's best known for his hidden sharp stars."

"Why are they chasing the old monk?"

"They cornered him here and asked for the return of someone called Holy Boy. But don't you worry. The old one is no ordinary man. Everyone here knows he was the headmaster of Xi-Ling, the true peoples' warriors, who were disbanded by Emperor Ghengi."

"Thank you, farmer," Luka said.

"Shut up now and watch."

In the ring, Abin twirled his sword and thrust it with fury, trying to fillet Gulan's left shoulder. With a puff of air, Gulan stiffened his sash into a long pole and deflected the blade with a distinct *clink.* The contact of the embroidered silk against the steel edge of the sword shocked Abin's right arm with pain. He withdrew his weapon, alarmed by the inch-wide chip in the steel, once again reminded why he had aligned with the royal court against Xi-Ling. Abin tightened his thighs around his horse and unleashed a hidden dart from his saddle.

Gulan heard it before he saw it. He might be weak, but he was still nimble. Twelve years behind the prison wall had clarified his mind and perfected his *Yin Gong* to the point where he could react with pure, effortless instinct. Gulan made a V with his middle and index fingers and trapped the oncoming dart's neck. "Another piece of royal crap," Gulan said, eyeing the black horse carved into the wood. He threw it on the ground and stepped on it, breaking it into three pieces.

Luka watched from the sideline with his heart in his throat. *Gulan's enemies are my enemies,* he thought. *I can't let him fight all five by himself.*

Luka saw his chance when Babu pulled on his horse's reins. As his stallion reared up, the soldier drew his spear to pierce Gulan's back. Without another thought, Luka called on his *Yin Gong* and leaped awkwardly ten feet into the air. The crowd gasped at the little boy who flew over their heads.

Little did they know that the most surprised among them was Luka himself. Lightness of body brought on a lightness of heart.

What an indescribable feeling—it set him completely free! But the matter afoot was urgent. Luka ended his flight and stumbled clumsily into the ring to the shrieks of the onlookers.

"Crazy boy!"

"The horses will trample you to death!"

Luka ignored them all and stepped between Babu's horse and Gulan's back. Nearly an inch shorter than the spine of the animal, he faced the pawing hooves. The plunging *qiang* was only a few inches from Gulan's scalp when Luka reached up, grasped the tip of the weapon, and pulled it to the ground, taking its master with it.

"The boy is a Wu Xia warrior too!" a man shouted from the crowd.

"Where did he come from?" shouted another.

"Haven't seen a boy this marvelous for a long time!" yelled a third.

I'm not marvelous, Luka thought. *The* Yin Gong *within me is marvelous.*

Luka stepped on Babu, making him eat dirt, and took one brief moment to celebrate before he turned to face Abin, the swordsman with the now chipped tool.

"Fugitive boy! Convict at large!" shouted Abin, infamous for his deadly three-step sword kill. Left, right, middle. An opponent might resist one step, two at the most if he was in the know, but never three.

Abin slashed left at the boy's head. Luka made a timely bow, the chipped blade hissing by his hair.

The boy is a learned hand, Abin thought, *but he will not live to learn more.* He chuckled and pulled his sword back to cut Luka's neck with the other edge, the good one. His horse, a Gobi Desert stallion, danced to his command. But the blade didn't touch the boy. Luka flew up and nearly kicked the weapon out of Abin's hand.

"Arghhhh!" Abin screamed. The boy was begging for his third step. He took aim at Luka's face and pressed a hidden trigger on the ornate handle of his sword. Out flew a nearly invisible hook attached to a string, aimed straight for Luka's eyes. Had it made a successful run, it would have gone into his right eye and out his left. That was how Abin had gained the nickname of Eyeball Collector.

The rising dust and the glaring sunlight made the hook even trickier to catch. But Luka could hear the metal zip through the air, tiny and mosquito-like. Then he saw it, coming nearer and nearer.

"Don't catch the hook!" Gulan shouted. "Guide it with your will back to its owner."

Will, Luka thought. *Will? Where's my will?*

As if Gulan could read his mind, he shouted, "Open up your Vision."

Luka closed his eyes and the Vision was right there, magnifying the hook in its flight. Luka *willed* it toward the horse. Obediently, the hook made a U-turn and shot back to the horse, looping many times around the animal's front legs before sinking into its knee.

Luka could have kicked himself for having made such a *willing* as the poor innocent animal crashed to the ground, bringing with him his screaming master, Abin.

Luka made another *willing*, staring at Babu, who was fighting Gulan. That was all it took for the hook to dislodge itself. It looped around Babu's neck a few times before making its final strike into his shoulder.

Good thing I never touched it, thought Luka. It would have crawled all over him like creeping ivy.

"Who asked you to come in?" Gulan shouted at Luka. "Get out!"

"Your battle is mine. We are one!" Luka shouted back.

"With three on the ground, you can go now. Grab that white stallion and head for the west," Gulan ordered.

Before Luka could reply, Gulan made a big loop at each end of his long sash and tossed it up in the air. Coaxing it with his fingers, he teased the double loops to follow the two remaining men on their horses. The sash made its final catch, netting the two bad boys and stringing them together off their horses like landed, gasping catfish.

The crowd cheered for Gulan as the five Mogoes squirmed on the ground.

"Kill the Mogoes!"

"Long live Xi-Ling! Welcome back, Grandmaster Gulan!"

"Emperor Ghengi is in trouble!"

"Gulan will save the people!"

Gulan gathered his clothes, dusted off the dirt, and bowed to those who had recognized him. Then he lifted himself weightlessly, mounting a white stallion, which seemed calmed by his presence. He shouted to Luka, "My boy, get on that black stallion and follow me."

Luka ran to the black horse, but it seemed driven mad without his master. It galloped around and around in a circle. Luka chased it and got ahold of the reins. But the horse was no pushover. It snorted at Luka and reared up. It had been ages since Luka had ridden and the horse seemed to know that. Yet while the sheer size of the beast dwarfed him, Luka was not scared.

"Come on, boy!" Gulan urged him. Luka knew he had every reason to hurry. The Mogoes were on the ground but were not dead. But the animal wasn't cooperating. Gulan rode back and with one sweep grabbed Luka and set him on the horse.

"Now take the reins and hold on tight," he yelled to Luka.

They rode off, heading west.

"You were masterful there!" Luka shouted after he had caught up with Gulan at the edge of the town.

"You were not so bad yourself."

"I love my new *Yin Gong* powers. Thank you so very much, Grandmaster."

"And I love what you're using them for." There was a youthful air about the old master. "But they know you have escaped and who you are. We must get out before the city gate is shut."

"Why did you ask me to run?"

"I could not bear to lose you again."

"But I would have lost you."

"I will always find you. Don't you ever forget that." Gulan tossed him a smile and urged his horse forward. Luka shook his reins and rode after him.

PArt 3

野洞寺院武俠

GULAN AND LUKA rode the whole day through an ever thickening forest. The path had disappeared and grass swayed as high as their horses' bellies. The trees grew taller and the foliage darker, blocking out the sun from this secretive leafy world. By nightfall, a howling wind chased among the lonesome tree trunks. Sometimes it sounded like someone laughing, other times like someone crying. Even the horses trotted with their ears erect, listening to those howls. Then the terrain rose and trees thinned. Their path ahead was blocked by a menacing cliff.

"Widow Cliff," Gulan said, tilting his head. "We have to retrieve the sacred manual to wed *Yin Gong* and *Jin Gong*. I hid it up there in a cave."

"Really?" Luka strained his neck back, trying to take in the size of the cliff, but felt dizzy just looking at it. The rocks seemed to soar right into the sky, and the summit was too high even to see.

"We'll also need to fetch some gold ingots for the long journey ahead."

"You hid gold there, too?" Luka asked.

"Right before we were disbanded, our brothers agreed to have one hundred pieces of gold hidden up there to be used only for emergencies. If you take one, you must return two. That way the treasure will only grow with time. And that is not all. It is also the only safe spot at which to leave messages for our brothers who are scattered throughout this land."

"What are we going to do with the horses?" Luka asked.

"They have served us well. We will let them go free." He removed the saddles from both horses and they bolted off.

"Where will they go?"

"Beyond the forest live some of the most skilled herdsmen around. They will treasure them like gold."

"Goodbye, horses." Luka waved to the stallions, which disappeared into the forest.

"The cave is hidden in the waist of the cliff, one hundred yards straight up," Gulan said with pride. "No one except Xi-Ling warriors has ever been there."

"How did you find it?"

"It was a monkey cave, and I hope it still is. The tea monkeys live there. They are trained to pick the rarest tea leaves that grow only on the most dangerous cliffs where no man can reach. They also collect precious *yan gao.*"

"The swallow spit that's smeared along the cliff walls?"

"It was the old emperor's favorite delicacy, you know."

"But how are we going to get up there?"

"You will see." Gulan grabbed a long, hairy vine hanging from above, shook it, and gave a few whistles.

Something began to descend along the face of the cliff toward them, spinning and swaying as it came lower and lower. It was a large bamboo basket fastened to a knobby vine that dangled from the cave's mouth. The basket was well cushioned with fluffy hay and leaves at its bottom.

"That is how we'll reach the cave," Gulan said.

"But who will pull us up there?"

"The monkeys."

"Why would the monkeys do that?"

"Long ago, we saved their ancestors by hiding them in this cave, away from the mountain predators. These white tigers had eaten nearly all of them. Safe in this cave, the tea monkeys multiplied all over this side of the mountain. The tigers can only look on with hunger and envy. You climb in first," Gulan said.

Luka did as he was told but the basket began to shake and threatened to tip over. "What's happening?"

"Oh, I forgot. The monkeys don't like strangers." Gulan gave another sharp whistle.

The basket instantly stopped shaking and Gulan climbed in beside Luka. Then the basket crept upward, jerkily.

"Someone's in a bad mood." Gulan frowned.

"Maybe they're trying to tell us something."

"Maybe."

As they dangled higher and higher, the wind picked up its tempo, swinging the long vines that crawled along the rocks. Everything on the ground seemed to shrink. The giant trees became young yearlings and huge rocks became rolling pebbles.

Luka felt tiny, like a bird in its leafy nest, holding tightly to the rim. Their basket spun with the wind and swayed with each rough pull.

"Torches! I see torches coming through the forest," Luka cried midway up. He spotted four columns of fire squirming toward them on the ground.

"Stay calm and don't rock the basket. We're almost there." Soon a knobby rock jutting into their path stopped them dead. "Here is the cave," Gulan said, tying the vine around the rock.

The mouth of the cave was hidden behind a thick tapestry of leafy vines and was guarded by an old tea tree with long beards.

"Strange," Gulan said. "I wonder where the monkeys are." He pushed aside the vines and walked in slowly with Luka trailing him.

The cave was windy and chilly even though the air outside was warm and muggy. Luka could feel sweat dampening his hands as they walked along the chunky walls. The ground was covered with pebbles, round and smooth, some dry leaves, and soft weeds.

"What is that smell?" Luka whispered.

It was more like a stench, Gulan thought, but all he said was a colorless, "Old death."

Luka jerked suddenly.

"What's the matter?"

"My arm. My arm . . . something is crawling up my sleeve." He shook his arm wildly but it had reached his armpit.

"Be calm and don't move," Gulan ordered, sticking his hand under Luka's shirt and yanking the creature out from under his arm.

"Ouch!" Luka screamed. The creature's many legs had clawed into his skin and each one was like a thorn being uprooted.

"There." Gulan threw it on the ground and stepped on it.

"What is that?"

"A centipede as big as a baby snake. The arm will swell a bit but it will go down soon."

Luka got chills just thinking about that thing on him.

"No more shouts or screams. You might wake up the giant snakes here."

"Where are they?" Luka whispered.

"Everywhere. Hold on to me. Our gold ingots are only around the corner."

Luka stayed behind the grandmaster, who seemed to know his way even though the darkness was absolute. When they came to a bend, Gulan asked Luka to stay put while he measured the distance with his feet. Ten feet in all, Gulan remembered. From the right shoulder of a little Buddha statue, he picked up two limestones, rubbed them against each other, and with the spark lit a candle. Seven candles had been burnt, Gulan counted. That was a good sign. That meant seven of his Xi-Ling warriors had been here and must have taken the gold to rebuild their training camp. But where were his monkeys?

"Luka, come and let me show you the treasure of Xi-Ling."

The flame, the size of a soybean, lay bare the mystery of the cave. It was a passage crushed pathetically between two giant rocks. Cold sweat from the walls had trickled down from cracks above. Centipedes crawled all over the ground among the pebbles, and wild thorny weeds poked in all direction.

"This way," Gulan said. He held the candle in his right hand and guided Luka with his left. They had taken only two steps when a puff of wind killed the light. Two eerie eyes gleamed at them in the darkness. Then, as quickly as they had appeared, the eyes were gone, leaving behind only scratching sounds of escape into another cave above them. Gulan made the fire again, revealing a wooden tray full of brilliant ingots, each piece lying snugly in its own little crib carved into a tray.

Luka's eyes grew wide.

"Eight pieces taken, but only seven candles burned," Gulan muttered. "Something is amiss here."

"What could that be?"

"I wish I knew." Gulan rolled up his sleeve. As he reached for an ingot, a huge monkey leaped down from above and wrestled Gulan's hand away from the gold.

"I knew it was you." Gulan didn't panic, nor did he resist.

The monkey shut the lid and sat on it.

Luka was ready to fight, but Gulan pulled him back. "Stop. He is our old friend."

The monkey stuck his wet tongue out at Luka and shook his head.

"Look at this." Gulan touched a long, hairless scar under the monkey's knee. The monkey seemed soothed by the caress and licked Gulan's hand. In the simple gestures, Luka felt the wordless love that passed between man and beast.

"This was from a Mogo's burning arrow. That's why we call him Scar."

The monkey nodded his shaggy head.

"Now are you going to let me have my gold or what?"

Scar shook his head violently.

"No?"

The furry head shook again.

"Why is that?"

The monkey jumped off the box and led them to another hidden nook. There lay a neat pile of bones stacked as tall as Gulan's shoulders.

"All of your family have died?"

The monkey nodded.

"I'm sorry." Gulan studied the bones, patting Scar on the head.

How could it be that all the young ones had perished but the oldest was still alive? Then Gulan saw that the bones were chipped in one way or another. "Someone has killed them all."

Scar lowered his head with sadness. There were sores on his neck, and patches of hair had been torn from his flanks. The eyes were no longer dark with bottomless curiosity. The young and lively Scar that Gulan had known was no longer. Still more alarming, all the signs here pointed to danger. This cave was no longer safe. They had to move quickly and get out before evil struck again.

"Scar, we are in a hurry. Please let us get our gold so we can be on our way."

But the animal did not step aside. Instead, he threw himself at

Gulan and wrestled him to the ground—and Gulan allowed him to. Understanding from his years alone in the dark cell what loneliness meant, to men or animals, Gulan wrestled playfully with him for a few seconds. Scar licked and nudged and tickled him till Gulan was giggling. But when he tried to release himself from the hairy embrace, Scar became deadly serious in nailing him to the ground. "Luka, get two pieces of gold and we will be on our way."

"Yes, Grandmaster."

The monkey let go of Gulan and threw the boy onto the ground.

Gulan was forced to shoot a dot of *Qi* into Scar's *bai hui,* a spot on the top of his balding scalp. The monkey froze instantly, staring fixedly at the wall with raised eyebrows.

With trembling fingers, Gulan opened the box and murmured to himself, "Forgive me, Xi-Ling heroes, for laying hands on our treasure." He pinched one ingot from its wooden crib, but to his surprise, a tiny scorpion lay motionless beneath it, as if it had been crushed by the weight of the gold.

Why would an insect choose to die here? he wondered. Gulan lifted the second piece and found a dead scorpion lying beneath that, too.

A trap, he thought, slipping the gold into his pockets. And he was right. The fresh air suddenly revived the dormant creatures and their legs began dancing wildly. They scrabbled out of their cribs. Before Gulan could move they had already dropped onto his boots, one on each foot, and in a blink disappeared under his pants to crawl up his legs. He had to stop them. As Gulan released his *Qi* to strike them dead, he felt a faint scratch.

"What's the matter, Grandmaster?"

"Mogo scorpions have stung me."

"Where are they? Let me kill them."

"They should be dead already." Gulan shook his pants but nothing came out. He rolled his pants up, inspecting his legs, but there were no new cuts or hints of blood. "Trouble," he muttered.

"Where are they?"

"There." He traced his fingertip along a slow movement just under his skin. One lump crawled up his left leg, the other down the right.

"How did they get inside you?"

"They dove into my old wounds."

"What are you going to do?"

The grandmaster looked undisturbed. "Don't worry. Remember what I taught you. I will cleanse them out with *Yin Gong*. They will come out where they went in, except dead. If that doesn't work, we'll surely find a cure in a book called *Evil for Evil.*"

"What is that for?"

"To find cures for all sorts of curses, terminal diseases, poisons, and spells."

"Why don't you cleanse them out now?"

"No time. We've got to go. I hear horses coming." Gulan knelt beside Scar and pressed a point just under the monkey's belly, but Scar just sat there. He beat his chest with his paws in the most sorrowful manner. Gulan tried to stop Scar from hurting himself more, but the monkey started slapping his own face.

"What makes you so upset with yourself?"

Scar continued.

"Stop it."

Finally, he did. Walking on his hind legs, Scar then led Gulan and Luka through the dark tunnel all the way to the mouth of the cave. He pointed at the wall, where someone had carved a message. With the flickering candle in his hand, Gulan studied each word.

> *Once a day it'll breed*
> *Grassy scorpions with dark souls.*
> *Twice a night it'll feed*
> *On the intestines of thee.*
> *For the cure you shall see*
> *The Angel of Eclipse.*

"Angel of Eclipse!" Gulan squeezed out the hateful name through gritted teeth.

Scar was still crying.

"Who is the Angel of Eclipse?" Luka asked.

"Ghengi. A nickname he proudly gave himself because he was born under that birth sign. Someone from inside our group has brought him here. That explains all the dead monkeys."

Scar shook his head up and down and hooted.

"Xi-Ling owes you once again, Scar." Gulan knelt and stroked the monkey. "Now go fetch me my coupling manual and any tidings of our fellow warriors."

Scar disappeared and returned with a scroll and a wrinkled

paper on which were scribbled large characters. A cliff with a river below was drawn beneath them.

> *Up the cliff, down the river,*
> *In fog, follow the monkey.*

Gulan was happy. "It's the handwriting of Lin Koon, my loyal disciple and a brilliant master."

"'In fog, follow the monkey'?" Luka read again. "What does it mean?"

"Fog means doubt in your mind. In doubt, follow the monkey."

"We now have a destination."

Gulan nodded.

Back at the mouth of the cave, the torches were at the base of the cliff. Shouts from royal soldiers rose from the foggy bottom.

"Flames are burning our eyebrows," Gulan said. He meant that they were in deep trouble. Five columns of torches surrounded the foot of the cliff.

Soft pops sounded in the night. Almost immediately a sheet of arrows pierced the air. A dozen slammed near the mouth of the cave, tearing their possibly poisonous tips against the ancient rocks. They were trapped.

"We can always go up, all the way to the top," Luka said. But as the old man winced, he quickly saw that his way was no way. Gulan had never cringed like that, not even when passing *Yin Gong* to him. The scorpions must be hurting.

"What should we do?" Luka asked, supporting Gulan.

"When in doubt, follow what?"

"The monkey."

Scar was right there, pawing at Lin Koon's writing.

"But should we, Grandmaster?"

"Most certainly. It's called faith. And how can we not trust him? Scar has been waiting for us here in this dark cave, surrounded by the bones and ghosts of his entire clan. Imagine the faith it took to wait for our arrival. Scar, lead the way."

Luka bowed to thank the monkey. With a friendly hoot, Scar lead them back into the cave.

As they advanced into the depths of the cave, the shouts of Mogo soldiers dimmed to a hum. The cave narrowed and the weeds thickened. The air thinned, making Gulan breathe shallowly, and the temperature fell, until chills ran down their sweaty backs.

The cave finally shrank to a little crack. Only with the aid of the slippery moss covering the walls were they able to inch along some more. When they could go no farther and the air seemed all but sucked out of the little space, Scar pulled aside a rock. A ray of moonlight beamed through a hole.

"We're out!" Luka cried as he helped Gulan to the ground.

"This is the back side of the cliff," said Gulan with weak cheer. He took in a long breath. "But do you know who owns this land that we are standing on?"

Luka and Scar shook their heads.

"Washandra warlords."

"Ghengi's allies!" Luka exclaimed.

"They must have been alerted by the Mogoes." Gulan sniffed the air. "Washandra are near."

"You can smell them?"

"The Washandra mercenaries are dark like ghosts, small like dwarfs, and deadly like daggers. They have one vice, which has often given them away: all Washandra men only wash themselves three times in their life. At birth, on their wedding day, and before burial. You can smell them several *li* away."

Luka sniffed around him. A rotten smell hung thick in the air.

"There is more than one column coming our way." Gulan's hairy nostrils flared.

Luka closed his eyes and twitched his nose. "Six or seven *li* away."

"Wrong. The wind is blowing toward them, making them seem farther than they really are. *Yin Gong* sensoria must always take their surroundings into account. For instance, the mountain air is always thinner than the air on the plain," Gulan said. "They are two to three *li* west of us. Scar, go scout a safe path into the forest. We can still make a clean break from them."

"But Grandmaster, you must cleanse yourself of the scorpions first, as you said you would."

"We cannot afford the time now. You see that patch of clouds in the distance? Once it covers the face of the moon, darkness will prevail and we will be lost in the forest."

"But—"

"I shall use every second that I can to send you as close to

Xi-Ling as my heart wishes." The determination in his voice reminded Luka of Atami, hard as a rock. "Scar, be our scout."

The monkey peeked into the forest for a moment before jumping up into the nearest tree. He straddled a high fork, gazing ahead with gleaming eyes.

"When in doubt, always follow Scar."

Luka nodded, and they headed for the dark trails.

At the beginning, the trees were short and foliage thin. Soon the trees grew taller, piercing the sky, and the branches thickened with grotesque shapes and tangles. Some shadows looked like people hanging, others like animals dangling. Still others like monsters striking and beasts gnawing. Gusts of cold wind howled like weeping ghosts. The moon shone farther and farther away from them, while the forest loomed bigger and more sinister and Luka felt smaller and less sure. Soon, near complete darkness possessed the leafy space, swallowing them like the mouth of a giant whale.

Gulan was right with him, trotting along much faster than Luka's youthful feet. Scar swung gracefully from tree to tree in search of a path out of the forest. Their progress was only interrupted once when Scar swooped down and landed in front of them, refusing to let them go another inch farther. Gulan dragged Luka to hide behind a boulder. What they saw next taught Luka a lesson he would not soon forget. Within minutes, half a dozen white tigers lumbered by, sniffing here and there. Luka stopped breathing as he watched the deadly cats pause near them, sneeze, and turn around, heading east.

"Wow!" Luka whispered. "Did you make them turn around and leave?"

"No, Scar did. Can't you smell it?"

Luka sniffed. "Someone farted."

"Scar did that to drive them away."

Scar grimaced, then led them on the road again.

For the next ten *li*, Gulan sensed new movements under his skin—slimy, squirming movements. The scorpions were breeding, Gulan realized with alarm.

His breathing was getting labored and his legs felt heavier but he dragged on, for he could tell that the distant footfalls of the Washandra were getting closer and closer. Every second he pushed forward could mean the difference between life and death for the boy he was protecting.

After another *li* of hurrying, Gulan finally collapsed against a tree.

"Grandmaster!" Luka rushed to his side.

Cold sweat crawled down Gulan's sunken cheeks. His lips trembled and his teeth clinked together.

Luka wrapped his arms around Gulan. "It'll be all right. I will help you cleanse yourself."

"Good," Gulan whispered. "Get rid . . . of those demons. . . ."

The moon pierced the canopy of treetops, shining light on Gulan. Sitting on a sheet of rock, he looked like a silver statue with legs crossed, eyes closed, and hands reaching for the sky. His dry lips chanted *Ying Gong* verses in weak whispers.

"My body is the temple of *Yin*. . . . Evils shall cease at its threshold. . . . Demons shiver in its presence. . . ."

His arms danced in intricate movements, like two willow twigs in the wind, fanning his *Qi*. His body swayed.

Zhou Xin Hu Yue, Luka thought. Inviting the Moon and Stars, the first step of *Yin Gong*. Gulan stood and embraced the silver touch of the moon, yielding to the sacred call. Perching on one leg with his arms stretched like the wings of an eagle, he spun east, south, west, and north. *Yu Zhou Zhun Huang.* Spiraling with the Universe. It was one of the most difficult steps, calling for earthly energy from the four corners of the land.

Luka cheered silently as Gulan began to enter the realm of ascendance. No scorpions would have a chance after that. The purity of his *Qi* would flow like the bluest river, cleansing everything from his body and from his soul. But instead of soaring and swaying, welcoming the arrival of the silver light, Gulan suddenly collapsed onto the rock.

"Grandmaster! What happened?"

"The scorpions have blocked my flow. They have broken me from inside," Gulan said.

Qi flowed in a circle, Luka knew. Any break would render *Yin Gong* a dead twig. The evil scorpions were still alive and multiplying and feeding. Soon they would eat Gulan from the inside, leaving behind only a tortured soul.

"Can I infuse you with my *Qi*?" Luka asked.

"Don't. An infusion now and you run the risk of the scorpions entering your body. Then all our dreams will be dashed." Gulan thrashed like a fish out of water. Luka held the frail body in his arms. The old man relaxed only temporarily before he convulsed and writhed again.

"Catch them, and squish them to death," Gulan gasped.

"How?"

"Look here."

A small ray of moonlight showed four moving lumps at work. They squirmed slowly along his thighs like rats in the whispering wheat fields, two in each leg, taking their time, nibbling along. The bigger ones, the mothers, led the way, and the smaller lumps, the children, trailed behind.

Gulan tried to catch them with his hands but the scorpions were faster than his trembling fingers. They lurched and careened around his knobby knees and raced up his groin and then down again. He almost caught one heading for his toes, but just as he pinched it between his fingers, it vanished, drilling deep into his calf muscles. The other three seemed to have been informed for they too crawled deeper into his flesh, safe from his fingers.

"Evil creatures," Gulan cursed. "Luka, ready your *Yin Gong*. Zap them with your power."

Murmuring a verse, Luka's fingertips gunned out four blasts of flaming *Qi* at the demons. The twin sets ran upward like ants fleeing a hot wok.

"Marvelous youth!" Gulan cheered. "No one is your peer, my boy. They won't last for long if you keep on doing that."

Luka willed another shot and the gang of four flocked together, huddling quietly under the loose skin on the left side of Gulan's chest.

"Are they dead now?" Luka asked.

Gulan slammed his hand down, meaning to squash them to death, but the demons suddenly leaped to life and fled in four directions all over his chest.

"There is only one thing to do," Gulan said. "Force them all into my left hand. Will it with your heart and shock them into submission with one blow."

The four all flocked into Gulan's left shoulder as Luka willed them to. With one last effort, he chased each of the insects into Gulan's fingers till their ugly forms hunched and squeezed into the pouches under Gulan's nails.

"Keep blasting your *Qi* on my elbow."

While Luka concentrated, Gulan grabbed his left arm with his right hand. With one powerful twist, he snapped his left hand off at the elbow. Blood gushed out from the neatly broken stump.

"Why did you do that?" Luka nearly lost his wits as the severed forearm twitched with life.

"To get rid of them for good. See, it's better than a knife job," Gulan chuckled at Luka's shock, marveling over his own bloody handiwork.

The break was clean, no dangling tissues or gory hanging flesh. The blood diminished immediately after the first gush.

"Put your palm here at my elbow while I punish these bad boys," Gulan said.

Luka followed Gulan's instructions, pumping warm flow into the arm stump to stop the bleeding.

"That feels right," Gulan said. "Look at them. Pathetic."

The scorpions were crawling out of the severed end of his hand like surrendered soldiers. They rolled blindly in the dirt and started attacking one another.

"Aren't you going to kill them?" Luka asked.

"No, they will kill themselves."

And they did.

The mothers first scissored the babies to death and devoured them hungrily. When the babies settled in their stomachs, they grieved and crawled around sadly. Meeting in a hug of death, they clawed each other's necks off.

Luka watched the horror in silence.

"Aren't they something?" Gulan said.

"They are like humans with emotions."

"The Mogo Empire is full of strange creatures," said Gulan. "Fortunately, we won't have to meet all of them. Now let me do some repair here."

The severed hand looked dark and lifeless now, but that didn't seem to bother Gulan a bit. "It still feels warm," the grandmaster said, aiming the parts at each other. He then forced them together, twisting the hand around and around till a small crackling sound was heard.

"Done," he said, smiling, and finished up by dusting a white powder over the wound. The oozing blood was soaked dry instantly. Gulan swung his reattached hand freely and curled his fingers. He looked satisfied. "That old trick still works. *Yunnan Bai Yiao* powder heals the skin and *Yin Gong* connects the bones."

"Wow, Grandmaster." Luka was amazed. "It looks as good as new."

"Not quite. I cannot do combat till sunrise." But combat would prove to be the least of his worries.

Within another *li* of walking, Gulan's breaths had dwindled down to feeble puffs. His limbs were shaking as small lumps squirmed across his ribbed chest. A pair of black scorpions ventured cautiously out from the tender craters of his leg wounds only to draw back under Luka's glare.

"I thought we got rid of them," Luka said.

"We got rid of the scorpions, but not their eggs, apparently," Gulan gasped. "Fortunately . . . the river is not far from here. . . . Can you hear its murmer?"

"We'll get to the river together. Please rest on my shoulder." Luka picked Gulan up and draped him over his back. The old man was as light as a feather and Luka's strides were long as he trailed the monkey. The river was indeed quite near and the murmur soon became a hiss.

"What do we do, Scar?" Luka asked, putting Gulan down.

But Scar had gone into the woods. In a matter of seconds the furry friend returned, dragging a little raft from a hidden cove. Luka jumped for joy. A river in the promise of night, and a raft in the grace of the moon.

Luka lifted Gulan aboard and the raft sank in welcome.

"Let's go, Scar." Luka beckoned the monkey.

Scar looked sad in the faint light as he shook his head and wiped his eyes.

"Why aren't you coming?" Luka asked.

Scar pushed the stern away from the shore without a pole or an oar and the raft started gliding.

"Scar!"

"Done his job. . . . Time to say goodbye . . . ," Gulan gasped as he lay limply on the rough wood. A light snore soon ensued.

The land had ended and the river begun. Luka's wet trail would soon dry and his pursuers be lost. Hope lifted his heart, but exhaustion knocked him on the head. He lay down next to Gulan, gazing at the fleeting stars. He let the current push his boat and the wind man his helm. Soon he was in the fluffy land of wrinkle wrinkle little star, ripple near, ripple far. His sweet breathing became a noisy snore.

The river soon picked up its tempo and the raft began to rock like a madman. Even then Luka would not have awoken were it not for the thunder that shook the raft. He jumped up and gazed around blindly. What he saw more than dismayed him. A thick mist hung like a cloud, and the thunder seemed to come not from the sky but from deep below him. Luka got a perfect view of what lay ahead just as they were about to plunge. *Why didn't anyone tell me there was a waterfall ahead?* he thought. It was too late to change course or turn around. Everything was going in one direction—down.

Luka's heart was thumping but his mind remained cool. He

woke Gulan and took a deep breath. Atami's words came to him: *Go with the flow and use the force to your advantage.* As the boat shot over the fall, Luka curled himself up like a shrimp, holding Gulan to him. But the force of the water flung them apart as the little raft spun and Luka tumbled. The force from above crushed him like an avalanche, plunging him farther and farther down. In a moment of silence, he was insulated from the world.

When he finally hit the surface, pain overwhelmed him and then all was dark. His last words were "Stay with the flow. . . ." His final thoughts were not of himself dying, but of a sad Atami, weeping and waving from far away.

野
洞
寺
院
武
侠

LUKA FLOATED UNCONSCIOUS in the robust river like a
dead animal, his arm draped over a piece of the broken raft. He
would have gone the way of the sea with the rest of the debris, but
a tall mountain that sat at the mouth of the river forced it to take
one last detour before merging into the sea. Luka was thrust into
a mossy boulder in the middle of the course and bumped east into
a tangle of grass. That brutal jostling hurt his head and the pain
woke him up.

He felt a sad emptiness, though he could not explain why. As he
bobbed in the river, he wondered why he was in the water and
what had brought him there. Nothing in the tranquil surroundings
offered any hint. He blinked, trying to bring back a memory. Memory of anything at all. But nothing came to his head.

What happened to me? he wondered as he tried to free himself
from the reedy tangle. The struggle only made him breathless, so
he let himself float, receding into the darkness.

When his consciousness returned, Luka was awed by the sheer
size of the mountain shooting up before him. He tipped his head

all the way back and still could not see the top. Its peaks were hidden somewhere high in the sky by a thin fog, and its base stretched far and wide, allowing the river only a tiny escape around its western waist. In his fuzzy mind, he thought it to be one of the northern mountains of his childhood. Yet unlike those mountains from his past, the one towering over him was lush with ancient trees and adorned with exotic cliffs.

Where am I? Clueless, he continued to float on the intertwining vines and leaves that covered the surface of the river. When a patch of fog passed, he spotted a curled-roofed temple, tiny and lonely, floating in front of the mountain's face. Thinking he was seeing things, he splashed his face with the cool water and looked again. But the temple was still there. This time he saw that it wasn't dangling in the air but linked to the earth by a thin path zigzagging downward like a slithering snake all the way to the river.

There is the temple! he thought. Yet he couldn't remember why he felt such fervor and joy. He paddled frantically with his arms and kicked toward the eastern shore, but the conniving vines roped him in. He tried paddling with one hand, the other holding on to the plank that had kept him from sinking, as he competed inch by inch with the falling darkness. An uprooted tree jostled him, swiping him farther east. Helplessly he floated. It would take another push, this time by a wineless barrel, to bounce him snugly into a horseshoe cove hidden at the foot of the mountain.

Luka celebrated his good fortune with weak shouts and a kiss on the rocky shore. He looked around at the little paradise shaded by a conspiracy of old trees. The water here bubbled, its utter clarity an eerie contrast to the muddy, churning river only a few feet away. He scooped a handful of water into his dry mouth. It tasted silky and sweet. It must be a sacred spring. No wonder the rocky steps ended here at its edge. The temple in the clouds was only a thousand steps away. His heart beat with hope.

He splashed about, untangling the slippery vines from around him. Then he heard footsteps coming from above.

"Sin! Sin! You are desecrating our sacred spring!" A monkish boy, ten at most, ran down the steps, carrying two enormous pails that hung from a bamboo pole draped over his shoulders. Luka looked up only to see the boy throwing the bamboo pole at him like a spear. He stopped the pole only inches away from his face. The momentum threw him back into the water.

What a powerful little monkey!

"Get out of my spring, you intruder!" the boy shouted, jumping over ten steps to land on Luka's shoulders. The boy was light, but his legs were like a pair of iron scissors that choked Luka's neck. "Get out! Get out!" The boy drummed Luka's head with his fists. Then he suddenly dived under the water, lifted Luka by his crotch, and tossed him up onto the rocky shore. The pain was drilling, but he ignored it for he was caught up by the magic of this young boy's strength.

"Surrender and confess," the kid shouted. "Why are you ruining our sacred well?"

"Peace and benevolence," Luka begged.

"Where do you hail from?"

"Where?" Luka still could remember nothing.

"I know who you are." The boy pulled out a bamboo flute hanging from his belt and blew a piercing sound. "You're that escaped convict on the run, aren't you? They said you might come from upriver." He jumped on Luka, sat on his chest, and landed punches all over his head and shoulders. Reluctantly, Luka marshaled his strength and tossed the boy off of him.

The two were soon involved in combat and the shorty was a formidable foe. His kicks were long and deadly and his punches were not just powerful but nuanced. Yet it was his foot scheme that impressed Luka the most. This was not a messy web of unskilled footwork but a calculated chess game, each move a preparation for the next. Whoever reigned over the temple had to be a peerless master. As Luka's strength waned and pain wracked every muscle, the boy tried to push him back into the river. Luka laughed hysterically.

"Why are you laughing like that?"

"Because you're letting me, a convict, go free. Isn't that a sin?"

"We want nothing to do with you." The boy pushed Luka back one more step.

Luka had to distract him or he'd be right back in the river. "Well, you must have a very lousy teacher."

"That does it! Nobody insults our teacher." The boy struck him three times, one punch to his forehead, two to his belly.

With difficulty, Luka summoned some *Qi*, which lessened the blows. "Ha! You punch like a girl."

The boy struck again. This time Luka was caught off guard but he quickly regained his balance. "You look like a frog with those kicks. Does your master also hop like a frog?"

"My master is a hero. How dare you call him a frog." The boy threw himself at Luka and choked him. Luka's head was filling with golden sparkles when he heard footsteps. Three boys jumped to the bucket boy's aid, nailing Luka down to the ground.

"Who is this intruder?"

"Looks rather familiar," said another.

"He's the escaped convict drawn in the fugitive notice we received from the village," the short boy said. Each of the four took a step back.

"Really? I have never seen a convict before," someone said.

"What should we do with him?" asked another.

"Dump him back in the river and never mention this to anyone, otherwise Ghengi's garrison force will be down our backs again," the tallest youth said. He gave Luka a cold look.

Luka could see four shiny shaved heads circled above him, each face looking rounder than the next. Their discussion grew heated and Luka would have liked to join in had a hand not covered his mouth.

"But we can't," the bucket boy argued.

"Why not?"

"He insulted me."

"What did he say?" the tall leader asked.

"He called me a frog."

"A frog is an ugly but good-natured and harmless creature that

Buddha loves. And you do look like a frog. What's so bad about that?" the leader said. "I say toss him into the river, now."

Luka mumbled.

"Wait," bucket boy said. "He also insulted our teacher, calling him a lousy frog too."

Silence dropped like a bomb. Everyone stared at Luka with dagger eyes.

"Did you?" the leader asked.

Luka nodded.

Several hands reached for him but the leader gestured them to stop. "Never, ever insult our master," he said. "Because when you do, you insult our tradition, our beliefs, and the glory of new Xi-Ling. Now you must come with us so that we can give you your due punishment."

Luka let out a strangled scream, struggling free from the sweaty fingers covering his mouth. "Did you say this is Xi-Ling?"

"Yes, the new Xi-Ling," said the leader. "We are going to teach you respect, convict." Two boys bound Luka's hands and mouth with cloth, swung him onto their shoulders, and started climbing the winding steps.

All the way up, Luka wore a smirk.

A FORBIDDING WALL stood atop the steps and surrounded the temple with secrecy. The young monks carried Luka into the grand yard by kicking open a squeaky narrow door, to the outrage of another teen warrior who stood guard. He ran after them, shouting, "No strangers! No strangers!" to no avail.

They hung him upside down by his feet from the branch of an old tree near a barn. When the monks had vanished, a cocky rooster and a clucking hen strutted up to Luka. They studied his dangling form for a while before they figured out what was wrong with the picture. Slowly they turned their heads upside down and found what they were looking for. The rooster clucked with satisfaction and the hen nodded with approval. Stepping closer, they started pecking on the boy's head. Luka shook his head violently but that only increased the birds' pecking. He closed his eyes, begging for the torture to end.

After what seemed like an eternity, Luka was awoken by a soothing voice, mellow like an old bell. "Oh, my Buddha. Release him immediately."

Luka opened his eyes to see first a few pairs of boots, then baggy pants, followed by yellow robes, culminating with seven nodding heads.

The upside-down figures were all tall with long necks and dangling arms. The speaker, an old monk, was visibly agitated as the others undid the ropes to let Luka down. He dropped to the ground, managing a little smile before he fainted again.

"How dare you torture an innocent boy like this?" the old monk said, smacking their melon heads one by one.

"But he was insulting you."

"Go inside the temple and wait for my punishment," the monk ordered, then knelt and untied the cloth strapping Luka's mouth and arms.

"Is he dead?" bucket boy asked, refusing to leave.

"We'll find out, Hu-Hu."

As the other young monks gathered around, their leader fished out a bamboo case full of needles. The long needles were springy and the short ones shiny with thickness. He selected the longest one and aimed it at the tip of Luka's right middle finger. All present knew what that meant. It was lesson number one in acupuncture. One little poke there and a dead man would sing. It was the tenderest of all spots on all ten fingers, with a direct link to the heart. All cringed as their master plunged the needle into the heart of Luka's fingertip. Most people would scream, but Luka didn't move. The old monk blanched Luka's fingernail bed and was relieved to see the redness return.

"The strangest thing I have ever seen," he muttered. "His color tells me that he has been drowned for hours, but redness returns when I press his nails. It could only be one thing." He flipped Luka over and sank a knee into his belly. Luka coughed up a gush of water before going limp once more.

"Is he dead?" Hu-Hu asked.

The monk shook his head. "Not at all. Limp is good. Stiff would be bad in this case."

"Please save him," Hu-Hu begged. "He was a good fighter, even weakened, and would make a good warrior."

"He's a convict!" another monk exclaimed.

"Warrior or convict is not my concern now. Even a sinner's life is worth saving. You all should have learned this by now," said the old monk.

"Please hurry, Master," Hu-Hu said.

A red bead of blood welled around the needle, encouraging the old man to spin it deeper and deeper. He was going for the heart. He was going for the soul. He was hoping to ignite the dormant life buried deep down below.

With his eyes closed, the old monk spun and spun like a knowing fisherman groping for that sly crab hidden in its muddy nest. His fingers knew the way. His mind knew the darkness. But it was hard digging. All he felt was mud blocking his reach. He was about to pull the needle out when Luka gave a little groan, followed by a string of screams. Then he slumped softly in the arms of the master monk, breathing evenly with sleep-like rhythm.

"He is alive! He is alive!" Hu-Hu shouted in relief.

"Shhh. Let him wake peacefully," the old monk said. He ordered a monk to brew some ginseng tea.

Luka awoke with a splitting headache.

"Where am I?" he asked, not remembering.

"In the palm of Buddha," answered a comforting voice.

"You mean I'm in heaven?"

"Well, you're halfway there," the monk said with a smile. "This is my humble temple."

"What am I doing here at your temple?"

"My student, Hu-Hu, fetched you from our river below." Hu-Hu's worried face was shoved into Luka's vision. "What were you doing there?" the old monk asked.

"I remember falling."

"Falling?"

"Yes. Something was pulling me down. . . ." Luka blinked. "Wetness and noise drowning me . . ." He went along slowly.

The old monk's face wrinkled and he nodded. "I know where you fell."

"Where?"

"Swallow Falls," he told Luka. "But no one has ever survived that fall." He patted Luka down his body, looking for hidden injuries, but he was okay. He grabbed Luka's foot and slowly tickled his sole with his long nail. Luka's toes wiggled beautifully, to the monk's satisfaction. But when he examined the foot more closely, his eyebrows rose. The boy had moles on his soles!

The monk checked the other foot, and there they were again, five on each foot, laid evenly in the symmetrical scheme of the celestial Phoenix Web.

"My dear Buddha!" The old master took in a long breath, his face tightening with ropy wrinkles.

"Am I okay?" asked Luka.

"It can't be true!" said the monk.

"What can't be?" Luka asked, worried.

The monk cupped Luka's face in his hands as if it were a precious golden bowl. His intense eyes narrowed and searched.

"Swordlike brows. A *tongtien* nose, long and straight. Long ears soaring above. A square chin. A full mouth. A face with celestial features," he said in wonderment. "You must be the boy."

"What boy?"

"The Holy Boy," the monk said. The other monks murmured.

"How do you know who I am?" Luka asked.

"I am Lin Koon, the headmaster of this temple. And you will be pleased to know that I once trained with the man who cared for you. Come and see." The old master lifted Luka to his feet and Luka wobbled, with Hu-Hu supporting his back, to a rock in a corner of the yard. At the top were carved the words HERO ROCK. Hundreds of names were chiseled below that. Koon traced his finger down to the middle and said, "Look, here is his name."

"Gao Shang Yu Zhen." A foolish monk from the high mountain. "Atami's formal name?"

"It is his temple name."

Lovingly, Luka also touched the name with his finger. As his eyes moved upward, he caught another name, Gulan. He touched it, and his memory came rushing back.

"You know Gulan?" the monk inquired.

"I do. I do." The dos really hurt his head, but Luka didn't care. "I remember everything now. We fell over the falls together." Luka explained as best he could. He told about his death sentence and meeting Gulan and their adventures.

"How did you find us here?" Lin Kong asked.

"Your message in the cave. And following the river. I was parted from the grandmaster when we fell down Swallow Falls. That was the last I saw of him. Please help me find him. Please."

"Say no more. We will search for him right away. The grandmaster should be able to survive anything, from what you have told us."

"But you don't understand. He was infected by Mogo scorpions back in the cave. He was dying when we jumped," Luka cried.

"Messenger!" Lin Koon shouted.

Branches and twigs rustled. A thin-lipped boy swung down from a tree and knelt before his master, waiting for a command.

"I want the temple on full alert. Gather everyone in the Combat Square immediately."

The messenger leaped back up the tree. Perched on the highest branch, the boy whipped out a little bamboo flute and a piercing melody shattered the mountain quietness. Hushed running footfalls were soon heard.

Master Koon led Luka through a maze of dark corridors. On the walls hung all sorts of weapons Luka had never seen before. A couple of students trotted past them, out through a door into the sudden glare of the setting sun.

"Wow." Luka could not help sighing. It was the most fantastic sight he had ever seen. No wonder the Combat Square, where the students trained every day, was the soul of a warrior temple. This one stretched proudly two hundred feet long and one hundred feet across. It was really a series of three rectangular platforms, each of which dropped down gently from one level to another. The stone surface had been smoothed by hundreds of years of stomping feet. And now all three levels were crowded with straight columns of young warriors standing at attention, awaiting their master.

Master Koon led Luka to the front podium. "This is the review podium where the honorable judges sit during a competition," he said, standing Luka to his right. "But today the honor belongs to you."

Koon turned to face his young warriors. "My students. Standing next to me is our fabled Holy Boy, Luka of Peking. The scrolls have long predicted that he would come with dark clouds but eventual victory. But hardly did I know that he would come to us bringing the good news that our grandmaster, Gulan, has been released from prison."

Students cheered.

Lin Koon waved for them to be quiet. "But our grandmaster is missing and greatly weakened by our enemy's creatures. The *Shui Gong* Warriors and I must find him, and quickly, yet I want the rest of you to take up your usual posts and be on the highest alert.

If Gulan and Luka are here, our enemy Ghengi and his forces will not be far behind. Now go!"

The students spilled off the platforms. Within minutes all had disappeared.

Luka followed Koon back inside. The old master led him through a long tunnel to a door that opened at the touch of his finger.

"This will take us to the Vault where Scholar is. He has knowledge of all the Xi-Ling treasures, and you can count on him to help locate Gulan."

It was so cramped inside the dark chamber that his shoulder rubbed Koon's. As soon as the door was shut, the floor began to fall. Luka grabbed Master Koon's arm.

"I should have warned you," Koon said. "The Vault is thirteen floors below the ground, deep in the heart of the mountain. It's safe from intruders, even under attack. You are the first nonmaster ever to come down here."

The landing was not as bumpy as Luka had expected. The door opened into a wide chamber lit with a dozen flickering candles.

A giant warrior blocked their way.

"Holy Boy, this is such an honor." The giant's voice was surprisingly gentle. Looking more closely, Luka saw a pair of smiling eyes and two dimples that nicely framed his gappy teeth.

"This is Scholar," Koon said.

"Honorable Scholar." Luka bowed, hiding his surprise. He had expected the scholar to be a dwindled old man with squinty eyes ruined by too much study. Who would have imagined a scholar to be so big and youthful?

"So polite and yet so extraordinary," Scholar said.

"What have you found?" Koon asked.

Scholar pulled out a pair of shining metal stars the size of Luka's palm. "These will aid us in our search."

"Xing Xing and Xong Xong," Koon murmured.

"In air it flies. In water it swims. The twin will not part. Far and wide they ring," Scholar quoted.

"How do they work?" Luka asked.

"Magically, Holy Boy. Let me show you." The giant pushed open a secret door hidden behind a tiger hide and led them outside onto a ledge overlooking the river. He threw one star into the air. "That is Xing Xing. It will go and search out its target and come back to tell Xong Xong, which you will keep in your possession."

Xing Xing flew out in a circle over the bay. It glowed with a light that was like no other Luka had seen. It peeped periodically, like a lost bird searching for its nest. Then, like a shooting star, it disappeared into the night.

"But how does it know to search for Gulan?" Luka asked.

"It's all recorded in the scrolls, my boy. The last generation of masters, including Gulan, had the mark of Xing Xing burnt into their flesh. Even without other instructions, it will search for its mark." Scholar bowed and handed Xong Xong to Master Koon.

"Thank you, Scholar. Once again you have justified your hidden existence in the Vault. We will launch our boats toward Turtle Brook." Koon held up Xong Xong and faced west.

"Turtle Brook?" asked Luka.

"Another branch that feeds into the river after Swallow Falls." Koon frowned and stepped forward. "We must act fast."

"Goodbye, Holy Boy," Scholar said. "Come back again. I have much to show you."

Luka bowed and followed Koon. They quickly made their way to the bay, where a dozen youths stood at attention.

"Into the boats now," Koon ordered.

Luka climbed into one of the narrow boats fastened by a thick rope to a secret dock. The old monk got in after him and gave the order to launch.

A boy shot a flaming arrow, which sliced through all the ropes, freeing the boats. Luka had to hold on to the sides as their little boat dipped and swayed with each steady stroke by the wide paddles.

A score of dark figures leaped off the cliffs and dived into the water. They swam beside the six boats.

"I'm grateful that you're sending out such a large force to look for Gulan," Luka said.

"For Turtle Brook, this might not be enough," Koon replied.

"What do you mean?"

"All the sea turtles, some as big as tables, swim up the bay to lay eggs on the sandy beach. Local villagers have long hunted them as delicacies. The gentle turtles have since banded together against human intrusion. They'll attack anyone venturing into their territory."

Lin Koon held up Xong Xong as if testing the wind. Quivering, it pointed to the west.

"Increase speed!" Koon shouted.

The swimmers lifted the boats with their shoulders and the boats raced ahead, skipping atop the whispering waves.

"These warriors are powerful," Luka said.

"They are my *Shui Gong* Warriors—Water Warriors. They were born by the sea and raised near the water."

Minutes later, they came to a fork. The falls murmured in the distance.

"Farther north is Swallow Falls. To the left is Turtle Brook."

Xing Xing was right there, flying back to guide them left toward Turtle Brook.

"I wonder how Gulan could have gone upriver instead of downriver as I did."

"The turtles must have taken him for revenge, mistaking him for a fisherman."

As they advanced slowly into the gleaming water, domed shadows gathered on the water's surface. "What are those?"

"Turtle patrols."

"They're huge."

"Bigger ones are yet to come. Everyone up in the boats."

The swimmers jumped into the boats.

"The turtles have formed a wall to block our advance," Lin Koon said. Ahead, a line of gleaming turtle shells were stacked one atop another.

"They must have captured Gulan," Lin Koon said.

"Can we go farther?"

"Not if you want him to live."

As Luka eyed the wall, Xing Xing suddenly dashed over the turtles and circled above a boulder that cropped up in the very center of the river. Unusually peaceful, the turtles made not a snap or a peep as they watched the blue star's midair dance. Its circles got smaller and soon the star began to beep. Xong Xong responded with delight by flipping madly in Lin Koon's palm.

"They found him!" Lin Koon cheered.

The star hovered lower and lower, as if succumbing to an invisible power, till with a brilliant blue glow it landed atop the boulder. It drew in the air like an illuminating pen, outlining the shape of a human body lying motionless on the rock.

"That's Gulan!" Luka shouted.

"They seem to be guarding him," said the puzzled Lin Koon.

Luka stood up. "Return my grandmaster, please. We come in peace."

To everyone's surprise, the wall of turtles began to disassemble. They swam together and formed a path, shell to shell, from Luka's boat all the way to Gulan's rock.

Lin Koon's jaw fell. "Unbelievable. I thought it was just a fable."

"What?"

"A turtle path, a path of faith that can be taken only by the most virtuous. They want us to walk on their shells to fetch Gulan."

Xong Xong leaped out of Lin Koon's hand and led Luka and Lin Koon along the backs of the docile turtles. They caused only a ripple here and there till they reached the rock.

"Gulan!" Luka cried. He held the poor old man in his arms and searched hungrily for signs of life. Gulan was dry, not even damp, and his eyes opened slowly.

"Grandmaster, are you all right?"

"I am. The turtles saved me."

"How did they find you?"

"I must have unleashed a cry of desperation. The next thing I knew, I was being carried by Ugly here." Gulan patted the rock beneath him.

"Ugly?" Only then did Luka realize that the rock was the shell of a large turtle. "He must be very, very old," Luka said.

"Old and wise. He was old when my grandpa was a little boy. My great-grandpa once helped him by extracting an arrow from his flesh."

"And he remembers you?"

"That's all they do. They swim and keep score of things."

"How do you know it's the same turtle?"

"Look at the carving on his shell." He pointed to a word. GULO. "My great-grandpa's name."

"Wow!"

"Now take your dagger and carve my name beside it," Gulan said.

Luka dragged the tip of his dagger along the ornate shell. Gulan smiled. "And why don't you carve your name on it too."

"Why?"

"So that it will live longer. Its life lasts only as long as its kindness to others. By carving your name here, you tell the world that this turtle has helped you."

"It will be my honor." He scratched LUKA in his boyish writing next to Gulan's name.

"Now it will live another two hundred years," Gulan said.

Luka kissed the old turtle gently on his shell. A thick head the size of a large wok emerged from the water. Its wrinkly loose skin piled around its neck like a tree trunk and two eyes rolled slowly in their teary sockets.

"Now he has seen you and will remember you for as long as he lives."

Lin Koon bowed, then took Gulan into his arms. "Welcome back, Grandmaster," he said.

"It's good to be back, Lin Koon."

The two men hugged tightly and Luka could feel the deep bond and love between them. It was evident in the care with which Lin Koon carried Gulan off the turtle and the gentleness with which he laid him in the boat.

Before they departed, Gulan waved to the turtle. "Goodbye, Ugly."

In their wake, hundreds of turtles followed them to the river fork in a lingering farewell. When they had waved goodbye to the last turtle, Luka inquired, "Grandmaster, how is it that I didn't drown?"

"I had unabled you, so that your body would shut down on the surface yet still maintain life within. Master Koon didn't tell you that?"

"No."

"Well, only his needles could have undone what I did." Lin Koon and Gulan exchanged a smile.

"How can I ever thank you enough, Grandmaster?"

"It is nothing, my boy. I had to save you so that you could come back to save me."

At sunrise, the boats eased into the secluded cove at the foot of the mountain. Three boys jumped out from behind the trees, each wearing a suspicious expression. With alarm, Luka recognized them as the very ones who had gagged him and hung him upside down.

"You have met these three before. They are my nephews," Master Koon said. "By height, starting with the tallest, these are Yi-Shen, Er-Shen, and San-Shen."

The master's nephews, Luka thought. His mouth was still sore from the gag and his ankles still raw where they had hung him, but he jumped off the boat and bowed in their direction. "It's an honor to meet you again, my *shi xiong.*" The term literally meant *elder brother masters,* a carefully chosen phrase that indicated the intimate relationship they shared.

"Who are you calling *shi xiong*?" barked Yi-Shen, the tallest boy, who had a crooked nose.

"Yi-Shen, be quiet," Master Koon said. "Grandmaster is recovering."

The three cast disdainful looks at Gulan, whom the swimmers carried.

"I am sorry if I have offended any of you," Luka offered. He knew kung fu brotherhoods were tight cliques and that any outside attempt to penetrate them was viewed with hostility.

"You'll have to be cordial to one another because Luka will be your *shi di*"—fellow disciple younger brother—"starting today," Master Koon said sternly. "Don't be a disgrace to me. Bow back."

The tallest took the lead, giving a miserly shallow nod, and was followed by the rest.

"Thank you, my *shi xiongs,* I'll do my best to deserve your trust," Luka said.

"We'll see to that," Er-Shen muttered.

"Youthful and unwise." Master Koon shook his head. "Please forgive their ignorance. They have not seen the world as you have and have much to learn from you." He kicked the heels of the smallest, San-Shen, which got the three going up the steps.

The door opened and a little monk welcomed them. His big eyes had a touch of fear and loneliness in them. "Welcome, my holy guests," he said, bowing his head. "My name is Do-Do. I am the door boy."

Before Luka could reply, Yi-Shen kicked the boy out of their way.

Why were these boys so ill-behaved, even outright hostile? Luka sighed as he followed Lin Koon into the temple.

"This is the Deferential Hall, where young disciples learn to fear our ancestral heroes."

The atmosphere certainly inspired fear. Wooden statues of ancient warriors stared at them with monstrous faces, octopus arms, spider legs, lion heads, and dragon bodies. Luka made a mental note: no visit to DH alone. "Why do some of the heroes have animal bodies?" Luka asked.

"Ancient Xi-Ling warriors came from dispirited animals lost in the wilderness. Some of the finest warriors had features of both the animal and the human. There is so much to teach you."

"But for now, Master Koon, I beg you to find a cure for our grandmaster. My learning isn't the most urgent matter. His recovery is."

"You are young but wise. I'll do my utmost to search for a cure. But it won't be easy."

"I'll care for him day and night. I also ask that you give me the most arduous and heaviest chores around the temple to lighten the burden of our living here. And I'll work double shifts for Gulan's rations as well."

"You will not have to do any more or less than anyone else here. This is your home," Master Koon said.

They entered a hallway. The windows were long and tall, and opened invitingly to a thick forest noisy with birds.

"See that?" Master Koon pointed at the ceiling. Luka looked up and saw that it was thick with creatures. They were bats! Gigantic dangling bats, swinging with the light breeze, covered the entire ceiling. At the echo of Koon's voice, several bats darted at them. Luka yelped.

"They are harmless," Master Koon said. "My friends of the night." The bats flew back to their dark perches on the ceiling.

Master Koon showed them a little room around the corner from those ratlike creatures. "Gulan will stay here in the safest room near the bats' nest. There is a secret way out of the room that drops you a thousand feet into the river and takes you out to Lan-Lan Island, just off the coast, in case of need." He gestured for the Water Warriors to lay Gulan on a bed by the window overlooking a courtyard, and whispered in their ears before they were dismissed.

"Tonight all worries should be put aside. Celebration is in order," Master Koon said.

"A celebration? For what?" Luka asked.

"Your arrival and Gulan's return. Xi-Ling has not been so blessed since the days of our former glory."

"But the grandmaster is so weak."

"I have sent for Scholar to come up with something to refresh Gulan's weakened state so that he too can enjoy this great occasion."

Heavy footsteps sounded in the corridor. It was Scholar, who was armed with so much bulky equipment that he had a hard time passing through the narrow door. When he finally squeezed himself in, he went straight to Gulan, ignoring everyone and everything, including a little table that he knocked over, and went to work on saving the life that was slipping away.

野洞寺院武俠

SCHOLAR WORKED A miracle on Gulan. By sunset the grandmaster awoke refreshed, his skin all smoothed out. If there were any scorpion eggs left in him, they were not to be seen, at least not for now.

"Attend the welcome dinner? Why not?" Gulan said to Master Koon. "Whatever you have given me has quieted the scorpions."

"It's ginseng," Scholar replied. "It's mixed with *dangui,* a pinch of three-footed chicken brain, five and a half ounces of powdered rocks called *lauxi,* two sloshes of potent liquor that we brewed here, fat sloshes, and—"

"Enough." Master Koon cut him short. "Grandmaster doesn't need to hear all that, Scholar. You are just going to wear him down."

"My apologies, Grandmaster," Scholar said. "I beg that you please give me some more time to tackle the thousand pages of *Evil for Evil.* I am certain that scorpions have no place to hide in the glare of Xi-Ling wisdom."

"Take your time tackling the nine volumes of *Evil for Evil.* Better you than I," Gulan chuckled. "Now where is that dinner you promised?" Gulan got off the bed and walked without any help. Luka and Master Koon rushed to his side, but Gulan pushed them away and declared, "I am ready to face the next generation of Xi-Ling students."

"So you are." Master Koon knew his teacher too well to say any more. He stood behind the grandmaster and gave Luka a wink that said they'd let him be brave but watch discreetly over him.

"It's being held in the Worship Hall, Grandmaster," Master Koon said.

"My favorite place." Gulan took the lead, whistling down the corridors. When they arrived at the entrance of the Worship Hall, Gulan paused and knelt for a long time, head bowed and hands clasped in silent prayer. When he was finished, he stood. "Nothing has changed. Everything is only more glorious," he said.

They sat at the table of honor, right at the foot of a huge Buddha, and Luka admired the beauty of the ancient sanctuary. The ceiling was an ornate dome covered with mystical drawings of flying humans and animals in bright colors, and the circular walls were covered with elaborate woodcarvings of monstrous sea creatures and mountain animals. Two striking dragons dipped their heads down from the roof, guarding the entrance. A dozen lion statues sat beneath them.

"The carvings and murals reflect the scene of our first Xi-Ling swearing-in," Gulan said proudly.

"Those dragons are so lifelike," Luka said.

"That's because they are alive," Gulan said, "though they are not dragons, not yet. They are only giant snakes."

One of them turned to give Luka a lazy stare. "Do they eat people?"

"No. They are serving their sentence of eternal *zhaohua*—redemption—here."

"They are redeeming themselves?"

Gulan nodded. "They used to be bad snakes, but now they're vegetarian. They will not devour anyone with a Xi-Ling mark."

Good to know, Luka thought. He was tempted to ask when he was getting his Xi-Ling mark, whatever that might be, but swallowed the question.

"What is that?" Gulan pointed at two signs that hung on the Honor Wall. One read XI-LING BENEVOLENT ORPHANAGE. The other, XI-LING BAY TOWNSHIP OFFICER. There were traces indicating that a third sign had hung there, but the sign itself was gone. Only the nail remained.

"In name, Grandmaster, I am the principal of the orphanage, a township prefect, and the secret head monk of this temple," Lin Koon explained.

"Secret?"

"As you know, ever since that Mogo Ghengi took over our country, the worship of Buddha is forbidden."

Gulan swiped a finger over the statue behind them. "No wonder the Buddha statue is so clean, without any dust."

"Yes, Grandmaster. I have to cover it up most of the time. A sin that I pray every day for Buddha to forgive me for."

"And who gave you the order to wear those other secular hats?"

"The current ruler." Master Koon bent his head.

"You mean Emperor Ghengi?" Gulan said.

"Grandmaster, please don't judge me by what I have had to do, but by what I have accomplished."

"And what have you accomplished?"

"The evil Ghengi rule rendered this part of the country poor, and the famine has been most devastating. Orphans were everywhere, starving and being beaten to death. I begged the local county magistrate's permission to set up this orphanage not just to save the children but also to save the temple. They suspected my motives, but after the many riots by hungry orphans, they realized that something had to be done. Finally, in the spring of the second year of Ghengi's reign, I got a county directive to operate this orphanage. And ever since then I have picked dying boys off the streets. I do the feeding but Buddha does the healing. The orphans can come and go as they wish, but all have stayed. So, Grandmaster, if you think what I have done is in contradiction with our Xi-Ling principles, I stand ready for punishment."

The grandmaster sighed. "No, my dear Lin Koon. You make me proud."

"You are not angry with me?"

"My Xi-Ling pride might be a bit hurt, but the lives you have saved have redeemed you tenfold. How can I accuse you of anything? You have been the one doing the good deeds, upholding the spirit of Xi-Ling, while I have been selfishly tucked away in prison honing my *Yin Gong*."

"But Grandmaster," said Lin Koon, "you went to prison to save all of us. You inspire me not only with your bravery and selflessness but also with your wisdom. You are soft and supple, facing forces that outweigh our strength. In so doing, you gave us time to heal and grow, and that is why Xi-Ling is still here today."

"Oh, Lin Koon." Gulan put his hand on Master Koon's shoulder and pressed for a moment. "Now tell me what is the third sign that you have removed."

"You will see," Master Koon said. He turned to Scholar. "Please show Luka the parchment."

In his big hands, Scholar held a small bundle of yellowed paper, ancient and moldy-looking. On bent knees, he showed it to Luka.

"What is this?" Luka asked.

"The papers that predicted your arrival, yours and Gulan's," the giant said.

"Our arrival?" Luka reached toward it with both hands but Master Koon slapped his wrist. "Don't touch. It may fall apart."

"This is hundreds of years old," Gulan said. "Look at the handwriting. It is all in *li shu,* the most ancient and ornate style of writing, with curvy strokes and fancy loops, much like a drawing. And the signature here says that it was scribbled by a grandmaster like me a long, long time ago."

Luka was stunned. His arrival here had been predicted hundreds of years ago.

"Everything is as predicted, even this dinner," Master Koon said. He gestured toward the huge sheet of rock that served as a backdrop for the Worship Hall, where trickles of water splashed into a little pond. "The water comes from the top of the mountain and finds its way here. One drop falls every second, in storm or drought. See here, the water level nears the mark of the moonrise. It's almost time."

One drop, two drops. At the third, balls of fire burst from the two giant snakes' eyes.

"Wow!" Gulan wore a childish grin. "They've never created such a pure fireball before."

"The purity of the flame is the purity of their hearts," Master Koon said.

"What was the fire for?" Luka asked.

"Qui xie," Gulan said. Driving away the evils.

"And cleansing the stale air," Master Koon added. "Please continue the ceremony, Scholar."

"Enter the students," Scholar announced.

The doors swung open, and a hundred boys rushed in to bow before Gulan.

One by one, Gulan examined the boys with an adoring smile, as if they were his own children. Gulan acknowledged each with a special nod or a wink, or sometimes with a simple lift of his fingers. "As you said, they are all fine, fine boys, Lin Koon."

When all were seated at their tables, Lin Koon stood up. "Tonight, as the good books predicted, we have reclaimed our past." The students cheered.

"To honor our grandmaster's return," Master Koon continued, "I hereby rescind my position as the head of our temple and rein-state Gulan as our grandmaster above everyone else beneath his grace, our Buddha."

"Grandmaster! Grandmaster!" The boys shouted and cheered.

"As part of our grand tradition here, may I present to you the new name plaque." At Master Koon's signal, two young boys carried in a brand-new wooden sign bearing eight brilliant red characters—GULAN DA SHI; CHI MIAO ZHI ZHU. Grandmaster Gulan, the head of this temple.

On tiptoes, the boys hung the new sign on the empty nail and bowed to a beaming Gulan.

"From now on," Master Koon said, "his words are the truth to be obeyed by all. He will supervise all facets of our lives here. More importantly, he will seek among you one taker of his ultimate art of *Yin Gong*."

Gulan gestured with his hand for Lin Koon to stop.

"Is anything the matter?" Lin Koon leaned over and whispered.

"Indeed," replied Gulan. "I have already passed the art to our Holy Boy."

"You have? But why such haste?"

"Haste? All my life I have been waiting for a boy like this to come along."

"Aren't you worried about the purity of our tradition?"

"You mean the purity of his blood?" Gulan asked.

"Yes, he's half Mogo."

Gulan drew a long breath. "True, but he was raised in our tradition. He is the fruit of Atami's sacrifices and the future of China."

"Forgive me for doubting you, Grandmaster."

Master Koon bowed to Gulan, then stood Luka up beside him and announced, "I thought our blessings were doubled, while in fact they have been tripled. Our Holy Boy has been chosen as the taker of *Yin Gong*. Therefore, according to our rules, I now present to you our new junior master."

In the stunned silence, Yi-Shen stood up. "How about me? I thought I was the junior master."

"You are now the deputy junior master," Master Koon said.

"Forget that. I was the junior master before you came," Yi-Shen spat at Luka, "and I will be the junior master after you are gone."

Luka was taken aback. He didn't know what to do, nor what to feel. "Really, Master Koon, I don't mind being the deputy junior master. Let him keep the title."

"Tradition is tradition. Our rules clearly state that the taker of *Yin Gong* is to be the junior master, who will eventually rise up to be master, and, with Buddha's blessing, achieve the final glory of grandmaster. It's an honor not to be refused." He turned to Yi-Shen. "Sit down, Yi-Shen, and say no more. Now let the celebration dinner begin."

A team of young cooks, each carrying a tray in one hand, brought fruits and vegetables out to the tables. Luka had never seen anything like it before. The watermelons were two feet tall, with yellow meat. Smooth-skinned strawberries generously covered one's entire palm. Seedless lychees dripped with sweetness like honey. Bees buzzed around the yellow tart but sweet loquats. And there were a few things he did not recognize at all.

Luka's jaw must have fallen quite a distance. Master Koon asked, "Is anything the matter?"

"No, everything looks fantastic."

"We grow them here with Buddha's blessing."

"No wonder they are uncommon."

"To say the least. And they are good for longevity. Look at me. I haven't been sick for ages. All because of the good food from the blessed soil."

Luka ate slowly, trying to appear decent and polite in this first dinner with his fellow brothers, but to his happiness the students all chomped down as if they were starving. The only ones not eating were Yi-Shen and his brothers, who huddled at another table in the farthest corner, guzzling their drinks.

Master Koon held a bamboo cup of yam liquor and shouted, "A toast to our holy friend."

All stood like shadowy puppies and raised their cups in celebration.

Luka downed his drink first and all followed cheerfully.

Luka leaned over. "Gulan, I didn't know what you gave me would bring me so much honor."

"The honor is all ours. I only hope it doesn't bring any trouble," Gulan said, casting a look in Yi-Shen's direction. "As an old proverb says, a good drink warms all hearts. Why don't you offer Yi-Shen a toast?"

Luka refilled his cup and raised his cup to Yi-Shen. "I'd like to offer a toast to Yi-Shen. May our friendship grow like a bamboo tree, reaching higher and higher each day."

"Oh, a goodwill toast, nephew," Master Koon said. "You must take it."

"I'll take any toast," Yi-Shen said. "But never from him." He and his brothers stood up and walked out.

"Then I toast to your health, Yi-Shen," Luka said, and emptied his cup with gusto.

Master Koon stepped in, accepting his nephew's toast. "And I toast to your health, our gracious Holy Boy."

Gulan watched silently.

As the dinner ended, Master Koon said to Luka, "As the new junior master, you will be living with the other students."

"But I must stay with Gulan to take care of him."

"I have assigned two guards for that purpose. Besides, it is a time-honored tradition of equality, and as their leader you must set a fine example by following the rules and ordinances."

"Luka," Gulan said, "go as Master Koon instructs you. I am in good hands."

"Besides," Lin Koon said, "you will need all your energy for your training, and a little bit of companionship with Yi-Shen will help mend things between you."

Luka hugged Gulan goodnight. "The future of Xi-Ling is full of unknowns," Gulan whispered. "Keep that in mind."

That night, Luka wrapped up his few belongings and followed Master Koon to the barn, where all the students slept. The master informed him along the way that he would sleep, eat, train, and work with the rest of the students from then on for the unity and prosperity of Xi-Ling. He had the title. Now he needed to earn the students' respect. He would need to be strong and artful, generous and nurturing. He would need to see far and hear wide. And he would have to start at the most basic level of training.

Yet Luka could think only of Gulan and his words about the unknown future of Xi-Ling.

As he followed Master Koon along the cobbled path, he heard a popping sound behind him. It was Do-Do, the door boy, who had leaped from his hiding spot high in the treetops.

"What are you doing here?" Luka whispered.

"I'm on night watch," Do-Do whispered back. "Trouble is coming your way." He seemed to have more to say to Luka, but Master Koon turned and asked, "Who is that?"

"It's me, Do-Do."

"Is everything fine?"

"All is peaceful, Master Koon."

"How about the coastline and upriver?"

"Quiet."

"Good. Off you go. And keep an eye on the barn tonight. I want a full report of any activity there."

"Yes, Master Koon." Then he was gone, climbing up the tree with the silence of a monkey.

Soon they came to a barn. Luka could smell cow manure and horse piss dense in the air. To the east, the shadows of cows' horns moved, and teeth rhythmically chewed the endless hay while long tails whipped. To the west, scores of Xi-Ling horses stood and slept, dozing while thinking. The serenity of the barn was disturbed only by the occasional baaing of baby lambs, whose fine hooves trampled the loose hay.

The door opened a crack. It was Er-Shen, holding a candle. "Uncle Koon, how can I help you?"

"Have you prepared the bed for Luka as I instructed?"

"Yes indeed," Er-Shen said. He led them past rows of bunk beds where boys snored to an empty bed by the window. The faint candlelight did not allow Luka to see much, but there was no need to. A bed was all he wanted. A pillow wasn't even necessary. All he prayed for now was to be left alone so that he could sleep till the sun shone on his ass.

He said goodnight to Master Koon, but the man was not done yet. He gave Er-Shen another of his "From Now On" speeches. The boy listened attentively but Luka knew well that no matter what the instruction, trouble was coming his way.

As soon as Master Koon was gone, the barn sprang to life. Everyone lit his bedside lantern and swarmed around Luka, bombarding him with words.

"The Holy Boy is here!"

"How do you like being the new junior master?"

"Shut up!" said someone. "I'm trying to sleep."

"Speech, speech," Hu-Hu shouted. The rest took up the chant.

Luka held up his arms and the noise subsided. "You are all my brothers. Let us live as a family. But for now, I believe it is way past bedtime. Let's go to sleep. That's an order."

They all groaned in disappointment and crawled back to their beds, except Hu-Hu and a fat boy, who dragged their beds next to Luka's. "This is Co-Co, the cook boy," Hu-Hu whispered.

"Hi, Co-Co. That was great food tonight," Luka said. "But why don't you move your beds back and let's all go to sleep."

"No, we want to protect you," Hu-Hu said.

"Protect me? I'll be fine."

"Fine? We don't want you dead, hear me?" The fat cook pulled his kitchen knife from under his pillow and waved it for effect. "They will do away with you." He cast a cold glance at Yi-Shen's bed in the far corner.

That got Luka's attention. "They will?"

"Of course," Co-Co said.

"The problem is," Hu-Hu explained, "Master Koon loves his nephews like sons. Make no mistake about that. Their father died because of Master Koon's tie to Xi-Ling and he feels guilty for that. He blames himself for the misfortunes of those kids, and with his soft heart, he could never bring himself to discipline them as he should have. At the beginning it was just a little more food ration, and less punishment, and so forth. The uncle gave them an inch and they took a foot, till one day the uncle realized that the more he taught the boys, the worse they became. Now the monsters are good only at fighting and nothing else. And they rule everything here. Whatever they say goes. This is their temple, their home, their everything. And you, my new junior master, have just peed on their homestead. Now you tell me you have nothing to worry about."

Luka was quiet.

"But we are all right behind you," Co-Co said, "and we are hoping that you will change things a bit around here now that you are the JM."

"Change things? Like what?" Luka asked.

"Small things. We have to hand our food over as levies to the master's nephews. We have to do little favors for them, like cleaning their night pots. Things like that."

"I don't know if it is my duty to interfere."

"Sure it is. You'll see what I mean tomorrow at the dining hall."

"Tomorrow is tomorrow. For tonight, think one word as you both sleep—*unity.*"

"Unity?" Co-Co said.

Luka nodded. "Yes, unity among us Xi-Ling brothers. Good night."

"Unity," Hu-Hu muttered. "He's crazy."

The following morning, Luka was awoken by something slimy on his face. He thought at first it was part of his dream about fishing and snaring a squirming eel. When something tickled his nostrils, he slapped his face and the dream was over. The eel turned out to be a dozen six-legged green snakes with snapping lobster claws crawling all over his bed and floor. Their three eyes stared at him from a central rectangular socket under their foreheads.

He'd been sleeping among them! Luka danced around like a girl until he reached an unoccupied corner. He heard snickering from the far corner.

"I thought you would enjoy meeting my pets, the clobsters," Yi-Shen drawled.

"You tried to kill me!"

"I didn't. The clobsters did." Yi-Shen laughed.

The rest of the kids were still asleep, snoring away like broken bellows. Luka snatched up a basket near his pillow and tried to herd the mutant snakes into it, but it wasn't easy. The shadow he cast over them seemed to frighten them and they ran amok, scrambling for the windows.

"Hey, you scared them. They're only babies," Yi-Shen said. "Next time I'll bring you bigger ones. And do you know why I'm going to such lengths to welcome you with these rare creatures from the Vault? Because I want to make sure that you enjoy our togetherness as much as I do." He laughed. "See you at the Combat Square. I look forward to beating you in every step of the fundamentals that you'll be learning and I'll be relearning with you."

He walked out and his brothers tossed another basket of baby clobsters toward Hu-Hu's and Co-Co's beds before following him.

Luka leaped in the air and caught the airborne basket before the lid was thrown open.

"What are you up so early for?" Hu-Hu asked, rubbing his eyes.

"Nothing, just gathering up some loose snakes."

"Ah!" Hu-Hu cried, hugging his blanket around him. "Those are not snakes. Those are clobsters!"

"What are clobsters?" Luka asked, gently shooing the little things into the other basket.

"Legend has it that some evil man married some poisonous snakes with lobsters. What are they doing here?"

"Having breakfast," Luka said. "Tell me where I should return them."

"They belong in the Vault. Only one boy could have gotten hold of them," Hu-Hu said.

Luka picked up the last of the clobsters and closed the lid. "The name of that boy will remain between us. Remember, unity."

"Aren't you going to report this to Master Koon?"

Luka shook his head.

"It's your call, JM. All I'm saying is if you don't fight back at some point, he'll just keep coming at you."

"Don't you worry. Since you know where they came from, could you please carry them back, my friend? I'm sure Scholar has good use for them."

"Is that an order?"

"No, a favor."

Hu-Hu grimaced and picked up the baskets in a gingerly fashion.

Once he was gone, Luka stretched and took a deep breath. He hoped for some delicious morning air from the sea and mountains, but all he smelled was dung from the animals housed next to the barn.

Luka waved down below but no creature returned his greeting. They were all too busy belching and mooing, baaing and crying for their breakfast. Others arched their thick tails, ready to relieve themselves. What an animal kingdom it was!

As Luka turned away from the window, the sweet melody of a bamboo flute played in the morning air. Luka stuck his head back out the window and saw a young monk sitting in the fork of a tall pine tree, dangling his feet.

"It's time to get up, everyone," the monk shouted. All the boys jumped up from their beds, grabbed their hanging weapons, and filed out. "My name is Di-Di," the messenger called out.

Luka caught the association when the boy waved the flute in his hand. *Di,* as in *flute.* "Good morning to you," Luka replied to the tree boy.

Di-Di swung like a monkey to another tree.

"Good morning, Luka," Master Koon said behind him.

Luka turned around and bowed. "Good morning, Master."

"You look refreshed. Did you have a good night?"

"I did," Luka said somewhat hesitantly.

"Yi-Shen and his brothers didn't bother you, did they?"

"Not really. How is Gulan?"

"Better by the hour. I don't want you to worry about him anymore. Concentrate on what he and I want you to do."

"Yes, Master Koon. I'll try."

"Be firm like a warrior. You must leave your worry behind. Here at the temple, we start every day with a prayer," Master Koon said. He led Luka back to the Worship Hall.

Inside, the rays of the morning sun filtered through the bluish incense smoke. Hidden under the clouds, a hundred young monks knelt obediently with their noses close to the ground.

The piety in the air filled Luka with nostalgia, for the whisper of prayers was his childhood lullaby and the tips of burning incense his calming lights. He could almost hear Atami's echo in the sanctuary under the domed roof. Where was he now? And would he ever return to his home temple, where he forever belonged?

As if reading his mind, Master Koon handed him a burning stick of incense and asked, "Luka, are you missing Atami?"

"Yes."

"This temple has a curse. A good curse. Once your feet have touched the threshold here, you will always come back, no matter how you have drifted away."

"Do you really think so?"

"I know so," Master Koon said. "Now, circle your face. Frame yourself in a ring of smoke until the incense burns down and the ashes drop to the floor."

"What does that gesture mean?"

"Circling signifies diminishing yourself and the dusting of ashes symbolizes your falling into Buddha's arms. From now on you are in harmony with the elements of the earth."

When Luka tried to catch a glimpse of the two giant snakes on the roof, he was surprised to find them missing. He looked around the ceiling. The lion statues were there but the snakes were gone.

He tugged on Master Koon's sleeve. "What happened to the snakes?"

"They come and go freely like the spirit of the mountain. They appear only on special occasions. Most of the time they lie at the foot of the mountain, where they think about their sins and wait for their redemption."

"What happens when they redeem themselves?" Luka asked.

"They will shed their skins and transform into heavenly dragons."

"Wow."

"Xi-Ling is a feast of knowledge. One has to nibble at it, one bite at a time. Even I learn new things every day." Master Koon pointed. "Just look at that bell. It is two thousand years old but the older it is, the farther it can be heard."

In the distance, a skinny rat of a boy climbed up a tree and swung onto the rope of the bronze bell. *Dong, dong, dong,* it chimed as he dangled back and forth. At the tolls of the bell, everyone rushed out of the Worship Hall. A few bowed to Master Koon and Luka, but the younger ones only chirped in their direction and ran off.

"Ah, the newcomers. They are always in such a hurry."

"Where are they going?" asked Luka.

"To morning practice," Master Koon said. He led them to the veranda overlooking the terraced Combat Square.

In the square, students were leaping noisily from one tree to another, but not everyone had mastered the flying art yet. One little boy, distracted by a passing bird, bumped into a trunk and fell to the ground. The whole class returned to help their comrade. Another flock of students was heading for the meadows, carrying an assortment of animals across their backs and shoulders. One fat boy held a wee piglet, while a really thin youngster carried a gangly young calf that looked quite content with its free ride to the grazing meadow across the brook.

From the kitchen, Hu-Hu lead his bucket team to the river to fetch water for the day. They sang buoyantly as they rolled down the thousand steps. Luka wished them good luck, for descending the stone ladder was not his idea of a fun practice at all. Along a short wall, a dozen boys were practicing *shatou*, Sand Head. They balanced themselves on their heads with their eyes closed, lost in meditation. Nothing in this world seemed to bother them, not even another class's syncopated Iron Fist punches against a dirt wall.

But it was combat training between two teams of boys that fascinated Luka most. Their weapons were shiny, and their shouts boomed in the empty valley. They kicked, tossed, struck, and spun, their shadows becoming a montage of spirited beings dancing in the rising dirt.

"I can't wait to join them," Luka said to Master Koon.

"You must wait. Grandmaster Gulan has ordered that your training be built from the ground up. The road to perfection will be long and thorny."

"So you'll teach me all the skills of Xi-Ling weaponry while Gulan recovers?"

"No, at least not yet. You will start where I start all my orphans."

"And where is that?"

"It's simple. Water, gold, wood, fire, and earth."

"The elements of the world," Luka said.

"Atami taught you well. They also constitute the very fundamentals of Xi-Ling art."

"But I need to train as quickly as possible so that I can go and save Atami. Besides, I can handle a lot more than that because I also have the power of *Yin Gong*."

"Grandmaster Gulan must have told you before that *Yin Gong* is only a source of power. Other skills have to be mastered to bring it to perfection." Master Koon pointed to an ancient pagoda perched on the edge of the temple. "One only sees the pagoda's glorious tip, not its solid foundation. But it is that foundation that has kept it grounded for hundreds of years. We need to build as good a base for you, so that you can soar like the pagoda. We're going to start with earth element today. Since the training is very hard, and will be even harder if you do it alone, I have asked Yi-Shen to be your companion as you learn and he re-learns the fundamentals, to help bring the best out of both of you. It is my wish that you two become my right and left hands. And Xi-Ling will thrive on the harmony between you. Let's go to the field now."

The phrase *learn and relearn* ricocheted in Luka's head. He was really beginning to hate that phrase. But he followed Master Koon, imagining what the field might look like. He soon found out.

"This is our field." Lin Koon gestured.

"This is it?"

"Not exciting enough for you?"

"Oh, no. This is very exciting," Luka said, trying hard to build up his enthusiasm.

The field turned out to be the thousand stone steps meandering down to the river from the mountaintop. His nightmare was officially here. Worse yet, Yi-Shen and his brothers were already waiting, each one on a step. Yi-Shen's crooked face bore his usual crooked smile, and he was chewing a green twig.

"Whatever you do, I'm going to beat you to the punch," Yi-Shen said.

"And whatever you do, I'll..." Luka stopped under Master Koon's stern look.

"The battle of words is empty." Master Koon whacked Yi-Shen's head. "The battle of strength is what I am expecting from you. Why don't you stop bickering, stop wasting your tongue, and let the earth training begin."

"Way to go, JM! Beat your deputy!" Hu-Hu shouted as he carried his big pails of water up the steps. Er-Shen and the other brothers grabbed for Hu-Hu, but he darted out of their reach, splashing water all over the sitting Shens.

"Enough, enough!" Lin Koon ordered. "Are you two ready?"

"Yes, Master," Luka and Yi-Shen said in unison. It was the first time they had agreed on anything.

"Earth nurtures men. Men prowl the earth," Master Koon chanted. "Get on all fours."

Luka plunged his open palms onto the soil and struck a tiger's pose. Yi-Shen cast him a nasty look, and followed.

"Run down the steps and back up, one hundred times," Master Koon said. "The earth regimen will make you strong like a tiger and supple like a cat. It builds your arms and toughens your thighs. In due course, your strength will be balanced evenly throughout your body like that of a four-legged beast. Do you want to be strong like a beast?"

"Yes!" they shouted.

"The first one to finish will have a breakfast of our precious stinking tofu. The other will have to make do with pickled peppers."

Both Luka and Yi-Shen swallowed mightily upon hearing that announcement. Men could live without meat, but not without stinking tofu—a fermented, rotten delicacy nurtured by squirming maggots. Although it sounded nasty, its pungent flavor melted your heart and made your tongue sing.

"Now dash!" Master Koon said.

Dash Luka did, almost tumbling down the stairs. It was harder than he thought to run the way cats did. Even harder down a forty-five degree slope. Yi-Shen whipped by, leaping down three steps at a time. Before he knew it, Luka was twenty steps behind. Yi-Shen paused and barked back like a dog, teasing him, but Luka was not ready to give up. He narrowed his eyes, studied Yi-Shen's supple moves, and soon caught the trick. It was all in the beat of the arm and leg movements. *Ta, ta-ta, ta. Ta, ta-ta, ta.* He'd made the mistake of jumping even-leggedly like a frog. Instead, he should be trotting like a horse. The former guaranteed a headlong tumble; the latter, a steady flow.

By the time Luka caught up, Yi-Shen sped down the stairs, negotiating four steps at a time. Soon, the boy sat at the bottom, waiting. As Luka limped to the last step, Yi-Shen said, "I am the king here in everything we do."

"We only have ninety-nine more to go," Luka said, looking at him sideways. "Make sure you don't turn into a queen."

But by the ninety-ninth trip, even Yi-Shen was crawling like an earthworm. Bounces and leaps were flattened to a mere paw-to-paw sticky climb. Determined as he was, Luka was doing no better. His hands were bleeding and his joints cracking like old bones. And his head felt like a windmill, spinning around and around. When he finally climbed up the last step of their last trip two steps behind Yi-Shen, he lay dead on the ground for twenty minutes. Yi-Shen, meanwhile, was so weak and torn that all he could manage in the way of insult was a feeble spit, which the sea wind blew back into his face.

"To your feet," Master Koon said, smiling. "Clean up and go to classes now. This afternoon, we'll climb to the stepless top of that nameless mountain to our west. Don't forget the weights to strap to your feet."

"Yes, Master Koon." Luka could only manage a small, sweaty smile before stumbling back to the barn to get ready for his morning class in the Art of War. The class was taught by none other than Scholar, who did not look happy this morning. He kept smoking a bubbling water pipe, his eyes downcast. Yet his hands trembled with deference as he read from the classic, Suntze's *The Art of War*, mandated reading among Xi-Lingers.

The class was attended by no fewer than fifty students. Many sought refuge near a window or a wall for some serious snoring while the boring class crawled on. Hu-Hu, Di-Di, and Co-Co swung down from a nearby tree, hogging up Luka's seat, which was only meant for two. Di-Di and Co-Co each ended up sitting with half an ass cheek on one end.

"I heard you got beaten?" Hu-Hu whispered.

"But only by two steps," Co-Co cooed.

"You are still my hero," Di-Di said.

"How did you know all that?" Luka whispered back.

"News in general gets around fast. Besides, there are plenty of unseen eyes and hidden ears in every corner of the temple," Di-Di informed him matter-of-factly. "In the old days, seeing a new lizard sitting on Scholar's head was the top news, but not anymore. You and Yi-Shen are the hottest thing now, and your rivalry makes it even juicier."

"But why is everyone so interested in us? Don't you have anything else to do?" Luka asked.

"Are you kidding me? We've got more chores than you can name, but gossip makes all the chores go by a lot quicker. And besides, we're all anxiously awaiting the day you beat him up till there's not a feather of arrogance left in that cocky rooster," Hu-Hu said.

"I am here to learn, not to compete or beat anyone up," Luka said.

"So are we." The three nodded in unison.

Pop, pop, pop. Three marble balls were shot one into each mouth, silencing Hu-Hu, Di-Di, and Co-Co instantly.

It was Scholar, who kept a bowlful of them on his desk, ready for any disruptive students in his class. "Do behave, my students," he said. "Or I won't remove them till tomorrow."

The three nodded.

"As you can see, I'm a little unhappy today," Scholar said. "And do you know why? Two of my baby clobsters are missing. They were gone all night and I don't know what happened to the two tiniest ones. They will die if I don't get them back soon."

The class burst into furious whispers. Luka was tempted to tell Scholar about his encounter that morning with the clobsters, but then he would have to tell on Yi-Shen and that was something he couldn't afford to do. Not only would the revenge keep coming, but he would also break the peace that Gulan wanted so much for him to keep. Luka remained silent.

"Anyone who knows anything, please let me know. It has taken me years to raise them, and I just want them back alive. No one will be punished." Scholar gazed in Luka's direction, making him fidget.

At that moment, the door was kicked open. In walked Yi-Shen with his brothers. "I know who has the two missing clobsters," he said.

Scholar had had enough. "Get out! You have taken this class ten times and have managed to fail each time."

"But don't you want to know where your precious clobsters are?" He stuck his smug face right up into Scholar's so that he could hardly breathe.

"Where are they?"

"In his pockets." Yi-Shen pointed at Luka.

Everyone's eyes turned to Luka, and the marble ball dropped out of Co-Co's mouth. He picked it up and put it right back in again.

Luka stood and patted his pockets up and down. "I don't have them," he said.

"Oh, you lying Holy Boy," Yi-Shen sneered. "Why don't you check your chest pocket."

Luka stuck two fingers into his chest pocket and screamed when something nipped him. When he pulled his fingers back out, two inch-long clobsters dangled from the tips. Luka danced around, shaking his hand, but the little suckers wouldn't let go. The whole class found it a riot, especially Yi-Shen.

Scholar took two giant steps toward Luka and whispered something to the little creatures. They fell into his waiting hands. Scholar whispered some more, cooing to them as the two baby clobsters sniffed and curled their bodies in his palm.

"Scholar, I didn't take them," Luka cried. "I don't know how they got there."

Scholar stared at Yi-Shen and said, "You don't know, but I do."

"What are you looking at me for?" Yi-Shen yelled. "He did it and he has to be punished."

"I said there will be no punishment. Their safe return is reward enough for me. You get out now so we can continue our class." Scholar slipped the clobsters into his chest pocket and gave Luka a little smile.

Yi-Shen and company exited, slamming the door behind them. Tranquility returned to Scholar's face: he was ready for class and he was ready for his students.

Their first lesson was the Empty Fortress stratagem. It was named after Zhu Ge Liang, a renowned strategist during the Three Kingdom Dynasty. Zhu Ge Liang's enemies once besieged his city with eight thousand soldiers, who threatened to topple the city wall while his own army was fighting far away. It was a desperate situation, with only twenty guards inside to protect ten thousand feeble women and children. But instead of resisting and sending out a smoke alert for outside help, Zhu Ge Liang opened wide the city gate. He sat alone in a cozy armchair by the gate and plucked away on his beloved *pipa* as if he had not a single worry.

The enemy was greatly puzzled and suspicious of the infamously tricky man. Zhu's calm was disturbing and his serenity troubling. They peeked through the gates at the empty city, but dared not take another step forward, fearing an ambush. Why else would the wise man risk his neck to sing those pretty songs with the gate opened so invitingly? As his songs grew louder, the enemy grew more fearful until they hastily withdrew. Without firing a single arrow, the wise man was victorious once again.

Luka was greatly inspired by the ancient lesson. At the end of the class, he announced to Scholar that this was his favorite subject and Scholar told him that he was his favorite student. It was not hard to believe, for Luka was the only one who had kept his eyes open. Scholar was so pleased that he gave him a smaller copy of Suntze's *The Art of War.*

"I'll cherish it day and night," Luka said. "But why didn't you wake the other students while you were lecturing?"

"Sometimes you find knowledge, and sometimes it finds you. Often I wonder whether I'm teaching the right students or if they're coming to the wrong class." Scholar paused with a frown. "Both could be right, or could both be wrong?" He lost himself in the pursuit of the answer to his own question for a moment. Luka could see the dangers of spending too much time alone in the Vault.

Scholar snapped out of his own reverie. "However the class might look like an empty fortress, my best reward is in knowing that there is one little Zhu Ge Liang like you out there, listening and learning."

Luka was warmed by the praise.

"Class is over," Scholar announced. He might just as well have said "Nap is over."

Everyone jumped into action, spilling out the windows and jamming the doors. Two boys, obviously first-time flyers, got stuck in the roof window.

Luka's three buddies grunted and gestured to Scholar, begging him to remove the marbles. Only after Scholar had put away his book and patted his two happy clobsters did he curl three fingers. Just like that, the marbles flew back into the bowl.

"Tha' wa' a goo' na'," Hu-Hu said, his numb mouth still sore. Di-Di pulled his lower lip to test its elasticity. Co-Co gyrated his whole mouth while mumbling, "I can't afford to lose my taste buds or all my cooking skills are down the drain."

"You aren't such a good cook anyway," Di-Di said.

"And you don't want me to be an even worse one, do you, skinny?" Co-Co shot back. He had a point.

The four of them sauntered out of the classroom only to be startled by Di-Di's shout. "The sun is overhead. It's lunchtime! I almost forgot to make the announcement." The messenger climbed on top of Hu-Hu's shoulders, then jumped to a fork in the pine tree, where he blew his piercing flute.

"Lunch hardly needs to be announced," Hu-Hu said. Indeed, everyone was already rushing in the same direction.

The dining hall was a mess. There were no lines and clusters of students fought for their food. The meals were not laid on the serving tables but distributed all over in large baskets and huge wooden barrels that hung far out of reach.

"What an unusual arrangement," Luka said, nearly tripping over the heels of a big boy.

"Another of Yi-Shen's evil ideas, that one's food ration is only as big and good as one's skill," Hu-Hu said.

"How did he get to decide that?" Luka asked.

"The junior master is in charge of the dining hall," Co-Co said. "We're lucky because we've all learned the Airy Skill," said Hu-Hu. "But those poor beginners haven't learned that yet, so they only get the soupy porridge. That's why they are called the Break-fasters. And we are the Lunchers."

"It's unfair that the little fellows should get less," Luka said, gazing at the pitiful flock of young boys mobbing the hot porridge barrel. "Something has to be done about it."

"Unfair? Wait till you see that." Hu-Hu pointed at the western corner of the hall.

It was the three brothers, doing what they did best, hassling and harassing. This time, they were snatching golden apples out of some young Lunchers' hands. The poor boys didn't even protest.

"What are they doing?" Luka demanded.

"What do you think they are doing?" Hu-Hu said. "They are taking their goodies and trading them for— Oops." Hu-Hu covered his mouth. "I shouldn't tell."

"I am the JM now and this is my territory. Tell me," Luka said.

"All right, all right. They use them as passes to the Vault, where many secret and magical weapons are hidden."

"Apples are passes?"

"Any food is good. Scholar needs food to feed rare animals and strange creatures that Lin Koon doesn't know about. There is such a shortage of food already, with more orphans coming than going."

"Those poor kids will go hungry just because the Shen brothers want passes?" Luka felt outraged. He remembered himself as a hungry child, begging for food and never getting enough. That had been bad, but it was worse to see boys robbed by the very ones who were supposed to protect them, if not love them. His blood boiled.

"What are you going to do?" Co-Co asked.

"I am the new JM, right?"

"Yes, you are." Hu-Hu nodded.

"It is my duty to fix things here, right?"

"Absolutely. Everything is leaking here. Everything needs fixing here," Hu-Hu said.

"Good." Luka grabbed Hu-Hu's chopsticks, and together with his pair, threw them with the swiftness of arrows. *Phew, phew, phew, phew!*

Everyone in the hall could hear the chopsticks whisking by, but no one could see anything but the fleeting shadows.

The four chopsticks hit their targets, sticking themselves in the heart of the apples the brothers held in their greedy hands.

"Arrgh!" Er-Shen screamed, and dropped his apple instantly. San-Shen still held his fruit, but his hands vibrated in tune to the tail of the stuck chopstick. None of them had any clue why the chopsticks had punctured their apples, except Yi-Shen, who quickly counterattacked with the apples that he had stolen from the boys.

He threw them with the same force Luka had thrown his chopsticks, but the apples hardly traveled at the same speed. Everyone not only could hear the apples, but they could see them too. And that was a big boo-boo in the world of Wu Xia, where the best were invisible, and even better, silent. But none of them had achieved that excellence yet, not even Luka with his *Yin Gong*.

Luka lifted a hand, and from his right palm sent out four tiny beams of *Qi*. The apples froze in their flight.

"Catch with your apron!" Luka shouted to Co-Co, who stretched out his apron from his generous waistline. The apples fell round and perfect into the cook boy's improvised net. Co-Co rubbed one of them with his apron and was about to sink his teeth in when Luka stopped him. "Not for you, fat boy. Return them to the young kids." With a shrug, Co-Co passed the apples back to the boys, but no one would take them.

Yi-Shen fumed with anger. "Holy Boy, you will pay for this. This time the entire temple will hate you and want you thrown out of here for good."

"And how are you going to do that?"

"Just you see." Yi-Shen jumped on the table. "Everyone! Since you all are so charmed with this total stranger, this so-called Holy Boy, now you're going to pay the price for your love—a little bit each day. Guess what it'll cost you today?"

"What? Tell us what, elder brother." Er-Shen urged him on.

"You all know what." Yi-Shen laughed like an animal.

This time it was San-Shen. "We don't know. Come on, tell us." They seemed to have a grand time playing the yo-yo of fake questions and answers.

"No, please, no!" a Luncher cried. "Please don't take all our food away."

"You guessed it. I will take your lunch away," Yi-Shen taunted with a wicked smile. "Let your hunger be a lesson to you all."

"No, please, no!" all the boys begged Yi-Shen. Some of them knelt, while others clasped their hands as if praying.

"Noooo? But I thought you asked for that," Yi-Shen said. "Let's dump it all and see how loving you feel."

Yi-Shen lifted himself up in the air and pulled out his sword.

"What is he going to do?" Luka asked.

"He's going to cut the ropes holding the baskets and dump all the food on the floor," said Co-Co, who had seen it all many times before.

Luka leaped into the air and landed with both feet on Yi-Shen's shoulders. He lifted the boy upside down and threw him all the way back to the eastern wall, where his ass was snugly framed in a window.

"You bastard!" Yi-Shen cried. "Come, brothers, get me out of here."

Luka hardly touched the ground before he bounced up again.

"Way to go, Luka man. You are very, very holy there. Can I help?" Hu-Hu asked.

"If you want to." Luka untied the rope from around the huge handles of one basket, lowering the steaming rice to the ground. He then delivered it to the stunned Breakfasters, who instantly filled their bowls with the rice. They ignored the shrieks from Yi-Shen, whose ass was still caught in the jagged teeth of the window frame.

"Are you crazy?" one of the older boys asked. "Master Koon will punish us all if he finds out."

"I am the new junior master, and I'll take whatever comes," Luka replied as he untied a second basket. As soon as he laid the basket of steaming vegetables on the floor, the poor students surrounded and devoured it, using their bare hands. They hardly cared what punishment might be coming their way. Food was good any time of the day, in any frame of mind. And within seconds it was gone, which left them hungrier for even better food.

Their eyes all focused on the barrel hanging from the tallest ceiling beam. It contained sauteed taros, glazed and mashed with scented peanut oil. This specialty was only for the ablest few, a dish for the beginners to sniff at when the breeze was blowing the right way, but never for them to taste. They started to clink their chopsticks against the rims of their empty bowls and chant: *"Taro, Taro! Can I have a bowl!"*

Luka gave them a knowing look. "You want taro?"

"Yes, we want taro!" they screamed back.

"Then you got taro!" Luka ran up the wall till he reached the ceiling, where he balanced himself on the narrow wooden beam. With two tumbles he was holding on to the rope that held the taros high and tantalizing.

He sniffed. Very good indeed.

"Watch out!" Di-Di cried. It was good of the messenger to warn him, but Luka had sensed it coming. One of the hard-shelled gourds abundant in the valley was flying toward his head from behind. Luka tilted his head to the left and the gourd smashed into the roof, its carcass dripping with teary guts. He couldn't let it go to waste, at least not totally. He caught the hard falling shell with his left hand and flung it back to wherever it had come from. Unfortunately, the shell missed Yi-Shen by an inch. His brother Er-Shen wasn't so lucky. His left face was whacked silly.

"It's time for the Freaky Fruit Fight," Yi-Shen, free once again, said to his brothers. Together, they dragged three baskets of fruits and threw them in unison at Luka.

Fruits were not merely fruits in the hands of a kung fu man. They took on the hardened cruelty of a deadly weapon, no softer than steel and no blunter than the sharpened blade of a dagger. Luka knew that, but he didn't panic. "Catch them if you can," he barked, "and feed them all to our hungry friends."

What followed was one amazing sight. Three pairs of hands ganged up against one nimble boy. Apples, pears, lychees, mangoes, and papayas flew wildly across the hall. In the chaos of blocking fruits with his head, hands, shoulders, elbows, heels, and toes, Luka tumbled, spun, leaped, and prayed all at the same time. He dodged with the spryness of a monkey and the suppleness of a tiger. Despite his gift, he was hit twice on his butt, by two apples. But he soon saw a pattern to the brothers' assault. They had been throwing missiles at him from the position of the Five Seas. The pattern was clearly the flow of the five sea currents. A Xi-Ling brother by the name of Hai-Hi had developed the strategem after studying the ocean for many years. If the scheme worked well, Luka had read somewhere, the objects thrown formed a fishing net that would catch the pursued from every angle. He also remembered that the only counterdefense to such an attack was the Seven Star Circular, a strategem that he had learned from his days with Atami.

The Seven Star Circular required him to leap continually in the pattern of the zodiac positions—east, north, south, then east again, before going west, landing only in the unseen gaps and tiny spaces left by the Five Sea attack. He tiptoed, glided, frog-leaped, and monkey-tumbled, zooming back and forth along the invisible lines illuminated only by the starlight within his mind. To an untrained eye, he resembled a crazy boy enflamed in a fireball.

Yi-Shen, recognizing the rare zodiac scheme, yelled, "Five Seas flood your soul. No man can shield our deadly blows!"

"Seven Stars shine on earth," Luka countered. "A thousand heroes hunt for devilish scourge!"

Shouted verses were part of Wu Xia combat tactics. Good verbal swordplay could shatter one's opponent's concentration and confuse his mind. Each word could punctuate one's own lethalness and accent the finesse of one's skill.

"All rivers die in the sea." Yi-Shen rapid-fired him with five jumbo papayas.

"All stars rise above the valley." Luka dodged.

"Your destiny's dark as the night," Yi-Shen said.

"Your fate flees in brilliant light."

"How dare you say I'm a flea!" Yi-Shen screamed. With no more fruits left to be thrown, Yi-Shen grabbed an empty barrel and spun it at Luka.

"How could you not be?" Luka balanced himself on one foot on the narrow beam and kicked the barrel back with the other foot, landing the barrel over Yi-Shen's head.

As everyone applauded Luka's victory, hurried footsteps approached along the cobbled path. "Clean up the floor and run for cover," he shouted from the ceiling beam.

When Lin Koon arrived at the door, all the boys had fled through the windows. He stared suspiciously at Luka up on the ceiling and the barreled Yi-Shen sitting on the floor.

"Why is the dining hall so empty"—he swept his eyes around—"and clean? What are you doing up there, Luka? And what are you doing under that barrel, Yi-Shen?"

Yi-Shen struggled out from the barrel, throwing it toward the corner of the hall. "He took down all the barrels and gave all the food away to the first graders."

"Is that so, Luka?" Lin Koon asked sternly. "Why did you do that?"

Luka jumped down to kneel before Master Koon. "Xi-Ling Brotherhood is about equality, respect, and loyalty. The eating system was unfair."

"Unfair to whom?" Master Koon asked.

"Those young, weak, and hungry."

"We have to ration carefully so that we don't run out of food when the winter comes," replied Lin Koon. "If only you could understand the shortage we face here, having to feed more and more . . ." Lin Koon's tone was apologetic. "Besides, as he explained to me, Yi-Shen's method encourages them to learn faster and to improve."

"There must be a better way," Luka said.

"But I thought all was going well?" Master Koon said.

"It was going well! It *is* going well!" Yi-Shen shouted.

Master sighed and turned to Luka. "Since you are the new junior master, it is up to you to make any changes you see fit."

"You are a heartless uncle," Yi-Shen shouted. "I saved you so much food, and no one was complaining."

"No one dared complain," Luka said.

"See, see? He's getting cocky now. Uncle, I'm still your favorite nephew and my father died for you. Now not only do you give him my job but everyone is covering up for him."

"What do you mean?"

"He stole the baby clobsters from the Vault."

"I didn't!" Luka said.

"Who did?" Master Koon asked.

Luka and Yi-Shen pointed at each other. "He did!" they said.

"That's it!" Master Koon shouted. "I am punishing you both by doubling your practice loads so you won't have any strength left to make trouble anymore. Now bow to each other and make peace," Master Koon ordered.

The two boys bowed, glaring angrily at each other.

Fame was a double-edged sword. On the one hand, the lunch incident won Luka even more admiration from all. On the other, it only hardened Yi-Shen's determination for revenge. During the days when Master Koon was around, Yi-Shen confined himself to sending cold stares at Luka. But at night the real contest of wills began.

Every night, like the rhythm of the moon, one of the brothers would play a trick on Luka. Nothing big, but everything nasty. One night it was an earthworm crawling into his ear. Another night a praying mantis jumped up into his nostrils. And yet another, a rat was tied to his finger so that when Luka rubbed his nose, which was tickled by an ear of wheat, he swung the rat right into his mouth.

Luka would have fought back but the exhaustion of the day was so complete that all he wanted to do was to crawl back to his bed and catch another hour or so of sweet snoozing before the sun rose and his day began again. But more importantly, there was the rule of tolerance that Gulan on his sickbed emphasized daily: when you live under another's roof, tolerate. And when you can't tolerate, skip the boat. And this was Yi-Shen's roof, so tolerance it was. Luka saw his ability to tolerate the brothers as a test of willpower that would make a warrior or break a weak soldier. Yet determination was one thing and reality another.

Hu-Hu often asked, "When are you going to fight back?"

"Why? I'm in harmony with myself."

Pretending was fine, but it still ate away at Luka every night as he lay awake, waiting for sleep to befall him. A slow current of smoldering anger formed that made him want to stand over those rascals on the other side of the barn and shout at them till they were deaf. But he contained himself by telling himself that this was, after all, a much better place than prison. He believed in fate and fate had brought him here for a reason, good or bad. He would sigh and let his thoughts fly to his dear Atami. Where was he? Was he still alive? In the dark of the night, he felt fatherless, and the serenity of the temple only deepened his desire to one day climb over that mountain and run to embrace the one who had not only given him his love but also his life, his entire self. Then sleep would take him into her arms.

Though the loved ones in his thoughts might soften his heart, the characters surrounding him continued to make life, a nearly perfect life, imperfect. Yi-Shen's pranks kept coming. Luka thought, *If I'm not going to fight back, I'll have to defend myself.*

An idea came to him. *Could I learn to sleep with one eye open, guarding myself while asleep?*

The response from an enlightened Scholar was, "Of course. It's called Dangle Sleep."

"Dangle Sleep?"

"Yes, a nearly forgotten Xi-Ling practice first perfected by our tenth grandmaster in the year of . . ." Scholar scratched his head and squinted in the bright sun. "Bad head, bad head." He hit himself. "I can't remember."

"Don't do that," Luka protested. "You have the most amazing head on earth. If you hit it any more, some knowledge might spill out and be lost."

"But I want some out so I can remember important things. Now where was I?"

"The dangle thing."

"Right. It's rather simple, but few have attained the ability. It would be a very useful skill to have for a warrior like you, when you are all alone with no one to watch over you while you rest. That, I believe, is the greatest vulnerability that we face. You see, we had a famous Battle of Sleep when Xi-Ling lost two masters to the barbarians of Washandra. I am off the subject again, aren't I?"

"It sounds very interesting, but how do you practice the Dangle Sleep?"

"Oh, you dangle," Scholar said, as if it were obvious.

"How?"

"You dangle your legs over a branch, then you practice what is called partial sleep, much like a bat hanging from the ceiling or a horse sleeping while standing. The idea is to have your body parts take turns sleeping, always keeping one part awake so that enemy movement will be detected soon enough for you to make a safe retreat."

"Any simple or hard rules of learning?"

"No. That's why I called it a nearly forgotten skill."

"What a pity."

"But . . ." Scholar paused.

"But what?"

"Only one man now knows that art, as far as I know."

"Who?"

"Gulan, but he's too weak to be consulted on this now. Why don't you wait until I have given him his treatment? It's not something you want to try on your own," Scholar said.

How hard could it be? Luka thought as he left. Early that evening, he went to a quiet spot, hooked his legs over a tree branch, and tried to take a nap. No sooner had he done that than Hu-Hu and Co-Co appeared, peering at him upside down.

"What on earth are you doing here, JM?"

"Dangle Sleep."

"Don't break your ankles over this, pal. It was only a rumored art that nobody can confirm," Hu-Hu said.

"Well, I'm going to learn how to do it. You have any problem with that?" asked Luka.

"Edgy, edgy," Co-Co said. "But we have no problem. Do you mind us watching you break your thick head?"

"If you're going to do that, do you mind catching me if I fall?"

"Well, I do mind," Co-Co said. "I'm on my break from the kitchen, where thanks to your new fairness policy, we have to do a lot more cooking nowadays."

"I'll catch you," Hu-Hu said. "That is, if I can keep my eyes open that long." He sat beside Co-Co.

"Thanks, buddy," Luka said.

As Co-Co and Hu-Hu began to snore, Luka's legs grew numbed and cramped. His head got heavier and soon he too dozed off. He fell down onto Hu-Hu's legs, his head saved by Co-Co's fat belly. The three continued to snore.

"Luka, Luka!" Di-Di yelled, flying down from a tree.

"What?" Luka sat up and rubbed his eyes.

"Scholar is going to perform something on Grandmaster Gulan called the Last Resort," Di-Di said.

"What is the Last Resort?" Luka asked.

"Don't know," Di-Di said.

"From my experience," Hu-Hu said, stretching, "the Last Resort should be rethought. It always kills and never heals."

"What are you talking about?" Luka said.

"I know what he's talking about," Co-Co said. "Last year this time, Shoti, a second grader, was bitten by a snake, and Scholar pulled out the Last Resort. The kid bloated up and croaked."

"I need to go." Luka flew down the hill and rushed through the meandering corridors, not even stopping when sticky bats landed on his shoulders. He pushed the door to Gulan's room open, and what he saw made his heart drop all the way to his toes.

Master Koon and Scholar stood over Gulan's bed, while two of Gulan's personal guards knelt and helped pin down the feeble grandmaster's arms and legs.

"What are you doing?" Luka demanded.

"Shhh. Catching the scorpions," Master Koon said. He bent over

Gulan, holding a crescent-shaped steel blade in his right hand and a burning iron rod in another. His eyes searched Gulan's body while Scholar hovered on the other side of the bed, clutching what seemed to be the mother of all clobsters. It had a snake's body, a crocodile's head, a lobster's snapping claws, and a green tongue. The creature reminded Luka of the evil monsters mentioned in the Book of Hell.

"That's huge." Luka shuddered.

"This?" Scholar said. "You haven't seen the huge one yet."

"What are you doing with it?" Luka asked.

"It's the Last Resort," Master Koon said. "The scorpions were choking his throat and gagging him all day. Thank Buddha, Scholar has found a cure."

"You mean the clobster is the cure?" Luka asked.

"Holy Boy, this is not your usual evil-cures-evil thing," Scholar said. "This is big evil cure small evil. You see, the scorpions laid eggs in Gulan's veins and only the black blood of the clobster can cleanse them all out and get rid of them for good."

"How do you know it is the right cure?" Luka asked.

"Because it is the poison of all poisons."

"What if it kills the grandmaster?"

"He's moments away from death anyway. Why do you think it is called the Last Resort?" Scholar said.

"But your *last* Last Resort didn't work that well."

"Who told you that?" Scholar wrinkled his face up. "Do you think this is easy? This is a hard job and I'm so ignorant. . . ."

"No, no, no. You are the wisest man I have ever met. Just, please, be absolutely sure," Luka begged. "I don't want him to die."

"I have the book right here. This is the only thing I found for scorpions, in a tiny footnote," Scholar said.

"Time is precious," Master Koon scolded. "We must start now."

And indeed, time was precious, for Gulan lay there nearly dead, covered with pearls of cold sweat, stretched out naked but for a cloth draped over his groin. Pus oozed silently from his leg wounds and he looked like a sickly dog ready for slaughter on a butchering table. The only sign of life was the occasional scorpion tautening the loose skin, running for cover under the rising temperature in the room.

With one hand, Scholar held the clobster, while with the other, he aimed a long needle at the creature's belly. At the sharp poke, the clobster thrashed its claws, and dug its half-dozen legs into Scholar's shoulder. With a scream, Scholar shook the clobster onto the floor, where it quickly scuttled to a wall and crawled all around. Everyone in the room suddenly scrambled like headless ants, some trying to catch it, others trying to dodge it. Even Master Koon was frantic. It was Gulan who stuck his right hand out and caught the sucker by the neck.

"Puncture it, Scholar. What's taking you so long?" he asked.

Luka laughed. Even near death, the grandmaster was still the quickest and nimblest.

Scholar grabbed the clobster around the belly, but the creature was smart. It covered its soft spot with an armor of hard and slippery scales. Scholar plunged the needle there a few times but the needle kept slipping and couldn't penetrate.

"Read on in the book to see where to puncture, Scholar," Gulan said with his eyes closed.

"That's a thought." With one hand, Scholar zipped through the pages till a smile spread on his face. "The back of its neck. Why didn't I think of that?"

With one prick, black blood flowed into Gulan's mouth. After a little squirt, Scholar covered the clobster's wound with a cloth. "Too little, the scorpions will be nourished. But too much, the patient will *guitien*." Go back to heaven.

"How do you know how much is enough?" Luka asked.

"I don't," Scholar said. "The book suggests the Wait-'N'-See."

Gulan began to convulse. His body arched, and his mouth bubbled with black and red saliva. Then an exodus of scorpions came squeezing out of each wound in Gulan's leg. Master Koon scraped them up with the blade and tossed them into the fire. He then sealed each wound with the hot iron, leaving behind the thick stench of burnt flesh.

Gulan sagged limply and resumed his even breathing.

"All done. He will be up and walking in no time," Scholar said happily.

"Thank you. What are you going to do with the clobster?" Luka said.

"There is much I have to do to make it up to him," Scholar said. He bagged the creature and left.

"Can I please be allowed to stay just for tonight and watch over Gulan?" Luka asked Master Koon.

"No. Rules are rules," Master Koon said. "Besides, the two guards have been taking good care of him. Why don't you run along? It's almost bedtime."

Luka stood by Gulan's bed as if his feet were nailed to the floor. His heart was most unwilling but he had his orders. "Good night, Grandmaster," Luka whispered, and shuffled out.

That night, when the boys were all snoring away, Luka climbed out of bed and leaped through the open skylight to the roof. He swung onto the pine tree next to the barn, where he found Di-Di snoozing like a kitten in the fork of the generous trunk. He jumped to the ground and ran and soon was at the eastern window, looking at Gulan lying peacefully in repose. To Luka's surprise, no one was watching the old man as Lin Koon had promised.

"Water. Water," Gulan whispered weakly in his sleep. The sight of Gulan so thin and frail jabbed Luka's heart, nearly causing him to lose his foothold on the windowsill. Then he saw something that was even more disturbing. A shadow nimbly flew down from the skylight and landed softly by Gulan. The intruder had a cloth wrapped over his head and a shining sword at his side. At first Luka thought it was just a guard. But the shadow hid behind the table when Gulan tried to sit up, and Luka knew there was something seriously wrong.

Luka grabbed a tile from the edge of the roof and threw it through the window at the shadow. Surprisingly, the intruder sensed the coming object and did a sloppy butterfly dance, dodging the tile clumsily. The tile crashed onto the floor and woke Gulan. The shadow soared for the skylight from which he had come.

Someone has come to kill Gulan, Luka thought. He climbed up the roof and sat waiting by the skylight. When the shadow appeared, Luka pressed his dagger to the intruder's neck. For one brief moment they were face to face, only inches away, but the face behind the mask was not to be seen.

"Who are you and why do you want to kill my master?" Luka demanded.

There was no reply, only the hiss of breath, panting, with death waiting.

"Water." Gulan's voice floated up. Luka's attention slipped and in that fraction of a moment, the assassin grabbed the dagger's handle and twisted it around to point at Luka's throat. But Luka was quick and the dagger a true friend. Luka curled his finger and the dagger repointed its tip between the eyes of the assassin.

"Who's there?" Gulan said in a trembling voice. A vase came flying between Luka and the assassin, knocking the dagger out of Luka's hand. The shadow slipped out the skylight and was gone in a second.

"Luka, is that you?" Gulan asked.

"Yes, Grandmaster."

"What are you doing here?"

"I saw an intruder with a sword enter your room. Let me pursue him before he gets away."

"You're not going anywhere without your dagger, are you?" Gulan threw the dagger back to him. Luka caught it and slid down the roof, dangling at the edge like a drop of rain. As he cut his eyes left and right, he noticed an adult's boot wedged in a tree fork. Luka circled it suspiciously and sniffed at the inside. His nose picked up a pungent scent, not the usual foot smell, but rather the inky fragrance one smelled from a calligraphy scroll. He reached into the tip of the boot, pulled out a crumpled ball of rice paper, and tried to decipher the words in the moonlight. All he saw at first were some badly sketched drawings of two human faces, one small like that of a boy's, the other gaunt like a dead old man's. They both looked rather familiar. Luka rushed on, and what he read next made his stomach flip.

fugitive #1: **LUKA**

Age 12. *Escaped death row convict*

REWARD

Head – *1,000 lian of silver*
Live capture – *999 lian*
One foot – *200 lian (Must have moles)*
Matching pair – *299 lian*

fugitive #2: **GULAN**

Ageless wild monk wanted for numerous riots

REWARD

Head – 500 lian of silver
Live capture – 499 lian
Arms or legs not needed
All other body parts negotiable

Fugitives NOT dangerous!

Luka trembled with rage as the paper burnt in his hand, this paradise suddenly haunted with ghosts of Ghengi. Every man could be a spy and every soul a turncoat. Even a ghost would turn you in for a thousand lian of silver. He must find the intruder right away. Springing to a treetop nearby, he jumped from branch to branch and tumbled up to the mossy rooftop of the South Gate. It would be a perfect escape. One dive off the cliff and all traces of sin would be buried.

Opening his mind, Luka surveyed the dark waters two hundred feet below, searching for any suspicious ripples or questionable bubbles. But all was silent.

I have to check the other gates, he thought. Like a little ghost, he raced along the thorny wall built around the entire temple, *Yin Gong* dagger in hand. The young guards at the other gates weren't even awakened as he passed by. When he reached the North Gate, the last gate, without finding anyone or anything, he thought: *Maybe I've been looking in all the wrong places. Maybe the assassin is from within.*

He sensed footsteps coming toward him and hid behind a thick tree. Two figures entered the courtyard. It was Master Koon, dragging Yi-Shen along by his ear.

"Let go of me."

"When you tell me what you were doing there by the bay," Master Koon said.

"Swimming."

"Swimming with clothes on at midnight?"

"Yes, Uncle." Yi-Shen shivered.

Luka jumped out from behind the tree, blocking their way. "I know it's you," Luka said, pointing his finger at Yi-Shen. "You tried to kill Gulan."

"Tried to kill Gulan? Is that what you were up to?" Master Koon yanked again on Yi-Shen's ear. The boy screamed like a stuck pig. "Ouch! I don't know what he's talking about," Yi-Shen spat at Luka, who shoved the paper into his face.

"Where did you find this?" Master Koon swept his eyes across the page.

"Stuck in this boot I found here."

Lin Koon examined the boot. "Please do explain."

"I caught an intruder trying to assassinate the grandmaster a short while ago," said Luka. "He ran away in the direction of the bay after losing this boot, and here you are with Yi-Shen all wet and dripping without his shoes. I think he is the intruder that got away."

"This is too large to be Yi-Shen's."

"Not when you stuff this ball of paper at the tip. Adult shoe prints would lead the suspicion away from him."

"He's lying," Yi-Shen cried. "I was just out there swimming. That's all."

"I will look into the matters tomorrow. But punishment for both of you is a guarantee."

"But I didn't do anything wrong," Luka said.

"You both broke the curfew law." Lin Koon drilled a finger at Yi-Shen. "You for swimming while you were supposed to be sleeping." He turned to glare at Luka. "And you for sneaking around making up horror stories about murderers and assassins."

Luka bowed, tugging at Lin Koon's sleeves. "Master Koon, I told only the truth. I did see an intruder in the grandmaster's chamber. Please don't take this matter lightly."

"I don't. You take it too hard. First of all, Gulan is fine. I checked on him on my way here and will look again if you insist."

"But what about the notice?"

"Notices of this kind are everywhere in the towns and villages. People use them to wipe their bottoms," Master Koon said.

"They do?"

"I wouldn't pay any attention to it, my little emperor. You are safe within the walls of Xi-Ling. Now both of you go back to your beds and do not move an inch from the barn until you are told to do so." Then off he went.

Luka followed Yi-Shen back to the barn. For the rest of the night he sat on the bed, holding his knees, pouting, and staring at the stars through the skylight. *How could the head of the temple be so blind? The assassin is still out there among us and his complete disappearance only makes clear his extreme cunning and danger. This place isn't safe at all.* But there was nothing Luka could or should do as a guest under someone else's roof. Lin Koon's words were the temple rules and everyone had to abide by them.

The punishment next morning was soft, yet unbearable. Luka and Yi-Shen were to sit and look into each other's eyes.

"Till when?" Luka asked.

"Till you see a friend," Master Koon said, and left.

How about never? Luka thought. Lin Koon knew torture like nobody else. And there was no worse torture than staring at Yi-Shen's hateful face. His big nose was crooked like an old man's fingers, and his flappy mouth made him look like a sad clown. Last night's cold swim, lie or not, had given him a sniffle, which only made Yi-Shen even more disgusting. Even worse was having to stay silent or both would have to start the punishment all over again.

The morning hours went by swimmingly. Luka stared at Yi-Shen with swords in his eyes and Yi-Shen stared right back with arrows in his. Soon the ears joined in. Yi-Shen's moved like fans, back and forth. Luka's, the ones that Atami said would make him famous or infamous, moved up and down. When the ears got tired, they began to poke their noses at each other. Luka's thrust like a cannon, manly and upright, with a slight sneer. Yi-Shen's shoved forward like that of a sniffing dog. When the nose battle got tiresome, they went to bat with their mouths. Yi-Shen's teeth were collapsed together, as if in a rush to get out of his mouth. He also had the breath of a pig, for he rarely cleaned his teeth. He knew the power of his puff and blasted Luka with a choking stench.

Luka wasn't ready to throw in the towel yet. His square chin, a sign of longevity and stubbornness, was a sure win over the weak slope of Yi-Shen's. Luka's was a powerful shovel, while Yi-Shen's was a surrendering owl. But soon their muscles were exhausted and their jaws slackened as the sun waned. The boys were soon napping and the game of staring turned into a contest of snoozing.

"See, I knew you'd be friends at sunset," Lin Koon said, awakening them.

"But we're not," Yi-Shen declared.

"But you are. No enemies would nap together. Only friends do."

"We'll see about that." Yi-Shen rushed off.

Lin Koon shook his head and sighed. "He is the debt that I have to pay my dead sister."

"Thank you," Luka said.

"For punishing you?"

"For being evenhanded."

"He really isn't a bad kid," Lin Koon said. "The question is when are you going to get along?"

Maybe never, Luka thought, rushing off.

"I heard you," Lin Koon shouted.

Luka paused in amazement.

"Never say never." Master Koon laughed in the wind.

Luka shook his head, heading for the dining hall.

Everyone was staring at Luka and giggling behind his back, even his buddies. When Luka asked them what it was all about, their mouths sealed and they ran off laughing among themselves. Luka was too hungry to pay attention, though: he hadn't eaten the whole day and so gobbled down food like there was no tomorrow. He spotted Yi-Shen doing the same thing, accompanied not by his brothers but by new groupies. They chatted, laughed a little, looked Luka's way, and went on chatting.

Luka finished his meal and stormed off, his mind full of other more important things. What was wrong with these people? Someone had been here, invading the sovereignty of Xi-Ling and breaching the peace of the temple last night, yet no one seemed to care. Even Master Koon had barely managed to suppress a chuckle when the notice had been brought up. Of course, it was not their heads that were being offered as a prize. The price tag had bothered him the whole day and would make this a sleepless night. But he dutifully followed the sleep curfew call and lay down quietly on his bed with the rest of the boys. He put a quilt over his head and pretended to snore. Within a few minutes the boyish chatter faded away and dreams baked in the oven of sleep.

The full meal had made Luka drowsy but he was determined not to sleep until the thug was caught. That took care of his nightly calendar for the long foreseeable future.

Luka snuck out his bed, leaped through the skylight, and stole off to Gulan's chamber. As he was about to jump down to Gulan's chamber, to the west across the wide courtyard he heard the rustling of feet shuffling dry leaves. He cut his eyes there but saw nothing. Then a faint whistle came from the bamboo garden at the eastern tip of the temple. Luka soared high into the air but heard nothing else—until it came again. Someone shouted from the woods in the south only to be answered by another shout in the north.

For a moment it looked like the beginning of *Si Mien Mai Fu,* a Four-Corner Ambush he had been warned about in Scholar's strategy class. Then Luka heard the *pew pew pew* sounds of Xing Xing and Xong Xong, the devices that had been used to track Gulan. As the sounds came closer, a bluish light blinked in the dark. Xing Xing came into view to circle him.

Who has taken these precious devices out of Scholar's Vault? Luka thought. *And why are they tracking me?*

Xing Xing buzzed right in front of his face like an annoying insect. He swiped at it, but it dodged knowingly. *It is a distraction,* thought Luka. As Scholar had said, the only way out of the Four-Corner Ambush was to leap out of its Square of Death.

He shut his eyes, imagined himself an eagle, and glided down from the pagoda toward Gulan's window. Mid-flight he felt his face pressed against the square holes of a fishing net. When he opened his eyes, the net brought him down to the ground with a thump. Four shadowy figures threw a bag over him and instantly all was darkness.

Luka's shouts were muffled as he was lifted and swung over some bony shoulders. Off his captors ran with him, jostling him as they descended a long flight of steps.

Who were these people? Assassins?

Luka tried to be weightless, but being tangled in the net and suffocated in the bag was too much for him. He tried to break through the layers of ropes, but his power felt like a dimming light.

When his captors finally dumped him on the rocky ground, they untied the bag, and Luka crawled out. Rubbing his eyes, he found himself on the shore at the foot of a rocky cliff, facing the Xi-Ling Bay.

"Surprise!"

Half the boys from the temple were there, cheering in hushed whispers.

"Why did you bag me and bring me here?" Luka demanded.

Yi-Shen emerged from the crowd, smiling crookedly. "Welcome to the Snagon Race. This is how the challenger is supposed to be brought here after the secret ballot."

Still dazed, Luka threw himself at Yi-Shen, but a wall of boys blocked him. This puzzled Luka because usually they were on his side.

"You almost killed me," Luka shouted.

"Not yet," Yi-Shen said smugly from behind the protecting crowd. "But I will when the race begins."

"Snagon Race! Snagon Race!" the boys chanted.

"All right, all right. What is this Snagon Race?" Luka asked.

"You don't know what the Snagon Race is? Did you all hear that?" Yi-Shen said. "And he calls himself the future of Xi-Ling."

Luka wanted to do some damage to that battered nose but the crowd surged against him.

"Where are the referees?" Yi-Shen barked.

"Coming through. Coming through." It was Hu-Hu, fighting his way past the taller boys to get to Luka. "Let me through! Let me through! I'm a referee." A muscular boy snatched Hu-Hu's collar and tossed him into Yi-Shen's arms. Yi-Shen in turn shoved the thin boy at Luka.

"Hush, everybody, and let me explain," Hu-Hu said, straightening his collar. "The Snagon Race is an annual Xi-Ling tradition where one daredevil challenges another. The winner is given the title of Snagon king. Since Yi-Shen here was last year's king—"

"And will be king again this year and the next," Yi-Shen said.

"Yeah, yeah. You didn't have much of an opponent last year," Hu-Hu said.

"Shut up!"

"How am I going to explain if I shut up, you idiot," Hu-Hu shouted back. He shrank behind Luka to avoid Yi-Shen's waving fists.

"Go on, then," Yi-Shen said.

"Right, right. As I was saying, we thought, I mean, the entire temple of boys thought . . . we really did . . . it would be a great idea if you represent us," Hu-Hu said to Luka.

"Me?" Luka said.

"Yup!" Hu-Hu nodded.

"Why?"

"Did you all hear that?" Hu-Hu said. "Our great Holy Boy asked why we picked him for the race. Everybody tell him."

"Because you are the greatest!" the boys shouted.

"No!" Yi-Shen yelled. "I am the greatest."

"Yeah, yeah. You're the second greatest, okay." Hu-Hu faced Luka. "The vote was unanimous. You're going to win, I know it. This is a great honor. If you win, your name will be carved on the back of one of the snagons, and that will stay there for good, maybe even when they go to heaven."

"But I don't even know what a snagon is," Luka said.

Yi-Shen chuckled. "What a fool you are."

Luka threw him a dark stare.

"Of course you know," Hu-Hu said. "The two giant snakes hanging around the roof of our temple. Puff, puff . . . the fiery flame, remember?"

"You mean those fire-breathing serpents with legs?"

"That's right. Snake and dragon. They are somewhere in between. Sna-gon. Get it? They really aren't as scary as they look. They are gentle souls waiting for redemption even though they did some really bad things in their lives before. That's why they're kept in a cave most of the time, except for the special occasion of your arrival, of course. The race is one of the chores through which they redeem themselves. Innocent kids get to ride on them, but they can't do any harm. It's a time-honored tradition. And best of all, it's fun!"

"But I've never ridden one before," Luka said.

"You will soon," Hu-Hu said. "Come on. We all chose you because you're not only brave, gifted, and smart, but kindhearted. Smart and kindhearted boys do well. Only stupid boys like him"—Hu-Hu pointed at Yi-Shen—"get hurt."

"Hurt?" Luka squeaked.

Hu-Hu nodded. "Yeah, last year, real bad. And you know why?"

"Why?"

"Don't tell him," Yi-Shen said.

"I have to tell the Holy Boy. It's public record in this temple, okay? He got injured because he was hurting one of the snagons, trying to speed it up in the last race. So the snagon had to fight back. And thanks to you"—pointing at Yi-Shen—"the lovely Moo-Moo might be left behind a decade later on this earth to do some more redeeming."

All the boys shot Yi-Shen a dark look.

"Come on, let's get the race going," Yi-Shen demanded.

"Why are you hurrying me?" Hu-Hu asked. "Are you up to no good tonight?"

"No, he didn't do nothing tonight," said Er-Shen.

"What did he do last night then?" Hu-Hu asked.

"Nothing. I didn't do nothing. Come on, let's get the race going." Yi-Shen sniffed his drippy nose.

"I've got a feeling you're lying again," Hu-Hu said.

"Oh yeah? I'll beat you up if you don't shut up." Yi-Shen shoved his fist in front of Hu-Hu's nose, but Luka pushed him back.

"Hey, let the referee do his job," Luka said.

"Race! Race!" the crowd cheered.

"Thanks, Holy Boy. Looks like you're on. Are you ready?" Hu-Hu asked.

"I am . . ." Luka didn't get to finish his sentence. Hu-Hu grabbed his arm and raised it high.

"We have a race! May the best boy win!"

"Luka! Luka!" The shouts drowned out Luka's spluttering. "Down with Yi-Shen! Down with Yi-Shen!"

As the boys' shouts drowned him out, whatever Luka had to say suddenly seemed trivial and whatever obsessed him was put aside. What lay before him, the challenge to defeat his nemesis, seemed tempting. And besides, if Yi-Shen was the assassin, then what better thing to do than to engage him here?

"Now a couple of ground rules," Hu-Hu said. "Well, not *ground* rules. You know what I mean. Water rules. In a short while, the two snagons will be released, and you better believe that they will be happy to be released for this occasion. The goal of the race is to ride around that island." Hu-Hu pointed at a dark mass of land in the middle of the bay. "The first boy back on the shore here wins. According to the historical records I read this afternoon after I was voted referee, some boys reported rough spots just north of here, right behind the island. Trade winds occasionally pick up where this bay dumps into the sea, causing undercurrents, which might pull in the snagons. You'll have to be firm but not hard with them."

"What does that mean, firm but not hard?" Luka asked.

"I don't know. It was in a footnote." Hu-Hu lowered his voice. "One boy a hundred years ago wrote that the only reason he won was because he had found the shortcut."

"A shortcut?"

"Yeah, instead of going around the island, he rode his snagon through an underwater tunnel at the northernmost tip of the island and scored the biggest lead in history. Now let's talk about the nitty-gritty of riding those monsters. You'll be riding on their back but always grab the tenth scale."

"How do I know which is the tenth?" Luka asked.

"You rub its neck and the tenth scale will stick up for you to grab. Got it?"

Luka nodded. "How do I speed it up or slow it down?"

"Whoa, whoa, stop there. Listen up. *You* don't speed them up or slow them down. *They* do. Got it? It's their game. That's why it's called the Snagon Race, and not the Yi-Shen and Luka Race, you dummy."

Hu-Hu looked up the cliff, where San-Shen was dangling thirty feet up in a small tree near the cave. "He's the other referee." With a loud bellow, Hu-Hu shouted, "Release the snagons!"

San-Shen swung himself to the front of the cave and pulled a plank. With a burst of bluish flame, a giant snake the size of a small boat leaped into the air, its many legs extended like wings and its long whiskers blinking like fireflies. It swept its tail back and forth so powerfully that even Luka, standing thirty feet below, could feel the gust of wind.

"Wow. That's Pawpaw, the male snagon. Never tired of showing off," Hu-Hu said.

Pawpaw soared into the sky and spat flame. He looked like an upward shooting star.

"He really wants to go to heaven bad," Hu-Hu said.

Pawpaw then dropped in a freefall with the whipping sound of a speeding arrow. The kids shrieked in delight.

Just as he was about to crash into the water, he stopped and tumbled in dazzling loops of light. Slowly, he rose back to the cave.

"What's he doing?" Luka asked.

"Being romantic and polite and all that, waiting for the entrance of his mate, Moo-Moo," Hu-Hu said.

"A romantic snake?"

"In that cave, that's all they do, romantic things. She always does a beautiful and seductive dance as her entrance. Mind you, she's no shy girl."

But what Luka saw next wasn't beautiful or seductive at all. Rather, it looked sad.

Moo-Moo crawled to the mouth of the cave, also spitting some flame. But her breaths were more like tired coughs, all smoky puffs but no flames. Her head dragged on the ground.

"She looks a bit sluggish," Hu-Hu said.

"She looks drugged," Luka said.

"Let's cheer her up. Maybe she's going through a woman thing," an upperclassman said, and started shouting her name. The rest of the kids took up the chant. "Moo-Moo! Moo-Moo!"

The calls woke her up. She stiffened her neck and spat her smoke at Pawpaw. Then she simply let herself fall into the bay, her tail narrowly missing the shore.

"You did something to Moo-Moo!" Luka accused Yi-Shen, who looked down at his feet.

"You don't have any proof," Yi-Shen said.

"You were dripping wet last night."

"Enough! Let's get going!" shouted San-Shen, the other referee.

"But she is too weak to race, can't you see?" Luka said. Moo-Moo's head was barely above the water. "We have to stop the race."

"It's too late to stop them now," Hu-Hu said. "If they don't get to race, they won't return to their cave. They rarely get to go out. And besides, we want you to beat Yi-Shen."

"Race! Race!" all the boys shouted.

"Quiet!" Hu-Hu hushed them. "It's time for Yi-Shen, last year's winner, to choose his snagon."

"I pick Pawpaw!" Yi-Shen jogged to the water.

"I will take Moo-Moo," Luka said.

"But you'll lose to that scoundrel," Hu-Hu said. "You can contest the choice when there is an obvious disparity like what we have here."

"She is still my choice," Luka said.

"Well, if you won't dispute, I will," Hu-Hu declared.

"You can't," Luka said.

"Says who? I'm the referee, and I'll see to it that the race is handled evenly."

"You do and I'm walking," Luka threatened.

Hu-Hu gripped his own hair then flung his hands out. "All right, all right. Let's just do it." He called Moo-Moo and Pawpaw to the shore. The two snagons nudged their heads onto the sandy bank, facing each other.

It was the first time Luka got to see their faces up close. They had flat, triangular heads the size of small tables. Their foreheads were covered with hard green scales and their thick red tongues slipped in and out as if tasting the air. Their whiskers made them look like ancient catfish. But their eyes were wide-set and kind. What helped distinguish them was the red dot on Moo-Moo's forehead and the gold square on Pawpaw's.

For one brief moment, Luka thought Moo-Moo smiled and winked at him but he wasn't sure until Pawpaw gave him a cheeky grin. Luka didn't know what else to do but smile back. He liked them—especially when they turned their heads toward Yi-Shen and stuck out their fiery tongues.

"On your snagons now," Hu-Hu shouted.

Luka gently patted Moo-Moo's neck, which was as thick as a horse's back, and the tenth scale popped up. He clutched tightly to the scale as Moo-Moo sank under his weight.

Yi-Shen, however, was having a hard time and it was entirely his fault. Instead of patting Pawpaw gently, as he was supposed to, he smacked him with his iron hand. Pawpaw didn't like it, but there was nothing he could do, for he would have to control his temper if he were to redeem himself. So he turned sly. Instead of giving Yi-Shen the tenth scale, he stuck up the eleventh, a smaller scale without the ribbing that was necessary for a good grip. Yi-Shen kicked Pawpaw, who spat flames at the mean boy.

"One last thing. No weapons." Hu-Hu frisked Yi-Shen, removing a sword. "You know the rules."

"What about his dagger?" Yi-Shen yelled.

"Superceding rule. It has to stay with him at all times," Hu-Hu retorted, and turned to Luka. "And you know enough not to use it. Okay. Now charge!"

Pawpaw burst into action, arching his back like a bridge and shaking his tail crazily. Suddenly the bay ahead was his playground and the race was all he had in mind. With his nose close to the surface and his eyes squinting, he paddled speedily with his many legs, shooting forward like a giant eel. Yi-Shen shrieked with delight, holding the eleventh scale with only one hand, waving the other to the cheering crowd. In a blink, he was fifty yards ahead, leaving behind a deep wake for Luka to follow.

Moo-Moo, on the other hand, was like an old horse. She blinked groggily, splashed by Pawpaw's waves, and belatedly charged forward as well. But her charging was a *char-* without the *-ging* and didn't get her very far at all. In contrast to Pawpaw's sleek masculinity, she had a big, fat belly. With labored breathing, she lumbered and pushed clumsily against the water instead of slicing through it. Luka's heart ached for Moo-Moo as he felt her old bones crackle into action. It wasn't fair to have her race on a bad day like this, Luka thought. He wished he could stop this race but the determined Moo-Moo was paddling hard. Still, she was at most half as fast as her mate.

The crowd cheered, seeing her finally take off.

Moo-Moo might be in a hurry to catch up, but Luka wasn't. He was just happy that he was her rider and not Yi-Shen, who would certainly have beaten her badly trying to speed her up. His goal was not to win but to protect Moo-Moo, and whatever she was willing to do was fine with him.

"Don't rush, Moo-Moo. We've got the whole night ahead of us," he murmured, rubbing her neck. The whisper was meant for him but Moo-Moo heard it and she stopped paddling entirely.

"All I ask is that you take it easy, but if you want to stop altogether that's fine then. I could sit on your back and enjoy the moon all night long."

Moo-Moo twisted her head around and winked at Luka with a snakish smile, all cheeks, no lips. Then suddenly she shot ahead into the air, leaping without touching the water, all her legs flapping like wings. Wind blasted Luka's face, numbing it with delight. He shrieked with joy.

"Yeah, Moo-Moo! Way to go," Luka shouted, wishing she would never come down.

His shout only fanned her craziness further. She slithered in the air as if she were on the ground. For one second Luka thought that maybe she had been dragonized. And that thought was good because if it was true, it meant that Moo-Moo was near the end of her redemption.

Behind them, the shouting and roaring continued from the shore. Luka thought the cheers were for Moo-Moo, but he didn't see the tall figure that had rushed from the temple to the edge of the bay. Nor did he hear Scholar's shouts of "Please, come back!

Moo-Moo has been drugged! The wrong drug! And she is going to kill you!"

Moo-Moo sliced through the water, jumped above the taller waves, and skipped on the thin air, hissing with delight. The laboring of her breath eased and so did Luka's concern. Maybe it had all been just a show by the smart snagons to fool Yi-Shen.

The shore raced by and the waves splashed on Luka's face. What a ride! Luka lovingly rubbed Moo-Moo's scale and she charged on with more vigor. Halfway to the dark island, she caught up with Pawpaw, and that sent Yi-Shen into a frenzy. He pulled out a long stick from inside his sleeve and shook it twice in the air. It shone with a reddish light.

Scorching Whip! Luka remembered Scholar's warning about its use. *One lash and a dead horse would fly for the mountaintop.* "Don't do it," Luka yelled. "You are breaking the rules."

"Ha!" Yi-Shen laughed. "The heck with the rules. I'm going to win at any cost." He struck Pawpaw over and over again on the most sensitive part of his body, his forehead. The sight of the bleeding and shrieking snagon angered Luka, but it angered Moo-Moo even more. She swam ahead of Pawpaw, then circled behind. The kindness in her eyes vanished. She bared her teeth at Yi-Shen and bellowed an angry roar.

She is going to kill him, Luka thought. *I can't let that happen.* His death would set her redemption back for good. But before he could act, Yi-Shen hurled the Scorching Whip into Moo-Moo's open mouth and set the volcanic mouth aflame. White heat rippled all the way to the tenth scale, where Luka was sitting.

Thrashing in pain, Moo-Moo dipped her head into the water. When her pain eased, she went limp, afloat on the surface.

"I told you I'm going to win," Yi-Shen said. "Now that your Moo-Moo is down, Pawpaw will bring me home to victory."

But Pawpaw was faring no better. The Scorching Whip had taken the life out of him also. As his bleeding reddened the water around him, he began to sink, taking Yi-Shen with him. The boy released the eleventh scale, but his seat held on to him. The more he twisted, rocked, and pulled, the more deeply he became rooted to his seat.

"I'm stuck!" Yi-Shen yelled. "Please help m—" He disappeared, leaving behind a chain of bubbles. *He is going to drown,* Luka thought, *all because of his own cruel stupidity. Should I save the boy and the snagon's soul or should I simply leave him to the hands of fate? The world certainly will not miss the boy, but will Pawpaw be wrongly blamed and forever condemned?*

Only after Yi-Shen's last bubble rose to the surface did Luka throw his dagger at the sinking snagon. The dagger swam through the dark, thick water, and cut the eleventh scale off Pawpaw. Luka dove into the water, fetched up the freed Yi-Shen, and swam with his limp body back to the island. Upon his arrival, he was surprised to see Scholar gliding down from the sky on the legs of a giant bat. It dropped Scholar onto the island shore and flew away.

"Please save Yi-Shen," Luka said, dragging Yi-Shen onto the sand. "His lungs must be filled with water."

"Hah! The bad boy deserves it." The usually congenial Scholar surprised Luka with his harsh tone. "First he drugged Moo-Moo, then he wounded both snagons with the Scorching Whip. Toss the boy to me."

Luka did, from ten yards away.

Not bothering to catch him, Scholar let the boy fall to the rocky ground with a big thump, which caused Yi-Shen to cough. Water flowed out from his nose and mouth. Scholar stared down at the groaning boy in disgust.

"What did he drug Moo-Moo with?" Luka asked.

"A drug that would arouse her killing urge. But he overdosed her, making her sleepy until the fresh air stimulated her. She should have killed you."

"Why didn't she?"

"Maybe she can tell good from evil now. And that's a good thing, considering what she is capable of."

"Quick," Luka said. "Let's find Pawpaw and Moo-Moo."

"I've already summoned them here." Scholar led Luka to a little cave near the shore, where the snagons were intertwined like two strands of a very thick rope. The giant popped something into his mouth, chewed, then spat some dark gunk into his palm.

"Gross, spit."

"No ordinary spit, my Holy Boy. It's dark medicine made from special charcoal. As soon as I found the whip missing, I immediately mixed the antidote." He smeared it on Moo-Moo's mouth and gave some to Luka to put on Pawpaw's forehead. When Luka rubbed it in, Pawpaw healed rapidly until there wasn't even a scar left. "What would have happened without the medicine?"

"The wounds would have rotted through to the bones."

Back to health, the snagons nudged each other affectionately, their long, flowing whiskers sparkling with light again. They stuck out their tongues and licked Luka's hands. He was almost certain they smiled at him again.

"Let's go," Scholar said. They hopped on the snagons' necks—Luka on Moo-Moo, Scholar on Pawpaw—and rode from the cave into the bay.

"How about Yi-Shen?" Luka asked. The boy still lay on the cold shore.

"I was thinking of picking him up tomorrow," Scholar said, "but you're right. We have enough room for another." He rubbed Pawpaw's neck and a new eleventh scale popped right up as if it had never been cut off.

Scholar fetched Yi-Shen by his collar and propped him again in his old seat, the sticky and tricky eleventh. "Hold on tight, Yi-Shen. The race isn't over yet."

That woke the boy up. "Huh? Are we still on? Come on!" He kicked Pawpaw's neck but the snagons ignored him and swam side by side, racing down the homestretch. "Why are you sitting here with me?"

"So Pawpaw doesn't turn around and kill you for what you did," Scholar said.

The boys booed when Pawpaw reached the shore first. "I won! I won!" Yi-Shen shouted.

"Not yet!" said Hu-Hu the referee.

"My snagon got here first," Yi-Shen yelled.

"No, no, no. I want to see your feet on the shore. That's the rule."

Yi-Shen tried to get off the eleventh scale, gyrating his bottom and twisting his waist. "I'll get there first," he cried, but his ass was glued. The sticky seat was stickier than ever.

Luka jumped off Moo-Moo and landed near Hu-Hu, who pronounced, "Our Holy Boy is the winner!"

The boys surrounded Luka and lifted him onto their shoulders, cheering. But as an angry Lin Koon approached, they abruptly dropped him and fled.

"You two," Master Koon said to Yi-Shen and Luka, "will be punished severely this time for violating the curfew rule two nights in a row and disobeying the temple's No Snagon Race policy."

Luka's head bent down in shame but jerked up again as something frightening caught his eye. "What are you doing here?" Luka demanded, rushing up to the two guards who were supposed to be watching over Gulan. "Shouldn't one of you be on duty?"

"We had to watch this race. Besides, he is resting peacefully," one said while the other rubbed his nose.

"Yup. No way we were going to miss this for anything."

Luka parted the crowd with both hands and raced toward the temple. He ignored Master Koon, who demanded, "Come back here. Where do you think you are going?"

Time was running out. He could feel it. Luka ran up the winding steps and threw himself over the South Gate. He heard a pair of lonely footsteps on the roof tiles of Gulan's chamber. Soaring to the roof, he spotted the shadow from the night before, now crouching at the chimney. Before Luka could reach him, the assassin had dropped down the narrow mouth of the chimney. Luka flew behind him, stretching himself long. But all he got was a boot. The matching boot!

Luka stuck it in his belt and jumped headfirst into the chimney after the shadow. They fell from the chimney base into Gulan's room in a puff of soot and fought noisily from wall to wall. His opponent's strength and deadliness didn't surprise him as much as his moves did. When Luka struck out with a lobster hook, the intruder countered with a shrimp leap. When Luka kicked out with a dragon sweep, the boy leaped away with a mantis hop. It was the response to Luka's last move, the typhoon thrust, that stunned him: the assassin countered eloquently with the thunderbolt. But that was an invention of Atami's. No one else in the world was supposed to know that.

Outrage filled Luka. This shadow was not only an assassin but also a shameless thief! Luka fought on even more fiercely, but as his opponent neatly countered his every move, he began to feel as though he were fighting himself. Every move was right from the Book. Who was this man?

When Luka finally landed an unexpected blow to his chin, the assassin let out a cry of pain. It was the voice of a boy!

The cry awoke Gulan. "What is going on?"

"Don't worry, Grandmaster," Luka shouted, dodging a left temple hook by his opponent.

"Luka, is that you?" Gulan asked.

"Yes, Grandmaster."

His opponent suddenly froze. "You're Luka?"

That boyish voice sounded familiar. "Yes, I am." Luka reached out and seized the assassin's throat in his mantis claw. "Who are *you*?" Luka asked.

"I'm, Ma—" He coughed and choked in Luka's tight grip.

"Ma what, you assassin?" Luka shook him.

"I'm not an assassin!"

"Who are you?" Luka demanded.

"Ma . . . Ma . . . Mahong!"

"Mahong?" Luka could not believe his ears. "I thought you were dead."

"And I thought you were."

Luka ripped the mask off Mahong's head, wiping the little face. "Is that really you?"

"Yeah, it's me, Your Holiness."

Gulan wobbled over with a candle, and in that flickering light, Luka saw the soot-streaked face of his dear friend Mahong.

"I can't believe it!" Luka said.

"Can't believe what?" Gulan asked.

"It's Mahong!"

"Who is Mahong?"

Luka and his old friend laughed hysterically as they wrestled, knowing no better way to express their love for each other. They rumbled on the ground to the utter puzzlement of Gulan.

Lin Koon darted to the doorway with Scholar in tow. "Is everything all right? We heard fighting," he said.

"I am as confused as you are." Gulan gestured to the two wrestling boys.

Lin Koon broke the two apart. "Who are you?"

"I am only a messenger," said Mahong.

"And a dear friend from my past." Luka beamed.

"Friend from your past?" Gulan asked. "And messenger from whom?"

"Atami," Mahong said, trying to gather his breath.

"Atami?" Luka asked, shaking Mahong's neck violently. "Is he alive? Is he all right?"

"Calm down, Luka. That's no way to treat a messenger, especially one with good tidings." Lin Koon broke the boys apart. "Now, my boy, please state the message from Atami."

"The good news is Atami is alive!" Mahong said.

Luka's legs collapsed and he knelt on the floor. "Oh, thank Buddha!"

"But the bad news is that he is dying from an arrow wound poisoned with Clob's venom."

"Oh, Buddha help us," Scholar sighed.

"What is a clob?" Luka asked, clutching the giant's sleeve.

"A formidable sea monster, and the thirteenth prince of the Oceana king. Remember those clobsters?"

"Yes, of course."

"Clob is the father of all clobsters and lives deep in the Pacific Ocean," Scholar explained. "It is the biggest of them all. Unfortunately, its venom is known to give such excruciating pain that all poisoned by it beg for death."

"The giant is right," Mahong said. "Atami is now reduced to flesh and bones and begs to die day and night. His painful cries can be heard throughout the whole prison. But Ghengi wants the secret of *Jin Gong*," Mahong spat. "And, as you know, Atami would rather suffer forever than give the treasure of Xi-Ling to that Mogo. But Atami has grown frail, and could die in a matter of days. That's why I am here to summon help from all of you."

The entire chamber was quiet. Only Lin Koon seemed suspicious. "Did anyone follow you here?" Lin Koon asked Mahong.

"I think not, head monk. I tried my best not to cause any suspicion," Mahong replied.

Lin Koon sized the boy up, a frown deep in his forehead. "What is it that we can do to help, messenger?"

"It's really simple. I need Xi-Ling heroes to help me fight Clob and fetch its blood so Atami can drink it because, as you know, Clob's poison can only be cleansed by its own blood. And the timing is perfect," Mahong said, rolling up the sleeves of his robe, which was two sizes too big. "The best time to approach the beast and get its blood is during Clob's monthly Bride Feeding, and the next one is happening two days from now."

"Why is that?" Lin Koon asked.

"At the Bride Feeding, Clob will chew up the pretty girl Ghengi selects for him. That's when a red glow will light up its middle eye, opening up its only spot of vulnerability. We'll drill that eye for the blood that Atami needs."

"How did you come to know all that?" Lin Koon pressed.

"An old warden told me before he died."

"And you believe a warden's words?" Lin Koon asked.

"Sure I do. I did favors for him and he did favors for me. He was kind to me and my brother. Never said a thing about us taking lessons from Atami and all. You might not know it, but everybody in prison knows everything happening outside the walls. For example, there were even notices of Gulan and Holy Boy's escape floating around in there. That's why I decided to look for you, and the first place that came to mind was this Xi-Ling temple."

"You were so brave." Luka patted his buddy, who nodded in agreement.

"Stop congratulating each other and listen to my questions carefully," Lin Koon said, annoyed. "Was that you who was sneaking around last night here?"

"Yes, it was," Mahong replied.

"If you were so sure of everything, why did you sneak around like a ghost?"

Mahong looked around the room. "Because I was instructed by Atami only to contact Gulan and no one else. And the best time to do that was at night, when all of your guards were asleep."

"Asleep?" Lin Koon frowned.

"Yeah, that's how I got in. Atami didn't want me to contact anyone else because of the way I look and speak." He rubbed his nose. "People don't trust me."

"Why don't people trust you?" Lin Koon asked.

"I don't know, maybe because of my street ways. Some people just look at me and call me a thief."

"Are you a thief?"

"Not since I met Atami in prison. Why are you asking me all this?" Mahong seemed irritated.

"Yes, why, Master Koon?" Luka protested. "He is my friend, a loyal friend."

"Why?" Lin Koon said. "One thousand *lian* of silver is why. That much money must be very tempting to you, thief."

"What are you saying?" Mahong's hands curled into fists.

"You came here for money, didn't you?"

"No, I didn't!" Mahong shouted. "I came for my master. I came for my friend."

"You can't accuse my friend like that," Luka said, only to be hushed by Lin Koon.

"What prison did you say you escaped from?" Lin Koon asked.

"Water Prison."

"How did you manage to escape?"

Mahong sniffed at his clothes and shrugged. "Underground."

"You lie!"

"It's true!"

"Water Prison is the most guarded prison in this land. No one has ever lived to tell the horrors that lie inside those walls. They must have let you out with this news about Atami as bait."

"It's no bait. I came here on my own to tell you the truth," Mahong said.

"Truth? I think not," Lin Koon said. "Scholar, tell Luka the real truth about Clob."

"Well, if my memory serves me right," Scholar said, "no one has ever been able to defeat it since its birth, not because it's huge or powerful, which it is, but because its body is covered with impenetrable scales, a perfect and seamless armor. It has no weakness that I know of, and believe me, I know a lot after experimenting with its offspring. I'd like to look into this story about the middle eye before anyone acts on it, especially now that the taste of blood has worsened Clob to a disastrous degree."

Lin Koon grabbed Mahong by his shoulders. "See, your story is at best the bait to a trap. Tie him up and put him away." Two guards with ropes in hand entered and jumped on Mahong.

Luka stuck himself between the two guards and Mahong. "You can't tie him up. If you tie him up, you have to tie me up."

"Holy Boy, come here." The stern Lin Koon pulled him away. "There is a rule you must know about friendship. Best friends make the worst enemies because they know your weakness."

"Friends are friends. That is my rule," Luka said.

"How do you know your friend hasn't been corrupted by the lure of silver or compelled by Ghengi's torture?"

"I haven't," Mahong shouted. "I would rather die than betray a friend."

"Fine, then you won't mind coming along to our Honesty Chamber to take my Innocence Test, will you?"

Mahong straightened and pushed out his chest. "Not at all."

"He *is* innocent," Luka said.

"We'll see. Take him away," Lin Koon ordered.

"You can't take him away." Helplessly, Luka stood at the doorway as the two guards pushed and shoved his friend down the corridor. He felt like screaming. Turning to Gulan, Luka begged, "My friend is innocent. I can vouch for him with my life. Can't you see that he risked his own life in order to save Atami's?"

"Don't do anything rash," Gulan said feebly from his bed. "I'll tell you what we will do at sunrise. All under Xi-Ling's roof must act in unity. Capricious renegade actions can only bring disaster to us. That is temple rule number one. Now go back to your bed and sleep your anger away."

Luka kicked his way back to the barn. As soon as he entered, he was surrounded by Hu-Hu, Di-Di, and Co-Co. His good friends couldn't fall asleep like the rest of the snoring boys until they got all the juicy news. The Snagon Race and its victory was long forgotten. All his friends cared to know was who the intruder was and what his appearance meant.

"Who is he?" Co-Co whispered.

"A buddy from my past," Luka whispered back.

"We didn't know you had such an interesting past," Hu-Hu said.

"Are you going to fight that beast at the Bride Feeding?" Di-Di asked.

"How did you hear that?" Luka asked.

"I heard the whole thing at Gulan's skylight," Di-Di replied.

"Can you show me where the Honesty Chamber is?"

"What are you planning to do?"

"Free my friend and run away. Can you tell me a safe way out of the temple?"

His three friends pulled back. Worry creased their faces.

"Come on," Luka urged. "I can't let my friend be tortured. Besides, I have to go save my master, Atami."

Their faces grew even paler.

"Why can't you wait till sunrise for the grandmaster's decision? Then maybe the whole temple can go help you," Hu-Hu said.

"But the Bride Feeding is only two days away and it takes two full days of running to journey to Peking. It'll be too late to save Atami if I wait until morning. Come on, you've got to help me."

His three buddies shook their heads. "We'd like to help you but temple rules come first," Hu-Hu said.

"Which do you choose as my friends, loyalty or obedience?" Luka demanded.

"Loyalty," the three muttered.

"Then help me."

Co-Co stared at Luka and then said, "All right, the heck with the rules. Let's help him out."

Hu-Hu and Di-Di nodded. "We're in."

"I know a way out from the kitchen," Co-Co whispered.

"Good, where does it lead?"

"Don't worry about the details now. When you get your friend out, I'll be waiting for you by the kitchen. I guarantee that it'll get you out and far away."

"Fine," Di-Di said. "Co-Co, you go to the kitchen. Hu-Hu, you slip into Luka's bed and cover your face with the quilt. I'll take Luka to the Honesty Chamber."

"Wait a second," Hu-Hu said to Di-Di. "Why don't you slip into his bed? I know where the Honesty Chamber is."

"You've got to do it. Your pumpkin head is as big as his. Mine is too small," Di-Di said.

"Okay, bird head," muttered Hu-Hu.

The four said a silent goodbye by pressing their thumbs together, a sign of their enduring friendship. Then Hu-Hu crawled into Luka's bed as Co-Co, Di-Di, and Luka climbed out the window, going their separate ways.

Luka and Di-Di ran across the courtyard, rose onto the roof, and crawled stealthily from one dark path to another. After scaling a dozen rooftops, they finally arrived at the Honesty Chamber, in a tower that stood alone in the far corner of the temple grounds. The roof was embedded with iron thorns, and its tiles were mossy and slippery, slanting with sharp drops. The two boys negotiated the climb deftly, though Luka caught his robe on the thorns several times.

"There it is!" Di-Di said.

"Thanks, my friend."

"Don't thank me yet. Remember to go left after you exit the chamber. That way leads to the kitchen."

"I will. Go back to your duty now before anyone catches you, Di-Di."

"Be careful, Holy Boy. Promise you'll return or we'll be miserable here without you."

"I promise. Don't cry. Now go."

"You go. I'll watch your back."

Peeping through the lit skylight, Luka was shocked to see his old friend strung up, dangling from the ceiling like a leaf in the wind. No guards were around, so Luka slipped through the skylight and undid the rope around Mahong's waist and arms. In the candlelight, Mahong's eyes were half closed and his face was pale as a corpse's. Luka needled his thumb into Mahong's *ren zhong,* a waking nerve point hidden in the furrow above the upper lip, and Mahong stirred. The first thing that came out of his mouth was not about his suffering but about the only thing that mattered to this street rogue.

"You believe me, Luka?"

"Never a doubt. Let's get out of here. I will carry you," Luka said.

"I can walk." He rolled his oyster eyes a few times and shook himself from head to toe, calling back his dormant energy. "The Half-Dead Technique really works," he said, patting himself. "I'm as good as new."

Luka was relieved. "Atami has taught you more than he taught me."

"But you are still his favorite."

"Time to go." Luka grinned and opened the door with a squeak of its hinges. The corridor was dark and zigzagged like a maze. Remembering Di-Di's words, Luka turned left at the fork and continued along a narrow passage shaded with spiderwebs and creeping vines. At the end of the corridor, a door creaked open. It was Co-Co, waiting for them, holding an oil lantern in his hand. "Follow me and pay no attention to the nightshift tofu boys," he said.

Six boys froze at their appearance.

"Keep on working. Holy Boy is inspecting our oven," Co-Co shouted as he pulled open the chunky iron door to an old oven. "Get in and go straight east from here." Co-Co shoved them in and slammed the door, leaving Luka and Mahong in sooty darkness.

Luka groped around in the oven, searching for a way out, but no secret exit or hidden door was to be found. Co-Co opened the oven door again. "Sorry, I forgot to tell you about the wire."

"What wire?"

"Above you to the left," Co-Co replied. "Oh, I nearly forgot again. Don't make the mistake of going west."

"Why not?"

"I don't know. But a drawing there warns you not to." The oven door shut again.

Luka reached up and found the wire. When he tugged it, the oven opened on top and the floor began to rise into a wide space, where it swung like a pendulum, dumped them into a tunnel, swung back, and disappeared.

What a magical oven! Luka cheered.

Little creatures ran amok upon their arrival. In front of them was a wall carved with drawings of all the odd sacred creatures Scholar said lived under the Xi-Ling Mountain. On one end the word *East* was carved, with an arrow pointing to the left. To the right was a drawing of a moldy skeleton. It had to be West, the direction Co-Co had warned him about.

"Let's follow the arrow," Luka said, but torchlight appearing in that direction stopped them short. A half-dozen burly, well-armed guards were breathing heavily, staring down at them.

"We can fight them," Mahong said.

"But we can't fight *him*," Luka said coolly as Master Koon pushed past the guards.

"Luka, stop," Lin Koon said. "Mahong is our prisoner until he is proven innocent. You have broken a very serious temple rule by helping him escape."

"He has done nothing wrong. You have no right to imprison him."

"I have the whole tradition of Xi-Ling to protect. I have to put both of you in detention."

"Goodbye, Master," Luka said, pulling Mahong west. "We have to go now."

"I wouldn't be going that way if I were you," Lin Koon said just as Luka felt the ground cave in.

It was another trap, Luka realized as he and Mahong fell into a deep, dark well.

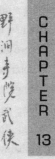
LUKA HAD THOUGHT that the Windowless Cave was just another pit, but he was wrong. It seemed interminable, and the deeper they fell, the colder they got. It seemed as if they traveled down the entire depth of the mountain before they finally landed. The damp, rocky floor was freezing.

"We're doomed," Luka said, picking himself up.

"Don't say that. Get us out of here!" Mahong groped in the dark.

"Scholar mentioned this place in his class. Do you know how many years Lin Koon spent and how much manpower was poured in here to sink a well this deep into the mountain?"

"Yeah, so what?"

Luka kicked around. "The old annual had a picture of this. I used to admire it so much because it was to be the most secure prison in this land. Even the most expert warriors could not fly out of here. The lead cover weighs one thousand *jin*."

"That makes me want to puke."

They heard a slam far above them. No doubt Lin Koon was

keeping a lid on them. "No prisoner," Luka continued glumly, "no matter how capable, could escape from here."

"Are we going to die in here?"

"Scholar said that it's freezing at night but when the day comes, the rising tide warms the base of the mountain. Prisoners supposedly have an abundance of sweet springwater that seeps through the rocks. That is, if they know how to tap them. But your fingers will probably bleed first."

"What do you mean?"

"You've got to dig for it," Luka said. "The source of water is somewhere in the wall but you'll have to find it. Everything here is a riddle."

"How about food? What do we do to eat?"

"Oh, that. If I recall, Scholar did say that if one was skillful enough, he should be able to find enough food here to sustain him for as long as he wished to live."

"How?"

"Again, it's all about ingenuity. There are holes to be dug with your fingers, and holes are good because they offer potential food."

"What kind of food are you talking about?"

"Rats and snakes. Vegetarians won't do well here. Occasionally you might have to make do with earthworms or scorpions—if they come down this far. I won't even mention the other creatures one might have to eat down here."

"How long are they going to keep us here?"

"I don't know," Luka said quietly.

"Well, I'm going to get out of here." Mahong crawled to the wall and started clawing at it with his fingers.

"That's no way to do it." Luka came and held him from behind.

"I am doing it and doing it till I dig us out," Mahong said.

"Don't worry, we'll get out."

"Don't worry, my foot." Mahong kept digging, but it was hopeless. He slammed his fists into the wall. "I want out of here. I want to see my brother. Oh, my poor brother."

"You will see your brother."

"No, I won't." Mahong slammed the wall with his fists some more.

"You will." Luka's voice was firm and assured.

"Really?"

"What was the first thing Atami taught you before any martial art?" Luka asked.

"What good is that now that we're trapped here?"

"Say it for me, brother."

" 'Be calm in the eye of the storm,' " Mahong recited softly, " 'or you will be torn apart . . .' "

" '. . . and cease to be.' "

"You know that too?" Mahong asked.

"We have the same teacher, remember? Are you calm now?"

"It's easier said than done," Mahong replied.

"Do you see the walls around you?" Luka asked.

"No."

"Good. So why should you feel trapped when you can't even see the cave?"

"You mean I should just forget about the surroundings and pretend that I am somewhere else?"

"Not just somewhere else," Luka said. "At this moment, you, the king of the street and the diligent student of Atami, are sitting atop a lofty mountain. A sea breeze is blowing and a bird is singing. And the darkness is only a cloud that lifts you up and keeps you floating in a dream."

"Thanks. I feel light-headed just listening to you."

"Now you're flying because the breeze has picked up and is carrying you toward . . . oh, an orchard, full of fragrant, ripening fruits. . . ."

"Sweet lychees," Mahong said dreamily, "dripping with honey."

"Then you come upon a rice field, greening in the spring sun."

"In darkness, I see light," Mahong said.

"Soon you hear the whispering melody of a jade flute . . ."

"I like the jade flute."

". . . played by a fair lassie . . ."

"I like lassies," Mahong said, "tender and plump."

"Very plump."

"Now I hear her," Mahong whispered. "I do, really."

Luka felt his friend's back soften and relax. "Mahong."

"Yeah?"

"Are you calm now?"

"I am the calmness, for I shall see no storm . . ." Mahong's voice trailed off as he started to snore.

Luka was left alone, tormented in the heavy darkness, until he too began to tear himself away from his surroundings. In the inner recesses of his mind, he saw the flowing hair of a woman, then a profile. It was Zuma, his mother. He reached out and held her hand and her skin was silky like the night, fragrant like a bloom. Before the bloom could blossom, Luka was asleep against the cool wall, his arms holding Mahong for warmth and security.

Luka was awakened not by light but by the sound of dripping water.

Plop, plop, plop.

The drops fell slowly, and each ended its fate in a lonely echo. But any sound meant life, and any movement meant hope.

"Water! Water!" Luka shouted, shaking Mahong.

"What water?" Mahong asked. He leaped up like a frog and bumped into the rocky wall. "Ow!"

"The mountain spring. Sweet like honey and rare like a fine aged wine." Luka reached out a finger, fetched a few drops, and fed them into his mouth.

"Where does it come from?" Mahong asked. He too reached over and scooped some drops into his mouth.

"Up there." The well trembled with the echoes of *UP . . . Up . . . up . . . up . . .* all the way to the very top. When the echo finally faded away, it was followed by a series of gagging noises. *Rrrbrt. Rrrbrt. Rrrbrt.*

"What is that?" Mahong whispered.

"Shh . . ."

Rrrbrt. Rrrbrt.

"Is it a frog?" Mahong asked.

Luka squeezed his shoulder.

Suddenly a ring of light appeared twenty feet above them.

"Light, light!" Luka shouted excitedly.

The ring lowered, cleaving through the darkness. When it landed, Luka and Mahong jumped back against the wall and stared at its source. It was a frog, big as a turtle, giving off a brilliant golden light. Even more alarming than its size was the third eye on the back of its neck. The golden frog croaked again and its neck swelled with air.

"Oh, my," Luka whispered. "Is this the Golden One?"

"What golden one?"

"Scholar told us about it in the class of good and evil. It's another creature serving its sentence down here. For his crimes, Buddha condemned him to darkness. But Buddha also gave him this golden glow so that he could be his own light. Are you the Golden One?"

Rrrbrt! Rrrbrt!

"You are!"

The frog nodded and extended a front webbed foot. Its two front eyes flickered with radiance.

"Oh, my Buddha, it's gazing at you," Mahong said.

"I think it wants to shake hands with me."

"Or maybe it's sizing you up for a meal," Mahong muttered.

Ignoring Mahong, Luka gingerly reached out and shook the frog's cold, damp webbed foot. When he tried to pull his hand back, the golden frog didn't let him go.

"Are you trying to tell me something?"

The frog nodded with a little smirk, a chinless frog smile. It then released Luka's hand, bounded toward the far corner where the water had gathered, and dived into the puddle. The golden glow lit the bottom of the puddle, and in that brilliance, Luka saw a hole the size of a small barrel.

"The way out!" Luka shouted.

The frog disappeared into the hole and the cave returned to total darkness. But seconds later, the brilliance of the Golden One appeared again in the same spot twenty feet above them.

Rrrbrt, rrrbrt, it gurgled, as if announcing its presence. Again it jumped down and plunged into the hole. In silence, Luka and Mahong watched the frog repeat itself several more times.

"I think we should follow it," Luka said. He dived in first, followed by Mahong. The water was sweet, and the golden frog's glow lit the dark hole like a torch. His third eye stared happily back at Luka.

The tunnel quickly slanted upward and the sides were ribbed in such a way that made it easy for them to follow. After climbing for a while, they came to the spot where the frog had first appeared.

"What do we do now?" Mahong asked.

This time the frog didn't leap off. It hopped across the cave and clung to the opposite wall, where one leg pushed aside some weeds to reveal another hole.

"Let's jump through. It might lead to something else," Luka said. But before they could, the Golden One fell and the light was snuffed out, returning the cave once more to darkness.

Someone was at the top of the cave, opening its lid and talking. "Where are they?" It was Lin Koon's voice. He lowered a bright lantern fastened on a long rope all the way to the bottom.

"I don't see anyone there," a guard said.

"But it cannot be," said another.

"I'll send Yi-Shen down there to check. Yi-Shen!" Lin Koon yelled.

No reply.

"Where is Yi-Shen?"

"He's been gone all night," someone replied.

"I'm going down myself," Lin Koon said, concerned.

Luka's heart skipped a few beats upon hearing that. They edged deeper back in the hole and held their breath as Master Koon, a rope around his waist, dropped down. He gazed carefully into every little nook and cranny along the cave wall, and it took a long while for him to pass the section where Luka and Mahong were hiding. Mahong, shaking violently, accidentally kicked a piece of rock, which fell all the way to the bottom, hitting Lin Koon on the head.

"Who did that?" Lin Koon shouted.

"Who did what?" the guard echoed him above.

"Pull me up! They are up there in the hole. That cursed golden frog," Lin Koon said.

"Where are they?" the guard asked, sticking his head in, trying to hear him better.

Luka reached out with his dagger and slashed the rope, dropping Lin Koon down screaming. Then he aimed his dagger at the mouth of the cave, hundreds of feet up, but whoever was there quickly slammed down the lid, leaving Lin Koon in darkness.

"Let's jump across and get into the hole now," Luka whispered to Mahong. Without a hitch, they landed at the hole and started crawling.

The hole got narrower and narrower and the dirt felt drier and drier as they clawed upward. Luka knew they were getting closer to something, but what was it? They finally came to a dead end, where three slabs of rock firmly blocked their way.

"We are truly doomed," Mahong said sadly.

"We are not doomed, we are dead." Luka threw his fist at the rock. "I can't believe we have gone so far only to be stopped by this wall. Why did the Golden One lead us here?"

"So we could live like him in darkness, condemned."

"Stop feeling like such a loser. You and I survived prison, didn't we?"

"Yeah, we did."

"Then we will survive this and find a way out."

"What do we do now?"

"Anything but go back. Let's break through." He slammed the rock again and again with his hands while Mahong pushed with his head and shoulder. But no matter how hard they tried, the wall remained a wall. Every knuckle on Luka's hands hurt and Mahong's head spun.

Three loud bangs suddenly came from the other side of the wall.

"Did you hear that?" Luka asked.

"Yeah, what can that be?"

It came again, louder. *Bang, bang, bang!* The rock collapsed and out came a beam of lantern light that revealed the last face Luka wished to see—that of a smiling Yi-Shen.

"What are you doing here, Yi-Shen?" Luka demanded, waving his dagger.

"Peace," Yi-Shen said, looking uneasy. "Scholar told me everything. You saved my life, now I'm here to save yours."

"Why?"

"You can call me anything but not ungrateful."

Luka's head didn't want to believe him but his heart yielded to the unexpected sincerity in the boy's voice. "How did you find us?"

"Scholar showed me the Golden One's Ring of Life. Let's go."

Luka, suspicious of Yi-Shen's sudden kindness, kept his eyes alert and his fingers on his dagger until they emerged at the mouth of a cave overlooking the bay. "This is the same cave where the snagons jumped out from last night," Luka said.

"And you're going to jump out of here as well." Pushing aside the hanging vines, Yi-Shen gave a light whistle. A little boat came into view thirty feet below them. "The red boat is for you. It will take you to Peking. There is a letter in the boat for you from Scholar."

When Luka and Mahong were about to jump, Yi-Shen stopped them and said, "There's something else you ought to know. About the Clob. You should go for the Red Pearl if the middle eye doesn't glow red."

"What Red Pearl?"

"The Red Pearl in its throat is its only weak spot then. But you cannot see it without climbing into Clob's mouth."

"How do you know this?"

"It's a secret that I paid dearly for. We are even now."

"We are even, Yi-Shen. Goodbye." Luka grabbed Mahong's hand and they jumped down into the red boat, which started to move without any detectable means of propulsion.

As the two raced into the foggy bay, the other boys appeared on top of the cliff and climbed in the trees, waving goodbye to them.

PArt 4

大戰海怪

LUKA WAS LOST in the fog, and being pulled by a mysterious force in an unknown direction didn't help either. He reached out with his senses, but all he saw was more fog and some wispy mountains in the background. Suddenly the boat started to spin out of control, landing Luka and Mahong on their butts.

"Ouch!" Mahong cried.

"What is it?"

"A scroll is stuck up my ass."

"The message from Scholar. Read it to me."

"Why don't you read it?" Mahong asked grumpily.

"I have to navigate," Luka said.

" 'Where there are . . . turtles, there is a way . . . ,' " Mahong read shakily.

"We are being pulled by the good old turtles. No wonder."

" '. . . Trust them, not doubt them. . . .' " Mahong stopped.

"Read on."

"I can't. It's so hard." Mahong hated anything to do with words. The thorny things seemed to walk all over his eyes.

"Okay, give it to me." Luka yanked the scroll out of Mahong's hand and swept his eyes across Scholar's scholarly writing.

Where there are turtles, there is a way. Doubt them not. Trust them you should. They will guide you to the secret Earth Heart Canal, a tunnel that for hundreds of years has been used by many a creature as a sea-to-land and land-to-sea passage. It will take you to Peking, where Atami is being kept in the Water Prison. You will have a fast ride since you are heading from the mountains down to the plains, but I cannot promise you a smooth ride. Nonetheless, enjoy it, for few humans have ever done so.

I have spent the night reading and it seems that Clob, though big, is only a baby in Oceana age. It was born a pampered prince, a little spoiled but always good-natured and kindhearted. It used to swim around the ocean saving fishermen from their wrecked boats, until the day Ghengi tempted it with its first drop of a virgin's blood. Ghengi wanted to cultivate a monster to help him rule the sea and dominate the coastal provinces. Clob became his victim. He fed it hundreds of girls that he took from the streets and villages. The innocent Clob soon developed the Blood Addiction. Now all it wants is blood, day and night. You are dealing with a crazed addict with unimaginable power, that of evil and madness combined. That's why I am begging you not to fight it until we are with you.

Oh, I also have spent the night looking into the middle-eye theory. It is true! The middle eye does show a brilliant red glow at the time of ecstasy. That makes it the only window of vulnerability for outside attack. Also, I would caution you not to wear any red because red is the color of blood and it stirs Clob to a murderous degree. I am telling you this not to encourage you to do the unthinkable, but just to be sure that if and when you are in need of my assurances, you will have them.

Last but not least, my readings also reveal that there is great hope that the marriage of Yin Gong and Jin Gong will be the only force capable of defeating Clob. But that will have to wait until Gulan and Atami are well enough to carry that out according to the Xi-Ling manual.

May Yin Gong be with you. And always remember, you are the one, my Holy Boy. The only one.

P.S. Xi-Ling is always behind you.

It was signed *Scholar* in the tiniest signature.

"Thank you, Scholar," Luka whispered.

"Good news?" Mahong asked.

"Couldn't be better."

When they came upon the island in the middle of the bay, they felt a sudden pull. An angry wave sucked them into the mouth of a dark tunnel.

"What is this?" Mahong shouted.

"I don't know. Just trust the turtles."

"But the turtles aren't going with us. They're all swimming away."

The tunnel suddenly narrowed to the width of the boat and flowing water pushed the leaky vessel toward its destiny. For the next few hours, they flew along the water, cold air blowing their faces and flapping their ears. Fear and darkness gripped them, but there was nothing to do but sit there and hold on for their lives.

"Where are we going with this crazy ride?" Mahong shouted.

"Peking, I presume."

"You presume? You mean we could be heading anywhere?" Mahong said with alarm.

The cave took a drastic turn, and the boat zigzagged out of the tunnel and into the morning sun.

"The sun is on our right. We're heading north," Luka shouted. The valley took another dip and dashed them into the mouth of a lower mountain cave.

"Hold on to the edge . . . ," Luka shouted, the rest of his sentence drowned by a thunderous noise that deafened their ears. Complete darkness blinded their eyes and the boat was thrust from one plateau down to another in a headless rush.

The rest of the journey was a very cold and painful blur. The boat was flying, no less, and dropping from one mountaintop to another, lifting his heart to the top of his throat. Luka's entire body was in revolt. His face was blasted by ferocious gusts of wind, blowing his cheeks full like apples, and his ass was smacked each time the boat hit the bottom of a mountain, only to arrive at the top of another, which only guaranteed another bottom.

Just when they thought they would be shuttling on forever, though, the valley came to an end and the boat capsized in a dark, sticky pond.

Mahong was the first to burst out from under the boat, and Luka soon followed, surprised that the pool was so shallow that the water only nudged their waists. "Mahong, flip the boat over."

Mahong gave one push and the boat flipped. They crawled back into it.

"What's this place and what's that awful smell?" Luka asked.

Mahong sniffed around like a dog and burst into echoing laughter.

"What's so funny?"

"We've just been dumped into a shit hole."

"Yuck, you mean those chunks of things floating in here are . . ."

"Yup, you got it. They are holy crap."

"A sewage dump?" Luka cried.

"Yup, and the finest of them all. The underground royal sewage, aka Royal Dump. Welcome to Peking."

"Peking already?" Luka smiled. "I never expected to arrive in a shit hole."

Mahong shrugged. "You could do a lot worse." He turned and pointed at a faint light in the distance. "That leads to the canal."

"You mean the big Peking Canal running through the heart of the city?" Luka asked.

"Yeah."

"Wow. Those ancient creatures were brilliant," Luka said. "They dug a secret tunnel through the heart of the earth and connected it to the canal through this stinking sewage system. But how did you come to know this place so well?"

"One of the outlets leads to the Water Prison."

"Is that how you got out?"

"Yeah, but don't remind me. It took me days of soaking in the river to get rid of the stench."

"You still stink."

"Now you do too."

"The whole place stinks." All kinds of things were clinging to Luka's robe.

"Stop being such a clean monk. Stinking is mighty good for you." Mahong fetched a wooden stick from the water and started to pole toward the opening.

"How?" Luka asked with disgust.

"It got me out of the city gate and it should get us in as well."

As they neared the mouth of the cave, water poured into the sewage, making it impossible to push the boat forward.

"Get down and push," Mahong shouted over the noise of the rushing water.

Luka jumped back into the water and they pushed the boat into the busy city canal. They soon joined a stream of little *shampans* and merchant boats heading for the city gate, which hung over the canal. Mogo forces rode around in dark painted military yachts, stopping everyone coming or going.

"The security is tighter today," Mahong said. "I wonder why?"

Luka ducked his head as two Mogo soldiers patrolling the river-bank on horseback looked their way. Luka's heart beat like the foot of a jumping rabbit as they inched near the gate, and the joy he had long imagined on returning to his hometown was replaced by sadness and fear.

On the left bank, a burly Mogo soldier poked his spearlike *qiang* at a crying child peddler. To his right, another Mogo, riding high and haughty on his black horse, was chasing a stray dog with his long whip. The dog, a puppy really, cowered and whined, bloody slashes on its back.

Luka tried to look away and ignore it, but he couldn't. He picked up a twig that had fallen into the boat and guided it with his *Qi* toward the Mogo. The twig zipped through the air and needled itself into the horseman's ear.

"Arrgh!" the horseman yelped as he dropped his whip and grabbed his ear. The puppy dashed away.

Mahong knew it was Luka. "What did you do that for?"

"I couldn't help it."

"Look at those notices along the bank," Mahong whispered, "and tell me you couldn't help it."

The notices were for his now famous thousand-*lian* fugitive award. They were posted not only along the bank, but also on the bridge, against thick tree trunks, and on the faces of buildings lining the canal. Luka stared at them with a little I-am-here-you-can't-catch-me smile on his face.

"Wipe that smile off your face," Mahong warned. "A Mogo yacht is coming our way. Do something."

"What?"

"Hold your breath for as long as you can and pretend to be dying."

The Mogoes bumped other boats aside, heading straight for the boys as Luka took a lungful of air and lay down stiffly.

One quick glance at him and a crazy idea came to Mahong.

Mahong shouted, "Coming through. Coming through."

"Hey, you little rascal, where do you think you're going?" demanded a Mogo soldier. He had a long, dark mustache and he pointed his sword at Mahong.

"Emergency. My little brother drowned. He's not breathing, can't you see?" He fell to his knees, squeezed Luka's face, and blew air into his mouth and nose.

"Alive or dead, we need to check your papers before you can get in." Two other soldiers jumped into the boat, nearly capsizing it. Mahong paid no heed to the Mogo and kept on blowing air into Luka's mouth, making his cheeks bulge like two baby apples. The soldier tried to pull Mahong up by his collar, but Mahong surprised him by begging, "You kindhearted Mogo, please save my brother. He is only twelve. Please blow some more air into his lungs." He shoved the soldier's face down into Luka's, which was smeared with manure.

The soldier jerked away. "What is that smell?"

"It was a tragedy. He fell into a manhole."

"You mean he's covered with . . ."

"Yes, royal crap."

"I'm going to kill you." The soldier wiped his face and neck frantically.

"Don't kill me. Not before I save his life. I'm begging you, please let us through so I can get him to my doctor. Please . . ."

"Get out of my way." The soldier whipped Mahong's head with his wooden choke stick, sending him rolling and cursing with pain. Pinching his big nose, the Mogo jumped back to his own yacht, dipped his face into the canal, and splashed it with water.

Mahong quickly poled their boat through the narrow city gate, bumping aside an onion farmer's sloop and an eelman's fishing boat. "You can breathe now, Luka. You're a good actor."

Luka exhaled a long breath. "Easy for you to say. 'Dying' almost killed me."

"You think blowing air into you was fun? Yuck! Your breath almost killed me." Mahong spat into the water and wagged his tongue. "Hey, am I right or what? Good old stench is king, isn't it? We got through!"

"You're still the best in the streets of Peking."

"You bet I am. Prison life hasn't slowed me down a bit."

Luka was trying to get up when Mahong whacked him with the pole. "Did I ask you to sit up? I said you could breathe now, not sit up. Keep your head down. The city is even more dangerous."

"What is that?" Luka asked, pointing to a bright red poster hanging on the stone bridge they were passing under. Two big words in the blackest ink screamed: BRIDE FEEDING. "Pole closer and let me read it."

"We don't have time for that. Rip it off and let's go. We have to disappear quickly."

Luka tore down the notice, which read:

BRIDE FEEDING

*Tender girl, rare beauty, meets
Prince of the Sea:*

Come witness Clob's monthly wedding at
Water Prison
tomorrow noon.

All citizens ~~required~~ invited under Mogo
Criminal Code. Absence not encouraged due
to overcrowding of jail system. Spontaneous
cheers a must, as required by Law of Bountiful
Joy. No tears allowed under Statutes
of Unnecessary Sentiments.

There was a whole list of provisions but Luka's action had already caught the eyes of another Mogo, who screeched from the shore, "Stop, ripper!"

"Is it against the law to remove the notice?" Luka asked.

"I guess so." Mahong shrugged.

"What shall we do?"

"Split up and we'll meet again." Mahong looked three bridges ahead. "There!"

"The market square?" A huge knob of boats, rafts, and *shampans* choked the already crowded dock leading to the spot where he had met the amazing Ma brothers years back.

"Run as fast as you can."

The shouting Mogo ran along the shore as Luka jumped from

one boat to another. The boy finally reached the opposite shore, climbed up, and grinned at the Mogo soldier—until he saw him smile back. That was bad. As Luka turned around, a huge horseman on a huge black horse approached. It was none other than the puppy-beating patroller, who now whipped Luka twice, once on each shoulder. Any other day, Luka would have knocked the man off his horse with one blow, but today his mission weighed heavily on his mind. Luka returned the stinging lashes with a cold stare and walked away.

"Stop and hand me back that poster!" the horseman shouted.

"You can have it when I'm done. Goodbye." Luka jumped up to the thatched roof of a bungalow, leaped into a tree-lined back lane, and disappeared.

When Luka returned to the market square, Mahong had donned a straw hat. His boat was hidden among hundreds of others vying to unload their morning catches at the dock.

"Where did you get that hat?" Luka asked, jumping into the boat.

"A napping boatman. Did you shake off the tail?"

"Most certainly."

"Don't be so certain." Mahong looked around. "It looks like a dragnet to me."

Mahong was right. Urgent whistles soon filled the air, and a fearsome ring of black-robed Mogoes surrounded the market square.

Mahong sighed. "You just had to read that thing, didn't you? What do we do now?"

"Let me think."

"Don't take too long."

Luka clutched his chin but nothing came rushing into his head. The animal cages looked too small to hide in, the wooden barrels were full of flopping fish, and the merchants would be more than happy to turn the fugitives in. And he had already seen the Mogo chaser pointing at him and whispering to his fellow soldiers. In the midst of all the chaos, an unmistakable voice rose above them all. It was a timeless voice of greed, calloused with raspy fringes. "Furs, furs. Best of the herd. Hides, hides. The toughest from Chinghai."

A smile cracked Luka's face.

"You're not thinking what I'm thinking, are you?"

"I'm thinking exactly what you're thinking."

"No, don't."

"Yes, do." Luka grinned.

"He'll turn you in."

Luka whispered into Mahong's ear, explaining about the letter written him long ago. This time, Mahong's face creased into a smile. "One man's fault is another man's gain. For a man that bad, he is way too superstitious for his own good. You played the dying pretty well last time. This time I want you to play a ghost."

"What ghost?"

"Your own ghost. Now go before the Mogoes catch you, and let me take care of the old man."

The man Luka had in mind was none other than Laoren, the notorious fur merchant. The old man had a few more wrinkles and his back was bent horizontally like a turtle's, which made it even easier for him to count his coins. His merchant eyes still glinted at the sight of money while sneering at anything and anyone that didn't smell of slippery coins.

Mahong sidled up to Laoren, agitating the roosters nearby. The disturbance alarmed Laoren, who turned around and stared down at Mahong. "Holy Buddha! Are you who I think you are?"

"Afraid so." Mahong winked and pushed the shaky fur rack, making it tremble.

"Buddha have mercy." The old man picked up the long stick he used to hook his furs with and struck at the boy.

Mahong caught it with his hand. "Still old and mean."

"I thought Ghengi killed you."

"Nope."

"What do you want?"

"I just want to mention one thing to you."

"You want money?"

"Nah."

"What then?"

"The letter." Mahong winked again.

"What letter? And stop winking at me, you rascal."

"The letter you wrote to the Holy Boy."

"The Holy Boy?"

"Yup. The boy that you helped push into Ghengi's hands."

"I made a mistake. And for that I have been praying day and night for Buddha's forgiveness. I could build a small hill with all the incense I burned for His Holiness. That's how pious I am."

"Pious? Praying and asking for forgiveness? People always act too late."

"What are you talking about?"

"The Holy Boy is dead," Mahong said.

"Dead?" The old man covered his mouth with both hands. "That can't be! There are still fugitive award notices everywhere. Why would the Mogoes be looking for him if he is dead?"

"A simple Mogo ploy so that they can continue to raid our homes and businesses and arrest people. Chaos is good for them, you know."

"I don't believe you." Laoren was getting angry.

"Come inside and see him with your own eyes."

"Didn't you say he was dead?"

"Shhh. Never use the *D* word before him or he will be gone just like that." Mahong snapped his fingers, startling the nervous man.

"You mean he's a ghost now?"

"Another big no-no. Never even hint at the *G* word. Those young and sensitive ones die hard."

"What is he here for?"

"For you."

"Me?"

"To give you another chance to repent so that you may enter heaven when your time comes, which is not too far from now."

When they entered his store, Laoren was surprised to find all the curtains drawn and the skylight covered. "Why is everything so dark in here?"

"Light is not good for him. Come out, you Holy Boy."

Luka jumped down from the rafters and appeared before the old man.

"Oh, my Buddha, it is you, Holy Boy." Laoren frowned and sniffed at Luka. "What is that smell?"

"Decay," Mahong answered.

"Decay?" Laoren trembled. "How are they treating you up there?"

"Oh, pretty good. Why do you think they let me down here."

"I've never met any . . . you-know-what before," Laoren said. "Can I touch you?"

"Sure." Laoren pinched Luka's cheeks and nose bridge so hard that the boy almost screamed.

"That hurt?"

"Not at all," Luka said through gritted teeth.

"He cannot feel anything at all. Hit him any way you like," Mahong encouraged.

"No, that's enough. Tell me why you would give a sinful old man another chance when it is my act that pushed you all the way down to the bottom of the well?"

"One word: shelter," Mahong said.

Laoren peeked outside. The Mogoes' horses were closing in. The old merchant thought hard, and his crooked old hands trembled. "The Mogoes are after you, aren't they?" he asked.

"Maybe," Mahong said.

"Yes, they are. Could you please help us?" Luka said.

"What if I don't?" the old man whispered, almost to himself.

"You might have prosperity." Luka touched a hanging fur.

"Or even longevity." Mahong fondled the old man's long beard.

"But you'll have no mercy from above," Luka said.

"And life after death will be painful," Mahong said.

The two worked on the old man like a pair of sages, but their words seemed to have no effect. It was only when Laoren turned toward the hidden shrine that peace descended on his wrinkled face. "All right, then. I am rich and have lived long enough. Come with me to the secret vault."

"Buddha will bless you." Luka grasped his hands.

"Yeah, yeah, yeah," Laoren said impatiently. As he opened a secret door behind a fur rack, someone pounded on the front door.

"Open the door! Mogo garrison forces!" boomed a coarse voice.

"Coming," Laoren answered, then whispered, "Go down the narrow stairs to my vault."

The secret door was so narrow that Mahong had a hard time squeezing through. Laoren grew more nervous as the Mogoes increased their pounding. Finally, they kicked open the front door and Luka had only enough time to give one last push. He shoved Mahong in to safety, but not himself. Silently he closed the vault door, then slipped inside a long fur coat hanging from the coat rack blocking the vault.

Laoren was horrified. The fur coat was long, but not long enough to cover Luka's feet. The old merchant coughed a few times in warning, then stepped on Luka toes.

"Why don't you fly away or disappear? Your feet are showing," Laoren whispered.

"I will," Luka whispered back as he summoned his weightlessness and lifted his feet.

Laoren shook his head and shuffled forward to meet the Mogo garrison force.

Through a buttonhole, Luka glimpsed the action unfolding in the store. Two Mogo soldiers slapped Laoren, sending him wobbling like a rocking chair. "Why didn't you open the door sooner?" a soldier shouted. "Are you hiding someone here?"

"No, no, respectful Mogo garrison officers. I have nothing to hide. Nothing can escape your eyes in my small store, not even a ghost," Laoren said as they walked to the back.

The Mogoes, long-chinned and flat-faced, came into Luka's buttonholed view. They poked here and there with their swords.

"Careful, please. They are precious furs," Laoren begged. "I'll brew you some tea in the kitchen if you two would care to sit down."

The Mogoes came closer and closer until they were only a thin coat away and Luka could hear their heavy breathing. As if sensing something, the fat Mogo sniffed up and down. His eyes narrowed; then he poked his fingers at the very coat Luka was hiding in. The coat was beautiful and shone with an unusual luster seen only in the finest of minks. The Mogo rubbed a few rich hairs between thumb and index finger and sniffed again. "What is that smell?" he asked.

Luka tensed.

"Oh, that is a special herbal powder that I dust on the furs," Laoren said, inserting himself between the Mogo and the coat.

"What for?" the Mogo asked.

"To keep moths away."

Luka's hand slid to his dagger.

"Moths, huh." The Mogo continued stroking the coat.

"Don't touch," Laoren said, shocked at his own firm voice.

"A Chinese ordering a Mogo? Sure, I won't touch it again. I'll just shred it with my sword."

"You'll be sorry if you do."

"Why would I be sorry, you old fart? Tell me." The Mogo pointed his sword tip at the old merchant's nose.

"Emperor Ghengi will punish you."

"Why would he do that?"

"Because it was on Emperor Ghengi's orders that I made this mink coat. Clob's bride will wear it tomorrow for her wedding."

Instantly the Mogo dropped to his knees and prayed in the Mogo language. Then he got up and shouted, "Next time tell me sooner. Clob is our sacred creature."

"Yes, officer."

"By the way, if you see this boy, report to me right away." The Mogo pulled out the fugitive notice.

"You mean the Holy Boy?"

"Yes, whatever his name is. Someone reported seeing him a short while ago near here. If I were you, I would keep the door shut and close early."

"That I will do, right away."

As soon as the Mogo was gone, Luka jumped out of the coat and hugged Laoren's mighty girth. "Thank you so much. Now mercy will befall you like abundant spring rain. By the way, that was a good lie."

"Save your life I did, Holy Boy, but lie I didn't. It's a regretful fact that Ghengi is forcing me to donate the fur for the bride tomorrow." Laoren's voice had a new edge. His eyes angrily pierced the dagger in Luka's hand. "Why don't you come clean and tell me the truth, Holy Boy." He clutched Luka's neck.

"About what?'

"Ghost? Look at you. You stink like a street mutt, and your cheeks turned red when I pinched you. And that dagger—I know that dagger. It belongs to Xi-Ling's grandmaster, Gulan. It's supposed to scare away ghosts and other evil. So if you tell me you're a ghost again, I'll kill you with this old hand."

"Sorry, let go," Luka choked in his grip. "You're right, I'm not a ghost."

"Why did you lie?"

"Because we were afraid that you would turn us in like you did last time."

That seemed to hurt the old man. He took the two boys by their necks to see the little statue of a boy monk sitting in the shrine. "That is you," he said. "I pray to you every day, hoping that I'll be redeemed and that I will not let greed blind my heart ever again. So don't lie to me. Tell me what you are really here for."

"To save Atami," Luka said.

"How?"

"We're going to fight Clob and get blood from it to cure Atami."

The old man shook his head in disbelief. "Are you boys out of your mind? Do you know how many boats Clob has sunk? How many children it has eaten? It comes and goes without warning. It's the biggest curse to us all. Nobody can fight it."

Mahong and Luka looked at each other. "We will," Luka said.

"Yeah, we have to," Mahong said. "And we know how."

Helplessly the old man sighed. "It's certainly heroic but I'm not sure it's wise." He sized up Luka. "Holy Boy, you have grown into a little man now and have a mind of your own. Someday this country will be yours. Who am I to doubt your wisdom."

"So you'll help us?"

"Not only will I put you up for the night, I'll also drive you in my carriage to the feeding site tomorrow. I have to deliver the fur there anyway."

That night, Luka tucked a blanket over his good buddy, then lay down back to back with him. Try as he might, though, Luka could not fall asleep. All he could think about was Atami. What joy it would be tomorrow to hold the dear man's face in his hands again, to tell him how much he loved him and how terribly he had missed him. All the years of separation would be over.

Big thoughts swelled like waves in his heart, and the quiet night seemed longer than ever. To calm himself, Luka knelt down and prayed silently to the east. He begged for the presence of Buddha, the invincible force that was his reason for being. He chanted for wisdom and fortitude. And he asked for forgiveness for whatever earthly sins he might commit tomorrow. With closed eyes, he felt the touch of Buddha's gentle hands over his face, and with it, an infinite love. In his mind's eye, a beautiful oval face with the smoothest skin came to him like a mirage. It was the face he had long ago imagined for the mother he had never met. Her mouth whispered, "I love you, Luka. I love you, child." Then slowly the whispers became "Save the girl. Save the girl."

What did that mean? *Save what girl?* Luka wondered as he fell deep into a dreamless sleep.

Before the sun rose, the sacred day had already begun under Laoren's roof. Laoren had been cooking up a storm for the two boys before their impossible fight. He usually made *yiutiao*, sweet fried dough, by twirling two strands together. But today he added one more strand for good luck. He'd once owned a three-legged dog that had lost its leg stealing a gold ingot that had made him rich. He'd liked the number three ever since.

Luka had been meditating in the vault since dawn, practicing the ritual of *Wu*, emptying oneself. Only then, when nothing would affect him, would he be a fearless warrior. All that remained was the purest *Yin Gong* flame, which burned brighter and brighter as time ticked and tocked toward the moment of truth. At the end of the ritual, Luka held his dagger high and murmured the Awakening Poem.

"The dagger that shines
The power that be
Be with me and guide my soul
Be with thee, Atami, and conquer the unforetold."

He had slipped in the "thee, Atami" part on the whimsy that *Yin Gong* would reach out and offer Atami the strength to survive the day. He was surprised when the dagger responded by glowing. He blinked, and was wondering if he was seeing things when he heard Mahong return from outside.

"What was that?" Mahong asked.

"You saw it too?"

"Are you calling upon Atami?"

"Why, yes. How did you know?"

"I saw your dagger glow. Don't do that again. Each time you call on him, he wastes another ounce of his *Jin Gong* answering and lives a minute less."

"How was your trip to the Water Prison? How's Atami?"

"It was tough. The security is real tight. Every block has three Mogoes strolling around. I had to take the sewage route. As for Atami, the poison has darkened all his skin up to his neck. He is wheezing and bubbly saliva is coming from his mouth. He doesn't have long to live for sure," Mahong said. "On a good note, Mahing, my brother, was glad to hear about you and our plan. He said everything is going to be fine on his end. He'll be sitting on full alert on the prison wall. The moment you get the blood, you rush the bottle to him so he can feed it to Atami right away."

There was a knock on the door and Laoren carried in a tray. His face was grim. "Let's eat my big *yiutiaos* and go," he said. His hands shook so much he nearly dropped the food on the floor.

"What's the matter, Laoren?" Luka asked.

"A boat was wrecked three miles off the coast this morning and three girls were eaten by the hungry Clob, who couldn't wait till the Bride Feeding today. The monster tore off half the boat and the girls' father lost an arm." Laoren shuffled out the door after dropping the news. The breakfast that followed was a very quiet affair.

The mood wasn't improved when Mahong wiped his oily hands on his robe and said, "This could be our last meal."

"Let it be, then," Luka said.

Mahong stood up solemnly. "Keep up your good spirit. It is time to battle." He burped. "Are you ready, Holy Boy?"

"Yes, I am."

"Are you prepared?"

Luka nodded. He whipped out his dagger and kissed it before slipping it back into its sheath, then patted the empty bottle stuck in his sash. Together he and Mahong marched out of the vault.

Laoren pulled up in front of the door and let the boys crawl into the carriage. "Stay covered till we get there, boys," he warned through the little window as the carriage trotted along the canal bank.

Before long the city was cast behind and the canal widened into a river. Through the window, Luka saw thousands of people, all sad and nervous, hurrying along the dusty road for the same destination. Farther ahead, a sprawling crowd had gathered, as if the sacred river goddess herself had summoned them there for her own burial.

"Where do you want to go?" Laoren whispered.

"As near as you can get to the platform," Mahong said.

"I'll try my best. We're coming to the checkpoint."

The carriage slowed and a Mogo barked, "Can't go farther. Stop!"

"Royal business," Laoren yelled back, waving a permit. "I've got to deliver the bridal coat right now to the Water Prison."

"Anyone in the back?"

"Oh, just some coats and two errand boys. I'm old. Can't carry them."

"Coming through. Coming through. Royal business," the Mogo yelled, parting the crowd with his sword.

Laoren got them as close to the platform as he could and knocked on the window. The boys slipped out like a couple of thieves. Before merging into the crowd, Luka bowed to Laoren and Laoren nodded back. The old man wanted to say something but the corner of his mouth quivered and he remained silent. He took a long final look at the boys with a rare glimmer of kindness and tender feeling, then drove on.

Luka grabbed Mahong's robe and elbowed his way through the mob to a grassy rising near the riverbank. A warrior was only as good as his footing, Atami had often told him. Footing here meant the landscape around him.

The river at this point measured about four hundred yards wide and its water was a dark blue. Dark from its unfathomable depth and blue borrowed from the not-too-distant sea. The formidable Water Prison sat like a haunted island in the midcourse of the river, untouched by land and guarded by imposing rock walls. Within those confines a feeble life was fading away.

In front of the prison stood the feeding platform with its rickety legs sunk into the riverbed. On it the despicable ritual would unfold and Luka would face his biggest opponent ever, the dark prince of the sea. Luka had prayed so long for the day when he could save his Atami. That day had finally arrived, and he was ready.

An eerie calm hung thick in the air. The peace was broken when a drawbridge from the Water Prison was lowered onto the feeding platform. A monkey-thin Mogo official rushed out and hit a gong. "All Chinese subjects must bow down in the presence of our glorious emperor, Ulanbaat Ghengi," he announced.

"Get down." Mahong pushed Luka's head down as the crowd bowed. Luka still managed to peek at the entourage of eight soldiers marching across the bridge, carrying a black sedan on their shoulders.

Ghengi. Luka's heart jumped.

"Calm down." Mahong pushed his head down again.

The evil Mogo stepped out of his sedan, ignoring the seat offered him by his officer. Ghengi's face wore an unusual shine and he looked taller and bigger than Luka remembered. A trailing black cloak not only concealed his missing right arm but also gave him a grotesque stature. He swept his eyes to the top of the watchtower, where an empty basket dangled high in the air, and squinted to the east, looking for the creature that was coming from the coast. Ghengi took in every element of his surroundings: the people, the river, the valley, and the blue sky with the glaring noon sun. He sniffed twice, his gaze darting toward Luka and Mahong. Luka's heart skipped.

"Don't move. Don't look away," Mahong whispered.

Luka stayed frozen in that malevolent stare for only two seconds, but it seemed an eternity.

"The man is possessed by evil spirits from his Mogo god. He can smell a breathing cow from one *li* away and a dead one from ten," Mahong said.

"You think he recognized us?" Luka asked.

"Don't move your lips." Both of them burned in Ghengi's frozen stare before his hawk eyes moved away. Ghengi shouted, "Light the cannon and welcome the sacred creature, Clob!"

Ten cannonballs were fired into the sky. The boom shook the ground.

"It's almost time," Mahong said. "Remember, the moment of vulnerability comes only after Clob eats the girl, got it?"

Luka nodded.

"Not the other way around, okay?"

"Yes, Mahong."

"Don't 'yes' me, old buddy. This is your life we're talking about. I've seen Clob at work before. Thirty men in one scoop and no trace of anything."

"Thanks for the encouragement."

"I am just trying to tell you. . . ." Mahong's voice was drowned out by music from the platform. Musicians were blasting away with a painful fanfare. Luka covered his ears with his hands only to have Mahong pull his hands away. "They'll put you in jail if they see you do that."

"But the music is killing my ears."

"I know, but do you see anyone else covering their ears? It's the law here."

"Why are they playing that?" Luka asked.

"They all think the music and cannons draw Clob out, but it really doesn't care. It only comes when it smells the blood."

A fat cow and three pigs were herded onto the platform before Ghengi. They were all wrapped in Mogo black satin and wore black ribbons on their heads.

"They're going to sacrifice them," Mahong said.

Sure enough, Ghengi himself pulled out a long whip and slashed the cow, ripping into the hide before kicking the animal into the river. The wounded cow should have bobbed up again, but not this one. It sank to the bottom and never resurfaced. Even the bloody surface water disappeared, as if a huge whirlpool were twisting in the depths.

Then it was the pigs, which squealed for their lives, knowing their fate. Punctuating each blow with his laughter, Ghengi whipped the poor pigs to the edge of the platform. One last vicious slash and the bleeding pigs finally leaped into the water. They floated with question marks in their scared eyes.

"Eat them! Eat them!" the Mogo soldiers chanted. "Clob! Clob!"

The shouting and the music grew even louder, jarring like a thousand saws sawing away at rusty metal, and more cannons were fired. Soon the water from the east rose like a tidal wave, and it looked as though a ship were racing beneath the water toward the platform.

In an explosion of water, Clob shot up into the air, waving its gigantic lobster legs. The length of its green body blocked the noon sun and cast a shadow on thousands of tiny human heads. It twirled mightily like a heavenly dragon, the flapping of its six legs creating a gust of wind that swayed the nearby trees and rippled the faraway water. Then it pounced down with its full force on the small pigs. The river sliced open with a big gulp, taking the enormous monster back into its bosom.

None was more shocked by Clob's size than Luka. *Huge* was hardly the right word. Clob was huge huge! He believed Mahong now about the thirty men.

"You did not tell me it was so big." Luka clutched at Mahong.

"Hey, hey. This is no time to be frightened. You can take him. Focus."

"It's easy for you to say." Luka calmed himself down and sized up the enemy that had resurfaced and now loomed before him. Clob's flat head resembled a deadly snake's and its fiery mouth still dripped with the cow's blood. Its three murky eyes, the size of big melons, were as blue as the sea from which it had come. Large green scales covered its entire body. But its scariest features were the two giant claws near its head. Clob looked exactly like one of Scholar's baby clobsters, only a thousand times larger and a million times more sinister.

Clob's entrance had splashed the platform and shaken its foundation, but Ghengi didn't seem to mind. He was laughing loud and long. "I have looked east, and I have looked west, my dear Clob, and I have found the best," Ghengi shouted. "Now what do you say you carry me around a bit before I show you the bride?"

Surprisingly, Clob swam docilely toward the platform, stuck its snake head up, and let Ghengi hop onto its nose.

"It is true. Ghengi has tamed it," Luka said.

"Clob will do anything Ghengi wants it to do as long as it gets the girls."

Ghengi wasn't a small man, but as he sat on Clob's flat face, holding on to a long antenna, he looked like a little boy. Clob swam up and down the river as more giant waves crashed. The beast finally rested its jaw back on the platform and flicked its forked green tongue. Its three eyes looked up the prison tower as it anxiously waited for the bride to descend.

"You can't wait, can you?" Ghengi rubbed its nose and Clob roared lustily. "Release the bride for my sacred beast!" Ghengi commanded.

A small door slowly opened. From within emerged a slender young girl wrapped in Laoren's mink coat. Like an animal, she was led by a thick rope tied around her waist, and she was rigid with fright. A soldier jerked the rope, pulling her toward the edge of the tower ledge. As she covered her face with her hands, she let out a nerve-ripping shriek. The faceless girl looked so alone, sad, and lost.

Does she have any family to cry for her? What is she thinking now that her life is only steps away from its end? Does she know why she has been chosen? And does it matter, anyway? All those questions pained Luka as he felt tears trickle down his cheeks.

"Hey, softie, are you crying? You're breaking the No Tears rule." Mahong wiped the tears off Luka's face with his sleeve.

"I can't help it."

As the soldier pushed the girl into the basket and lowered her inch by inch, Clob danced again in celebration. The lower the basket descended, the more wildly the creature thrashed in the water. When the beast jumped up again, its claw nearly caught the basket.

"Be calm and let me off so I can show your bride to the people one last time before you have her for good," Ghengi said. Clob threw the Mogo back onto the platform just as the basket landed. The ruler then yanked the girl from the basket and swung her to face the crowd.

"Lower your hands. This is your last chance. If you don't show your face, no man will fight for you." Ghengi turned to the people. "Anyone who dares fight Clob for her life will have a chance to own her forever. Come on, you hot-blooded young men. Any challengers?"

Nobody moved. "No takers? I don't blame you, young men. You haven't seen her face yet, and what a face she has."

"Show her face!" the soldiers roared. "Show her face!"

Among the loud cries and shouts, the girl's delicate hands slowly opened to unveil a painted oval face framed by a cascade of soft hair. No older than Luka, she was a rare beauty in every way, just as the poster said. But Luka found something familiar about her in the way she frowned at the sun and bit at her lower lip. His heart stopped.

"That's Hali."

"Who?"

"Hali, a kind orphan I met in prison. It can't be." The peace for which Luka had meditated all morning was gone in a snap. His heart flew out to her as the searing memory of that death camp came rushing back to him.

"Don't do anything stupid," Mahong said desperately. "We've got a plan, remember?"

"It has to be changed," Luka replied, his eyes fixed on her.

Mahong groaned in resignation and shook his head.

"Follow me," Luka said.

"Where are we going?"

"We've got to get to the river's edge."

The two ducked low and crawled like mice through the crowd. Arriving at the river, they waited in the water and hid behind the swaying reeds. Between the leafy blades, Luka saw Clob flick its tongue at Hali and lick its lips. She screamed in horror, but no one dared move to help.

The evil Ghengi wasn't done having fun yet. He started to remove Hali's clothing, first the mink coat, then the scarf. When Ghengi ripped her outer jacket off, revealing her thin red blouse beneath, the creature stirred with great anticipation.

"Come get her, you handsome groom," Ghengi yelled. He tore off Hali's red shoes and threw them at Clob. The creature snatched them with its right claw and chewed on them.

"Help me, please," she pleaded to the watching crowd.

"What? Are you afraid to die? You should be happy, my little orphan. You're going to be empress of the sea, at least for a month,"

Ghengi said, trying to kiss her neck. Hali slapped Ghengi right across his ugly face.

"You ungrateful child! I fed you good food and groomed you with the tenderest care." Ghengi ripped off her blouse, leaving her with only a sleeveless shirt that revealed her bare arms. The crowd gasped, for the local custom forbade girls from ever showing their bare arms. Even their hands were to be covered by long sleeves.

Hali crouched down on the platform, trying to cover her arms. "Don't shame me any more, please."

"Don't shame you?" Ghengi yanked down the slim strap off her right shoulder. "You burnt down my clothing factory. Many of our Mogo soldiers froze in the cold winter. You must pay for your sins!"

Luka jabbed Mahong. "Did you hear that? She's a patriot!"

"Yeah, loud and clear. But you still have to remember: no girl, no glow in the middle eye. No glow, no moment of vulnerability. You have to let the beast eat the girl first or you will never get the blood for Atami."

Luka was stunned. "How can you say that? No matter what, I have to save the girl first, got it?"

"And let Atami die?"

"No!"

"Then how do you plan to do both?"

"Remember what Yi-Shen told us?"

"What, if the middle eye doesn't work, go for the Red Pearl inside the mouth? You can't trust Yi-Shen. That sounds like an easy way to get rid of you."

"I have no choice."

"You're crazy! Clob will kill the girl and you, then Atami will die because of your stupidity."

"You call that stupidity? I call it faith. Remember the first vow of Xi-Ling? 'Trust your fellow warrior like your brother.'"

"You don't have a brother. You don't know what a brother is really like. And Yi-Shen wanted to kill you, remember?"

"But I saved his life and that changed everything. Now I have to save Hali. You would do the same thing."

"No, I wouldn't."

"Yes, you would. You did. Who went all the way to Xi-Ling, risking his life to save Atami's?"

Mahong knew any further arguments were useless. "All right, what can I do to help now that you've decided to kill yourself?"

Luka whispered into Mahong's ear and pointed to the red clothes floating at the water's edge. Mahong disappeared in that direction.

On the platform Ghengi was toying with Hali's remaining shoulder strap. His voice rang out over the crowd again. "Now you all will see how I reward my enemies. With an ugly, shameful, bloody death!"

"Get your filthy hands off me, you beast!" Hali screamed. Her spit, which he wiped off his face, didn't enrage Ghengi, but the word *beast* did. He slapped her so hard that she slid halfway to Clob's mouth.

Serenity within. Serenity within, Luka chanted repeatedly, striving to collect himself.

Eight Mogo soldiers on the platform ran back into the prison and drew up the bridge. Then Ghengi crouched like a mountain eagle and flew to the top of the tower, his cloak fluttering like long wings.

Hali was left alone to face Clob with only the deep water surrounding her.

The beast slithered forward. The cow and three pigs obviously hadn't been too filling, for bloodthirst filled its crazed eyes.

Without warning, its claw struck the platform, narrowly missing Hali. Hali scrambled backward until she too reached the platform's edge.

Sensing Hali's vulnerability, Clob calmed. It smiled in an imitation of kindness even as its claws flocked Hali toward itself. Then the smile faded as the monster's middle eye began to turn pink. That was it. Clob was about to devour her, Luka thought.

"Here," Mahong said. He crawled back from the thick reeds with a red shirt that dripped with water.

"Just in time." Luka draped the shirt over his robe, not knowing exactly how girls' clothes were supposed to be worn. Mahong, no expert dresser either, tied the loose hem around his waist. Luka looked like the fabled half-boy, half-woman.

"You can't even attract a cow looking like that," Mahong said.

Luka ignored him as Clob's right claw inched closer from behind Hali's back. It was now or never.

"Let's go!"

Luka called on his *Yin Gong* and rocketed to the dizzying height of the tower top. He suspended himself in the air, weightless, waiting for the perfect moment. Mahong trailed behind him like a flying monkfish, his baggy robe all askew. They passed before Ghengi's eyes like birds passing treetops.

When Clob raised its ugly head toward them, Luka plunged like a diver with his Iron Arms stretched and Steel Fingers curled into fists. He thrust with the force of his body weight and the blast of his *Yin Gong* power. From afar he looked like a desperate metal anchor reaching for the ocean floor. He was going for Clob's flat nose right where Ghengi had ridden. But it was not easy. Clob tried to slither away on the slippery platform, but Luka was nimble and flexible, following Clob's movements with his *Qi* until the confused beast tried to slip back into the water. But Luka wasn't going to let it swim away. His arms opened like a pair of scissors and closed in on the nose of the beast. Mahong flung himself onto Clob's left ear, clinging to its slimy earlobe.

Clob's nose was not only flat but also slippery, and it was impossible for Luka to get a good grip on it. He slipped down the monster's face, all the way onto its upper lip, his legs dangling before Clob's mouth. Not good. Any lower and he would be Clob salad meat. But Clob's randomly grown facial whiskers saved him. He grabbed the thinnest one and swung himself in a circle. Beneath him, the crowd were all stunned, but no one more so than Ghengi, who jumped up from his seat on top of the tower and glared at the two boys. His soldiers were lowering the drawbridge, ready to capture them, but Ghengi ordered them to stop. He had other plans.

Luka and Mahong were still spinning as Clob tried to fling them off. Even as the beast shook its head, Luka could see Hali clutching a wooden beam on the platform. Her clothes were wet, and her eyes were big from watching the unfolding drama, her own danger forgotten.

Clob, unable to rid itself of the two tiny nuisances, struck its own head with its lobster claws. But Luka and Mahong dodged the blows. The beast grew crazier—and that was what Luka wanted. The time had arrived. Luka gave the signal and Mahong flung himself from the ear toward Hali.

Clob's eye, the lazy middle one, froze at the sight of Mahong. Then the monster snatched Hali with its left claw before Mahong could reach her.

"Help! Help!" Hali cried desperately as the claw dug into the tender skin of her waist. She tried to push the pincer open with her hands, but only bloodied her fingers on the jagged blades. The more she fought, the higher Clob brandished her in the air like a trophy.

Trouble. Luka followed Mahong and landed squarely on the platform before the monster. They stood only as tall as Clob's nostrils.

"Hali! It's Luka," he cried, waving his hands.

Luka's red garment caught Clob's attention.

"Luka?" Hali asked with disbelief. "The death row boy?"

"Hali, I'm here to save you!" Luka yelled. Hali was truly a tiny twig dangling in the monster's pincer, but bigness was no threat to Luka. He was here to fight small. A flea-in-an-elephant's-ear and needle-in-the-sea small.

"Hali, stay calm. We're going to open the claw up for you."

"It'll kill you!"

"No, we'll defeat it together." While Luka rose up in the air just out of the monster's reach, Mahong climbed to the top of Clob's head and dangled a red shirt before the beast's nose.

"Come, you nasty creature, come get me," Mahong teased.

Clob only tightened its claw around Hali.

"The plan is not working. Let's open the claw, Mahong," Luka said, and planted his feet on the lower pincer as his arms pulled the upper one. But the claw just kept closing, no matter how much *Yin Gong* he summoned. Hali's screams were growing weaker.

"Hang on, Hali," Luka yelled.

"Go . . . please," she gasped.

"Watch your back," Luka heard Mahong shout from atop Clob's head, but it was too late. Clob's other claw caught Luka around his waist like a pair of giant scissors and yanked him away from Hali. He concentrated his *Qi* to his belly where the pincer gnawed him, but it was hardly enough to counter the enormous power of the huge claw.

"Now it'll eat both of us," Hali moaned.

"Don't worry. I want it to eat us so I can fight it from within."

"How—" Before she could finish, Clob waved its claws in victory while the crowd wailed. The louder the people became, the more Clob waved his prizes.

When Clob finally stopped tossing them, Luka's head was still spinning and Hali was puking. But that was hardly the end. Clob began dipping them in the water like two dumplings plunged into soy sauce—in and out, up and down. Hali coughed water from her nose and mouth while her body coiled in fright. But the cool water only refreshed Luka, stopping his dizziness instantly.

The Red Pearl inside Clob's mouth was Luka's last resort. And the only way to find that pearl of blood was to get inside the mouth. *To steal a tiger's tooth, one has to see its mouth open.*

Meanwhile, Ghengi had enjoyed the sight like a proud father, but enough was enough. It was past noon and it was time for the finale. "Eat them!" he shouted from atop the tower, reinforcing his command by shooting down a sharp star at Clob's head. The creature stopped the dipping and rolled its murky eyes up toward its master. When Clob's enormous mouth began to open, Luka looked inside. What he saw was a green cave—green teeth, green tongue, green gums, green everything. But there was no Red Pearl.

Have I been misled? Did Yi-Shen lie so I would die? Luka's mind raced as the claws lowered them. But he had no time to doubt. Faith was what he needed and faith was all he had left. And with that faith, calm descended on him. He heard Yi-Shen's parting words again: *You saved my life. And I'll save yours.*

He was only inches away from the green cavern when he felt the claw loosening. *Come on, Clob. Open your mouth wider,* he begged. And it did. The monster stretched its jaws to the fullest and let out an enormous growl, and in that moment Luka saw it, the Red Pearl, glowing at the root of its tongue, illuminating the entire mouth with redness.

Luka threw his dagger and it dashed headlong for its prey with a pure blue glow of its own. With a pop, it punctured the pearl, and as the red glow vanished, Clob began to gag as if choking on a fish-bone. The dagger was doing a fine job, drilling and spinning for the blood its master needed. Then suddenly, it stopped, and Clob's jaws clamped shut like a dungeon's door. Hali and Luka were locked inside, and their only light was the pure blue *Yin Gong* glow.

"We're going to die!" Hali said, crouching by Luka's leg. But dying was hardly his concern; not getting Clob's blood was.

"Be calm, Hali. We'll get out as soon as I fill my bottle with blood."

"How can I be calm? I can't breathe."

"Hold my hand and remember that death is fearful of life. We will win," Luka said. He willed the dagger to continue drilling, and it spun with new vigor, disappearing entirely inside the pearl. Silence followed, then a rumble.

Luka screamed, "Hear that?"

"The rumbling?"

"Yes, the rumbling!" Luka cried with delight.

In one blinding gush, thick blood burst out of Clob's throat like the Red Sea, shooting Luka and Hali out of its mouth and onto the platform. Luka was covered with gore and his tongue and throat had a fishy taste that burnt all the way down to his stomach. *I've drunk Clob's blood,* Luka realized as he spat and coughed. But the bottle in his hand was full and that was the only thing that mattered.

I did it. I did it! Atami could be saved now.

"Luka! That was fantastic!" Mahong cried from atop Clob's forehead.

The beast's head hung on to the edge of the platform as its tail dipped into the water. All three eyes were shut, with no sign of life visible.

Wow, my dagger has done it again.

"Where's Hali?" Luka wiped the disgusting droplets off his face and searched for her. Slowly, from a corner, Hali rose and stumbled toward him, so completely covered with gooey redness that Luka hardly recognized her.

"Are you okay, Luka?" She gripped his arm tightly.

"Yes, you?"

Hali nodded.

"We have all we need. Let's go now," Mahong said.

"My dagger!" Luka touched his empty sheath, puzzled when the weapon did not come at his call. "My dagger is locked behind Clob's mouth."

"Let's open it." Mahong stomped on Clob's head, trying to rouse it as Luka attempted to lift its jaw. But it weighed even more now that Clob was hardly breathing.

"We've got to go," Mahong shouted.

"No, I can't leave without my dagger."

"Ghengi is coming!"

"I still can't leave."

"I'll help you," Hali said. As she crawled over to Luka's side, Clob's eyes caught the redness of her shirt and began to open as if it were awakening from a slumber.

"Did you see that? It opened its eyes for me," Hali said. "Maybe if I dance a little, it'll open its mouth for me."

"No!" Luka tried to stop her but she was already waving her arms wildly in front of its sleepy eyes. "Clob, open your mouth. I'm all yours!" she shouted.

Clob groaned and moved its upper jaw but failed to open its mouth. Still the beast would not give up. The sight of Hali had stirred something deep inside it and finally Clob managed to crack open its mouth for a split second. That was all the dagger needed. It flew out into Luka's hand.

"I've got the dagger," Luka shouted to Mahong.

"Throw the bottle now," Mahong yelled. He dove into the water with Hali in his right arm and swam away, leaving Clob with a big question mark in his blinking eyes.

As his friends swam away to safety, Luka cast a quick glimpse at the shadowy boy straddling the prison wall. It was Mahing, and he was where he had said he would be. Luka threw the bottle, aiming with the help of his *Yin Gong* power, in the direction of the Water Prison.

Luka's heart jumped with a joy he hadn't known for ages. His mission was accomplished. Atami would be saved and Mahong and Hali had already swum away. But when he was about to dive away after his friends, he saw Ghengi's batlike shadow headed for the bottle. Before Luka could recall the precious blood, the evil man snatched it into his hand and flew down with his long cloak fluttering behind him. He landed before Luka, facing his son for the first time.

Luka stood firm. "Give me the bottle or I'll cut off your left arm the same way my master did away with your other one."

Ghengi laughed morbidly. "I think not. Cloak, remove yourself." The cloak strings began to squirm like earthworms, untying themselves from around his neck, and the cloak flew away to the tower like a bat. In that instant, a green lobster claw, a miniature replica of Clob's was revealed, grown from the severed stump of Ghengi's right shoulder. "You call this armless?" He waved the claw in the air.

"You *are* an evil beast."

"And a happy one." He laughed.

"I hate you."

"You won't much longer. You and Atami will both die today. Then I, Ulanbaat Ghengi, will be the Invincible!" His pincer snapped at Luka. "You know all this was staged just for you, Holy Boy. Will the blood of Clob really cure Atami's wounds? Yes. But is he ever going to get it? No." He waved the bottle. "You may ask why, why you? The answer is simple. I want you dead because you are the darkest of curses to all you touch. Your moles are daggers of your fate. They first killed your mother. Atami will soon follow—"

"And then you? Is that why you want me dead so badly? Is that why you have wanted to kill me ever since I was born?"

"No, no, much earlier than that. I wanted to kill you the moment Zuma's belly bulged with your life. I wanted you to end before you could even begin. That prairie witch was right. I should have done away with you long ago. But all will end today because your mother passed to you the weakest of all human qualities—goodness of the heart. And that will serve as your own death nail, a gift from her."

Luka took two steps back and struck a tiger's stance, his eyes focused on Ghengi's claw. "Remember the dagger that cut off your arm?" Luka dashed the blade straight at the root of the claw. The dagger hit the shoulder with a little *ding* then lurched around and around like an aimless dragonfly not knowing where to land. It struck the claw a few times, but the shining blade kept slipping off, not making a dent.

Ghengi roared with laughter. "Seamless Claw. Thank you, my Clob. You did it. You did it!" he shouted. "You made Xi-Ling power useless."

The dagger's glow paled and it swayed aimlessly in the air, puzzling Luka with its dimmed spirit. Luka recalled the dagger back into its sheath. "I'll fight you with my bare hands."

"And I'll fight you with my bare claw. Come and get the bottle, if you dare."

Luka gazed at nothing but the bottle in Ghengi's hand. It was a Xi-Ling technique called Smalling, which could reduce even the biggest opponent to a dot of weakness. Ghengi's ugly face faded with the rest of the background. In the eye of Luka's soul, the red bottle gleamed. And in the chamber of his heart, he yearned to reach out and take into his possession the only cure for his dying master.

Then came the rush of that precious heat, which spread from his tingling toes into his heels. Slowly the silver light, *Yin Gong Qi,* built into a flame that rose up his waist, through his chest, and into his arms. Finally the magic light surged into his fingertips and the rest of his body became as light as a feather. He shot up into the air and headed for one goal: the bottle in Ghengi's hand.

To Luka's surprise, Ghengi opened his mouth and blasted a cloud of chilling air that blocked his *Yin Gong* vision. In that darkness, the shining red bottle vanished. Luka thrust his fingertips at that invisible force, but the wall persisted.

I am Yin Gong, *the source of goodness, and you, the darkness, the origin of evils.* Luka's faith in the supreme power of *Yin* was absolute, especially at that moment. He utterly let himself go and blasted his power to counter that enemy force. But Ghengi's force was like a rocky cliff. It absorbed nothing and returned everything.

I am the moon, beaming the darkness of night, and you are the shadows that flee at my breath. Luka's faith carried him forward and smacked him into the evil man's chest. But Ghengi did not fall as Luka had willed. Nor did he falter as he should have. Ghengi ripped off his shirt, revealing a chest covered entirely with hard, shiny scales like those of Clob's.

The man has turned himself into a beast! Luka nearly threw up at the sight. *But he must have weaknesses. Man shields his front but rarely his rear,* Luka thought as he slipped between Ghengi's legs to slice his unprotected back. But his back was also covered with an armor of green scales, which deflected Luka's dagger.

Why am I failing in the face of evil? Luka lamented. *And why is my* Yin Gong *weakened into submission?* Then he saw over Ghengi's shoulders an even scarier prospect looming. Clob was rising and slithering toward them, its eyes bright with renewed vigor, staring angrily at the bottle in Ghengi's raised hand.

"High time you woke up, my sacred creature. You can have him now that he has taken your bride away," Ghengi said, sensing its movement.

But Clob showed no interest in Luka at all. Its three eyes were glued only to the bottle. "What are you looking at your own blood for?" yelled Ghengi. "Aren't you hungry, or angry at him?" When Ghengi smacked the beast with his claw, Clob's eyes filled with rage and its mouth cracked open. The monster then snatched Ghengi and rattled the Mogo in the air.

"This is no time to play, Clob," Ghengi roared, but Clob shook him even more. "Put me down now or I will never feed you again."

The beast paid its master no attention as its middle eye turned pink again and its mouth opened wide. Ghengi screamed. "What do you want from me?" It was like talking to a stone wall. "Help! Help!"

None of his soldiers came forward. Some of them even climbed farther up into the tower. The crowd began to rush away from the riverbank as if a disaster had just befallen them.

Luka could not believe his eyes. There were shouts from the crowd for Luka to flee, but Luka thought only of his Atami, dying in a rotten cell. He wasn't going to leave without the bottle. Luka rose to his feet, and faced Ghengi. "Doesn't look like any of your men are going to help you."

"Help! Help!" Ghengi shouted.

Luka shook his head. "Give me the bottle and I'll save you."

"How can you save me?"

"I'll stab the Red Pearl again."

"You're trying to trick me."

"Whatever you say."

Clob's mouth opened to its fullest and the Red Pearl glowed again.

"All right. Here." Ghengi frantically tossed the bottle to Luka. "Now throw the dagger." But Luka ignored him and turned toward Mahing, who straddled the tallest wall of the Water Prison. "Are you ready?" Luka shouted to him.

"Yes," Mahing shouted back.

But as Luka raised his hand to hurl the bottle, a wave of dizziness crippled him. His head was spinning like a windmill and the world around him darkened like night falling. Though he could still hear Mahing's echoing shout, "Throw me the bottle," he found not a shred of strength to lift his right hand. Though he could see Clob's gigantic claw open, throwing Ghengi away, he could not summon one single thread of *Qi* to move his body. *What is happening to me? Am I dying? What am I dying for? Have I been poisoned by Clob's blood or has my fate unleashed the curse to end it all?*

Mahing yelled, "Throw it now! Atami is dying!"

"Atami!" As the name passed Luka's parched lips, he suddenly remembered. *The blood. Atami. That's right, Atami. I need to throw the bottle.*

Lying flat on his back, Luka marshaled up his last ounce of strength and tossed the little bottle east where he had last seen

Mahing. It was his last wish and final gift for the man who was so dear to him. Now it was out of his hands. His wish had been fulfilled and his heart was content. He was deaf to the angry roar unleashed by the enraged Clob, which had witnessed its own blood flying away from under its nose, and blind to the gigantic jaw opening to swallow him whole. Finally the mouth closed around him, shutting out the daylight and cutting off all air. In that instant darkness, Luka knew his ending had begun.

Please, Yin Gong. *Please, my precious dagger.* The blue glow was nowhere to be seen. He willed once more for his dagger, his only hope in the face of hopelessness. And this time a blue glow cut through the darkness like sunlight. His heart leaped with joy at the sight, though his breath was running out and soon all would cease for him. The dagger flitted around him, but what should he will for?

Then, in recesses of his soul, Luka remembered Gulan's words spoken in the silver moonlight of his cell: *Your wish is its command. Will anything. All is for your asking!*

What shall I will that hasn't been willed before? And what could the dagger do but circle in shame at its inability to save its master? Then, in the wildest of all his wishes, Luka murmured the word "Grow." *That's it. Grow, please, and lift up this jaw so that we both can live to see the sunlight again or our souls will be trapped here forever.*

The dagger suddenly ceased circling and started to grow right before Luka's eyes. Soon it became a ten-foot spear, stretching defiantly against the crushing jaw. Clob was roaring and fighting to keep its mouth shut but the dagger kept growing till it bent to the point of breaking. Then the dagger straightened and cracked apart Clob's jawbone. Unconscious and limp, Luka fell from the beast's gaping mouth into the muddy water.

Clob let out an anguished growl for the spirited dagger had pierced through its middle eye, poking out of its socket like a thorn. The pain fortified its will for revenge and drove the mad creature madder. It dove for Luka and fished out his lifeless form, but before it could feed the boy into its mouth again, two shafts of light snaked into the sky like lightning. One shot from the hands of a lonesome monk in a tree to the north. The other zigzagged like a knobby vine from the deepest cell of the Water Prison. Clob glared at the strange lights as they danced their mating ritual around and around its head, searching for something. Then they found it. That pinnacle. The tip of that trapped dagger. With a clap as loud as thunder on a summer night, the ends of the twin lights met at Clob's forehead, causing an explosion of sparks and a fanfare of lights. The creature shook from head to tail and instantly was set aflame, looking like a fiery dragon ablaze, before collapsing into the deep water, taking Luka with it.

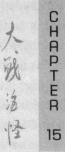

WHEN LUKA WOKE up several days later, he thought he was dreaming. He looked around and found himself lying in a big bed under a pavilion perched on top of a small hill that overlooked the Xi-Ling River. A dozen incense sticks burnt idly away around his bed, filling the air with that unique fragrance from his past. Why was he guarded with this fence of burning sticks? They were only meant for the dying.

He climbed out of this bed and felt light-footed, his heart filled with an unknown joy. *I'm not dead. I'm alive!* To prove his vitality, he hopped up and down on the bed and swung up into a tree branch that hung over it. The wind was sweet and the air fresh. Everything felt just right, as if he had woken up from the soundest sleep. *What has happened to me? Why am I up here away from the rest of the temple?*

As he scratched his head, two boys flew down from the nearby treetops, crashing him back into bed. It was Mahong and Mahing in Xi-Ling uniform, patting him from head to toe. "Holy Boy is awake! Everyone, come see him!" Mahong screamed, startling the birds in the nearby forest. Luka covered his ears with his hands, shocked by the loud voice.

"What are you shouting for? You're hurting my ears," Luka said.

"You don't remember?" Mahing asked, rubbing Luka's temples for him.

"Remember what?" Luka asked.

"Don't think too hard. Wait here," Mahong ordered, slapping his brother's hands away. "We've got to inform the entire temple. Let's go!"

The two rascals started to scramble away, but Mahong turned back. "You won't go back to sleep on us, will you?"

"No, I don't think so," Luka said, and climbed back up the tree branch.

"You hear that? He's thinking." He poked his brother and they ran down the slope.

A moment later, the entire temple was running toward him. In the lead was Gulan, tall and thin like a leafless tree, followed by Master Koon. Behind them were the Shen brothers, all pumpkin-headed and scruffy as ever. Hu-Hu still had his water pails, Di-Di carried a flute in his hand, and Co-Co's ladles dangled from his belt. Everybody looked as if they had just left what they had been doing.

"I told you he is alive!" Mahong pointed at Luka. "He's up there in the tree. Now do you believe me?"

Luka jumped to the ground and the crowd all dropped to their knees, alarming Luka greatly.

"What's the matter? I'm not dead. I feel great." Luka drummed his chest and took a deep breath. "Come over here, all of you, Hu-Hu, Co-Co, and you, Di-Di. Come!"

All the boys got to their feet, running and hopping toward Luka as if a dam had burst. The footsteps rushed like wild water.

"Holy Boy! Holy Boy!"

"Junior Master!"

They jumped all over Luka. Hu-Hu, Di-Di, and Co-Co wrestled with him, nearly suffocating him, but he was too happy to complain. Gulan parted the boys and rushed over, accidentally kicking aside an incense burner. "You've recovered, Holy Boy," he said with surprise.

"What happened to me, Grandmaster?"

"You've been in a deep sleep for six days. We thought you would never wake up again."

"I have?"

"Clob nearly killed you." He lifted up Luka's robe, revealing red, swollen claw marks.

"Clob! Now I remember! But who saved me?"

Gulan pointed to the river below. "They did."

Luka's eyes followed Gulan's finger down the cliff to the river. Two snagons rose from the water and dipped their heads to him.

"Moo-Moo and Pawpaw?" Luka bowed back to the snagons.

"Yes, they carried me down through the Earth Heart Tunnel all the way to Peking in time to aid you, and they fetched you up from the river. *Yin Gong* and *Jin Gong* were married right at Clob's head with the help of your little friend."

"My friend?"

"Yes, your *Yin Gong* dagger, remember?"

"My dagger. Where is it?" Luka patted his waist urgently, finding only his empty sheath.

"It's still trapped in Clob's head. When you wished it to grow, it did, but in so doing, it lost most of its power. The dagger could have escaped through the third eye with its remaining power, but it made one final sacrifice to bring *Yin Gong* and *Jin Gong* together."

"So did you kill Clob?"

"No, we tamed it."

"Why didn't you kill it?"

"Because even the worst creature deserves a chance at redemption."

Luka frowned.

"Someday you will understand. It will be a long while before Clob returns to the shore. Unfortunately it has swum away with your dagger still trapped inside its head."

"How am I ever going to get my dagger back?"

"Someday we will hunt Clob down."

"Oh, Master Koon and Grandmaster Gulan, I am so sorry. I have lost a Xi-Ling treasure to the beast."

"Xi-Ling treasures are known for their great sacrifices for their masters. It is up to us to be worthy of them and to bring them back home when we can," Lin Koon said.

"Can I keep the sheath?" Luka asked.

"Of course you can, but why?"

"Someday I will fill it again," he vowed, and bowed before them. "Are you going to punish me?"

"Why would we punish you?" Lin Koon asked.

"Because I broke the temple rule."

"Yes, you did, but no, we will not punish you. For you followed your heart, and that makes you the kind of warrior we want all of you to be—a noble warrior." Lin Koon swept his eyes over all the boys surrounding them, then pushed Yi-Shen forward. "Yi-Shen, it is time you apologized to the Holy Boy for the wrong you have done him."

"No, no, he doesn't owe me any apology," said Luka. "In fact, I must thank him." Luka extended his hand.

"Why?" Lin Koon asked.

As he took Luka's hand, Yi-Shen blinked at him in warning, and Luka knew that what had transpired between them in that cave would remain forever a secret. So he smiled back mysteriously and said, "It's between him and me."

Lin Koon frowned in puzzlement.

"Where is Atami?"

"Oh, he's coming. He has been fasting and praying day and night for you and passed out upon hearing of your awakening. But don't worry, Scholar is with him."

"I have to see him now."

"You're too weak. . . ."

Luka ran barefooted down the grassy slope toward the main temple. When he entered the courtyard, Luka spotted him, his dear Atami. He was just crossing over the threshold, supported by Hali on one side and Scholar on the other. He looked much thinner, all bones poking and skin hanging. But that face of his, gaunt in every sense, was still the picture of spring. His kind eyes were smiling, and the sweet dimples hidden in those sunken cheeks were budding. Joy was written along the deep furrows of his wrinkled forehead. He stumbled toward Luka, not caring that he was faltering, and nearly fell. Luka dropped to his knees and crawled toward him like a pious son. In the middle of the courtyard, the two met and embraced, melting into each other. One year of wandering had come to an end.

Atami pulled himself away and cupped Luka's face in his trembling hands. "Oh, my Holy Boy. It has been a long, long goodbye."

"Oh Atami, I didn't even get to say goodbye. I have missed you so much."

Like a blind man, Atami touched every feature of Luka's face and every limb, making sure that not a toe or a mole was missing. "I am sorry you have suffered so much. You risked your life to save me."

"It is my duty, Atami, for you are dearer to me than my own father."

"And you are as precious to me as my own son." Atami's tears wet Luka's shoulders.

"But I could not have saved you without Scholar's help." Luka hugged Scholar around the waist, his arms only reaching halfway around the giant's girth.

"My petty help is paled by your bravery," the giant murmured, hugging Luka so that the boy disappeared into his chest. "Xi-Ling has hope. Xi-Ling has hope."

"No more tears. Come meet this girl. I think you two have met before." Atami pushed Luka to face Hali. The two were red-faced and tongue-tied. Their hearts thumped as if they were meeting for the very first time. Hali, twirling her long hair and spinning on her heels, looked even more beautiful than before and smiled even more sweetly than he had remembered.

"Welcome to Xi-Ling, Hali," Luka said, reaching out to clasp her hand. Atami slapped his hand away.

"Welcome back to life," Hali said. "What took you so long, Holy Boy?"

Scholar explained, "Hali woke up three days ahead of you."

"You were also in a long sleep?"

Hali nodded. "And I've been feeling unusually good ever since I woke up. How about you?"

"Me too." Luka frowned. "Why were we both asleep so long?"

"Hali's sleep provided the only clue," Scholar was only too happy to continue talking. "You both must have accidentally drunk Clob's blood, only you probably took in more, which knocked you out longer."

Luka frowned. "What will happen to us with the blood still flowing in us?"

"Nothing and everything," Scholar sighed. "I am still researching the ancient scrolls for an answer. In the meantime, you two, do tell me if you notice any changes within yourselves. No symptom is too small to be ignored. But I won't worry about it till it worries you."

"I won't have time to worry about it," Luka said. "What are we going to do here now, Atami?"

"Oh, rebuild Xi-Ling. We must first find our eighteen lost warriors. Each is in possession of one unique Xi-Ling art. Without them, the collective wisdom of our tradition will be lost forever."

"Eighteen of them?"

"There is more. Twelve of our treasures are still missing, not counting your dagger. Each weapon is blessed with rare magic and unique power. And we know in whose hands each lies now."

"We can journey together to search for them from one corner of this land to another, like real wandering warriors," Luka said excitedly.

"No, no, no. There will be no more wandering for you, Holy Boy," Atami said.

"Why?"

"Why? Aren't you forgetting what you were born for? What you are meant to be? You are the Holy One, and you have missed so many lessons. You'll have to work extra hard to make up for the lost time. The ancient scripture lesson will start tomorrow at sunrise."

Luka meant to protest but the urge disappeared. *Tomorrow at sunrise.* He smiled, chewing the phrase in his mouth. A phrase that used to make his childhood days seem long and dull now echoed in his head like the gentle tolls of a golden bell, soothing his soul. In the depths of his heart, an old tender feeling was born anew.

Luka was home once again.

ABOUT THE AUTHOR

DA CHEN was born in the tiny village of Huangshi, China, near Xinghua Bay and grew up in the shadows of Southern Shaolin Temple. He came to America at the age of twenty-three with thirty dollars in his pocket and a bamboo flute.

Da Chen lives in New York's Hudson Valley with his wife and their two children.